The Shadows Beyond These Wheels

BROOKE L. SMITH

ISBN: 978-0-692-19897-1

DEDICATION

To my friends who helped me get through some of my toughest years yet.

CONTENTS

ACKNOWLEDGMENTS

My friends helped me stay positive and strong throughout the publishing process. My dad helped me realize that it was something that needed to be shared. My mom never gave up on me and knew that whatever I decided would be the best choice for me. My aunt helped teach me tips and lessons that I needed for my first book. My entire family has been super supportive and they all were excited for when publishing day finally came. My sister let me read her over 5 chapters and helped me figure out what I needed to add. Dasha Didenko, my friend since 6th grade, helped bring my characters to life.

1 MY BIKE

"For safety is not a gadget but a state of mind."

I believe that we all have places that comfort us. Whether it be your bedroom. That tree that no one goes under in the local park. The special hidden grove in the nearby woods. Heck, it may even be your car.

Unfortunately, some of us have our special spots taken away. I'm not sure if it's happened to you, but I know that usually we end up finding another place. A 'next best' one shows up. It's not exactly the same, but it will suffice.

For me, I had all of them taken away. They weren't physically taken from me, but they all became infested with bad memories, making me consider my once safe spots, lethal ones.

Over time I lost the patience I once had. I stopped caring. It's funny, really. I'd wake up. Do crap. Then go to sleep. I started questioning my family's bond. Eventually, only being on my bike made me feel alive.

My life stopped having meaning and I stopped caring. That was until I met 18-year-old Ricky Doone.

"Mom have you seen my helmet?" I called out, trying very hard to get my mother's attention away from her phone and on me. I knew that asking her where my helmet was would get her attention because she doesn't particularly love the idea of me riding.

Riding my motorcycle, that is. I knew exactly where my helmet was. I always knew where my helmet was because it was my ticket to freedom.

"You mean your ticket to death? I think it's on your dresser in your bedroom." She informed me, looking at me for only a second or two. I've always wondered how she read my mind.

"He'll call you back, Mom. He'd be stupid not to," I said, referencing the guy she'd been texting for the past 30 minutes.

"You really think?"

"I'm 99.9% sure he will."

"What about the .1% possibility he doesn't?"

"That is saved for the possibility of him dying before he can call you back, Mom," I said, trying to stay serious throughout the entire conversation. After only seconds, we both started bursting out laughing. Tears were actually coming out of my mother's eyes.

The man we were referring to was the new boyfriend she picked up from one of her business trips. He's not new in the sense that she just met him, but Jerry is the first guy she's dated since my dad left. They met and 'instantly had a connection' were her words. I, surprisingly, like him. He's great and seems to be a true gentleman. After all my mother has been through with my dad, she definitely deserves it.

I walked over and gave her a hug from behind the kitchen counter. I started to head for the door, having already grabbed my helmet from upstairs. As I said, I only asked Mom that question to get her attention away from her phone for a few minutes.

"You need to be back by 7," my mother shouted, hurrying around the corner of the kitchen to look me in the eye before I walked out the door.

"Yeah, yeah. I know." I smiled putting my hand on the doorknob.

"I mean it, Gwen," I heard her say as I was closing the door of our townhouse.

Our house wasn't anything grand. It did have this amazing bay window where I loved to sit. That was until my father left. He had carved our names on the inside, forever reminding my mom and me just how permanent his mark would be on us and our home.

Shaking my head, I hopped onto my motorcycle, fastening my helmet over my dark red hair with purple highlights. My hair was styled into an asymmetrical bob. I liked it. After a while I stopped caring about my long hair and decided to donate 8 inches of it. I was feeling, let's just say, in need of a change.

I kicked my bike to start it, only to learn that the noise I was hearing wasn't the bike starting but rather something being knocked around in the exhaust pipe. A few months ago, a little boy had stuffed acorns into the exhaust. I guess he did it again. I jumped off my bike to look for acorns, but before I knew what was happening, I was being pummeled with small pebbles and wood chips. I knew who did this the second it hit my face. It was one of the many pranks the boys from my high school pull on me.

You'd think that a girl would only have to go through this once, but for me, it was a weekly occurrence. Every week one of the guys from the football team would come to my house, usually with a buddy, and vandalize part of my house or one of my belongings. Usually it was spray paint on my garage or a rock through the window, but I guess, they've decided to change things up a bit. I had to lie to my mother and tell her that all of the pranks were just that. Pranks. Silly games that I had gotten myself into on purpose. Even though that's not true, I haven't really cared about what they do because I always get them to come back and clean it up. This all started because my brother was friends with a few of them. They decided that they would just make this a tradition. This time though it was different. This was the one stable thing in my life. This was *my* bike!

Usually, the guys hid behind this hill that looked onto my house so I immediately wiped the stuff off of my face and ran across the street, over to the field with the hill. I ran over to see Gary and Kent, on the ground, snickering loudly.

"Dumb and Dumber, what a pleasure to FINALLY make your acquaintance," I said, sarcasm dripping from every word that rolled off my tongue. They were the only ones on the team who hadn't messed with me yet. Well, them and their egotistical captain.

"Oh, just shut it, Gwen," Gary said, standing up. He towered over me in a menacing manner that would've made any other girl cower in fear. His nose was only 3 feet away from my face, but by this point, I was not planning on backing down.

"I don't plan to *shut it.* I've said it before but I guess I'll have to say it again, my brother isn't here! He hasn't been for years and you know it."

"Gw-"

"Yeah no, Gary, no. I'm not doing this anymore," I said, taking my helmet off and untying my riding gloves.

"Wh-what are you doing Gwen?" Gary asked suspiciously, backing up as he asked me.

"I'm beating-"

"Dude, RUN! We can't get into this with her!" Kent yelled, already 10 yards from where he once was only seconds ago. I watched as Gary took Kent's advice and booked out. I pretended to chase them for only a few seconds before I decided that I was ready to go.

I turned around and smiled thinking about how ridiculous they looked running away.

I hopped on my bike, for the second time now, and rode off. Trying to completely erase the memory of the two douchebags would be hard, but definitely not impossible. All I have to do... is ride.

I turned onto my favorite back road and drove off. I went off trail for a little while, expertly dodging boulders and small ponds that somehow found their way in front of me. The wind blew through my hair as I drove down the bumpy path, having no care in the world. You will never truly understand the feeling of riding alone until you actually do it. There are no words to explain how free you feel when you successfully conquer a turn that has tripped you up for weeks or when you hit a new record speed without even trying. It makes you feel like everything else-everyone else is irrelevant. They are irrelevant because for once they don't have anything to do with me or my bike. I guess they are the reason I enjoy being alone, but they don't make me feel how I do on my bike. No one else has ever made me feel this way. I love that I don't have to depend on anyone else. I have my bike and that's all I need.

Before I knew what was happening, the sun was setting. It was warning me that it was almost time to make my way home. I have this system set up on my phone that records and tracks wherever I go when I'm on my bike. All I have to do is turn the app on and set it on the stand I built into my bike. This app shows me the trails I take when I go through the woods. I usually don't use it when I'm on the road because the roads aren't where I get lost. I can always find my way back home when I'm on them. It's the woods that get me lost. It's the woods, because the woods are everything I am. Complex. There are no signs that tell you where you came from or where you are going.

I rode straight through the woods and ended up at my favorite pizza place. Granted, I was across town and my mom was cooking dinner, but I was hungry. Like I always say, a girl has got to eat when a girl has got to eat. There is literally NO getting around that... at least not when I'm involved.

I parked my bike a little distance from the restaurant, just so it wouldn't get scratched. I absolutely despise scratches. They usually leave me in a bad mood for the rest of the day.

I walked into the pizza shop and noticed the guys who were seated in the large, round, booth in the back. The restaurant was designed in such a way that there wasn't any privacy. You could see everything from the entrance to the bathroom doors.

I recognized the guys as none other than, Jay Allen (the quarterback a.k.a. football team captain), Gary Watson (vandalizing guy from this morning), Kent Holden (other vandalizing guy from this morning), Troy Miller (running back), Brett Townsend (wide receiver), and Zack Cline (middle linebacker). The infamous football boys of Rodger Wells High.... yippee! (That was, in every way, sarcastic).

I walked up to the counter, trying very hard to ignore the stares and whispers I was receiving from the boys.

"Hey Darren, how's Trina?" I asked, giving Darren a friendly smile.

Darren Brown. The sweetest man I've ever met. He is 26 years old and has a 4-year-old daughter named Trina. She is the most adorable thing on this planet. Darren's ex-girlfriend left Trina with him, and ever since, he has done a phenomenal job caring for her. She's healthy and happy. He's a true inspiration to me. He put his college plans on hold to support her and even asked Trina to call him Dad. He's incredible. I have known him since my mom and I ordered pizza on an extremely cold winter day. It was exceptionally icy and Darren slid right into our house with the pizza. The pizza was squashed between his stomach and welcome mat. It was okay, though, because we all hit it off. He ended up staying for two hours at our house that day. I got his number, he got mine and we've talked almost every day since.

"Oh, hello there Gwen! Trina, she's great. She just learned how to read this book I got her a few weeks ago so I've been reading it with her! It's amazing to see how much she improves every day!"

"Oh, that's great Ren! What time do you get off today?"

"I actually get off at 8 so in just a few minutes!" He said excitedly. I smiled and opened my mouth to say something when what he said sunk in.... it's almost 8 o'clock.

"Please tell me it isn't actually 7:55...." My voice drifted as I pointed to the clock hanging on the wall behind Darren. He turned around and looked at me with apologetic eyes.

"I'm afraid that I updated that clock this morning."

"Could I get an already made slice to go then? I really need to hurry. My mom told me that I had to be home by 7, but you know, that isn't exactly happening today." I looked up at him with a worried smile.

"How about this, I'll call your mom," He paused, waiting for me to nod, "And I'll tell her we were talking for about an hour and a half. She'll be glad that you weren't on your bike this whole time.... I'm guessing that's what you've been doing." He said as more of a statement than anything else, knowing already that my answer would be yes.

"Yup. But back to your plan. That sounds like a fantastic idea! Thank you! Thank you! Thank you!" I exclaimed, reaching over the counter and pulling him into a hug. He laughed as he wrapped his arms around me awkwardly, trying his best to hug me over a metal table. I pulled back and smiled at him, grateful for all of the lighthearted moments like these we have together. He chuckled one last time before reaching for the phone and dialing my mother. The number, might I add, that he has memorized by heart.

I listened to the sound of Mom's voice as she told Darren that it was okay I was here. Before he even set the phone down I let out a sigh of relief.

"Well, in that case, I'd like to order a small size of my usual," I said, happy that I could order the pizza I wanted. I love things that give me energy so usually I go for a pizza that has a ton of protein on it. My pizza usually has 3 different types of meat on it and extra cheese. Yum is the only word I can use to describe it.

I sat down at the little bar-like table at the front of the store. I wanted to be facing the opposite direction of the boys so I didn't have to watch them while I waited. Besides, the view of the outside world calmed me. I pulled out my phone and started playing Fruit Ninja. I'm not sure if you have a go-to game, but whenever I'm bored, I always open up this one.

"This seat taken?" I looked up to see a beautiful boy standing above me. The grin he had plastered on his face told me this conversation was going to be interesting.

"Depends on who wants to take it," I say smartly, enjoying how taken aback the pretty boy was. His eyes flash with an emotion I couldn't decipher as he sits down, not even waiting for my answer.

"The name's Trey Anderson III." His mouth slowly formed a smirk that, surprisingly, looked good on him. It didn't, for the first time in forever (cue the song from Frozen), make him look like a jerk. On most guys, smirks make them look like jerks.

"Interesting," I said, still looking at him.

"Well, Interesting, I really liked the bike out there and was wondering whose it was?" He said, acting as though my name was Interesting. I chuckled to myself at the thought. Interesting Brady.

If it were any other guy, I would've responded with a flip answer. I would've totally shut him down within a matter of seconds, but there was something about Trey that just... I don't know. Maybe it was the way his dark brown hair looked effortlessly perfect on top of his handsome face. Maybe it was the way his dark blue eyes searched my face for any clue as to how he was doing this far. I'm not going to lie and say that it wasn't working, because it was, and I liked the idea of meeting someone new. Someone who hasn't been poisoned by what they say at school about me.

"It's mine and the name's Gwen so I suggest that you stop calling me Interesting."

He leaned in closer before whispering, "And what if I don't?"

I chuckled. "Oh, you couldn't even fathom the consequences."

"A guy can certainly dream." He whispered once again. I looked him straight in the eye before picking up my phone and leather jacket from the table and walking over to the counter. I know about how long the pizzas take so my pizza was ready two seconds after I walked up there. I mouthed a thank you to Darren who, I knew, was watching the exchange. I winked at the boys in the booth and blew a kiss to Trey. He was still trying to recover from our conversation as I walked out the door.

I pulled my leather jacket up and placed the pizza in the basket on the back of my bike. As I was snapping on my helmet and kicking my motorcycle to a start, Trey was jogging out of the pizza place.

"Wai-"

That was all I heard as my bike started and drove me into the darkness. Like I said, I love my bike!

2 REALIZATIONS

"Decision is a risk rooted in the courage of being free." – Paul Tillich

"WAKE UP!" I woke up with a start as my mom's voice came echoing into my room.

"I'm up! I'm up!" I exclaimed, trying to convince her that she didn't need to yell anymore. Her high-pitched voice was enough to make the singing birds from Snow White explode. Plus, the walls in our house were so close together that everything sounded about ten times louder than normal.

I was pulling on a pair of jeans when my mom burst through the door.

"Honey, Jerry is coming over so I need you to be on your best behavior," she warned. Clearly stressing over the thought of my misbehaving while her boyfriend was over. The fact that she's known him for well over two years makes me question why she's asking me to be polite. I've met him before.

"When am I not?" I asked, trying to sound as

innocent and sweet as possible. She clearly saw right through that because she rolled her eyes.

I don't blame her though. I am definitely a wild card and if I were her, I'd be worried too.

"I'm making eggs for breakfast! Do you want bacon?" She yelled from the staircase.

"Always!" I answered, brushing my hair as I put on a beanie and went downstairs. I walked into the family room and noticed the giant object sitting in the middle of the room. It was suspiciously covered with a cream-colored blanket. I cautiously pulled off the cover and was thrilled to see a familiar display case I'd had my eye on for the past eight months!

My mom walked around the corner and clapped her hands when she saw me admiring the case.

"Isn't it wonderful?" Mom asked, standing next to me.

"It's amazing, but why did you get it?"

"I know how much you love your pictures, I wanted to get you something to keep them protected. Plus, I've watched you obsess over it for long enough now." Smiling, I leaned over and hugged her.

"Thank you! Where did you get it?" I asked, curious about where she found it. My mother looked at me with so much light in her eyes that I realized how little I talk to her nowadays. She hung off of my every word as though I was a ghost giving her advice for the future; like I would disappear at any second or something.

She walked over to the dresser in the front hallway and pulled out a piece of paper. She read it and shut it back in the dresser.

"Azul City Museum," my mother said, smiling at the

display case.

"Mom, that must have cost a fortune! You didn't have to do that." I was concerned about how much she spent on me. We don't exactly have a million bucks and that museum caters basically to people who do.

"Don't worry about it Gwen. I wanted to do this and besides, I was thinking that this would give you more of a reason to stay off your bike. I would hate to take away your riding time, not really, but I thought that your photography should become more of a priority."

I chuckled at how serious my mother was until I realized that she wasn't joking. I immediately dropped the smile that was on my face and replaced it with a grimace. I have had enough of her complaints about my riding. I live to ride. I love it, and nothing she says can change that. She has been pestering me since I got it two years ago. Every day she makes me feel badly about leaving her alone. It's not my responsibility to look after her! I am 17 years old, and I don't think it's fair that she makes me feel like I need to babysit her. She's 42!

"Mom why don't you like me riding?" I asked, trying to hide how frustrated I had become. I've asked her many times before. This time feels different, though.

"I just don't," she said, breaking eye contact with me as she said the words I've heard so many times before.

"Mom I'm not accepting that anymore. I can't handle you telling me something is bad when you don't even tell me why. I need an answer! Don't you think I deserve it?!" I was raising my voice now. I moved around to face her so she had no other choice but to look me in the eye. She sighed before telling me the real reason.

"It's because I lost my best friend to that God-awful

contraption outside. My best friend, Melony, loved to ride just as much as you do. One day a truck ran a red light and hit her. She went flying, Gwen, and do you know what the most awful part about it was?" At this point, I was the one hanging on her every word.

"I was there. I couldn't handle seeing that happen to you. The only problem is how much you love to ride. That passion is what makes me feel trapped. I want to take it away from you but then I would be taking away something you love and I...." Her voice trailed off as she whispered the last part and looked down again, her eyes filling up with tears.

I put my hand on my mother's shoulder and wiped away the tears that had fallen down her face.

"I'm not Melony, Mom. I am never going to leave you. You can't keep me from something just because you are scared of what happened years ago. It doesn't mean it's going to happen to me, Mom." She took my hand and then gave it back to me before adding, "It doesn't mean that it *won't* happen to you either."

I watched as she left to go to the kitchen. I sat there and looked up at the picture she had on the mantel of the last reunion she had with all of her high school and college friends. The date that was scrawled in the corner of the image was 12 years ago. I never realized this was probably the reason why they stopped seeing each other so frequently.

I don't remember much from that long ago, but I can see my mother leaving the house and coming back hours later with about 5 ladies I'd only met a few times before. I bet one of them was Melony.

A few minutes later, Mom came back with my eggs

and bacon. She sat down on the couch opposite from me and clicked the TV on, totally avoiding the conversation that was bound to happen between us.

After what felt like an eternity of brutal silence, she muted the TV. "You need to be ready for Jerry at 12." I nodded before finishing my food and walking to the kitchen. I placed my silverware in the sink and my plate in the dishwasher. I steadied myself as the thought of my mother watching her best friend die played through my mind. I could hear her footsteps behind me as she refilled her glass with water.

"Why didn't you ever tell me?"

"I didn't want you to worry about how I felt whenever you rode," she said quietly.

"But I've always been worried about you. I will never stop worrying Mom, you know me." We found ourselves in a tight hug in the middle of the kitchen.

"Please be careful, my Gwen," she whispered into my hair.

"Always and forever, Mom," I smiled as she pulled back and walked upstairs. I turned to the oven and saw that it was 10:37 on the digital clock.

I figured I could get one last ride in before Jerry got here, so I hopped on my bike and let the wind carry me and my thoughts away.

I went back to the trail I had taken the day before and replayed the conversation I had with my mother in my head. She said that she lost her best friend to a motorcycle accident. Okay I get that. But she let me buy my bike. Granted, it was my money but still, she could've said no. And then the way she 'gave' me back my hand like I had the plague. She looked so disappointed in me. I hate seeing her like that, but after everything that happened with my dad and Jett, the bike quickly became the only place I could go to feel free. I'm not sure if this makes sense but my bike is the only place where I feel safe. I understand that a motorcycle is probably not the safest spot for a 17-year-old girl but that doesn't really make a difference to me because that's what society decided. Society has made me feel like an outcast for 12 years and counting. Society has labeled me as 'EMO' and 'depressed'. I don't listen to society anymore. I don't stand for it. I don't trust it. I don't even like to relate myself to it.

At the fork in the trail I can either go right or left. Yesterday I went left so today I think I'll go right. I make my turn and space out again. The passing trees have a way of making me feel like life could just go on forever. Whenever I look at them I always get crazy ideas of tricks to try. They hypnotize me in a way that makes me feel safe.

"WATCH IT LADY!" My eyes lock onto a grown man yelling in the middle of the trail. I turn the wheel to the right and skid to a stop two feet in front of him.

"WHAT IN GOD'S NAME DO YOU THINK YOU ARE DOING RIDING ON PRIVATE PROPERTY?!" The man roared. I pulled my bike back a little to put some space between me and the infuriated man in front of me. I could easily drive away due to the fact my bike was parallel to Mr. Grumps. But I didn't.

"Sir, I am so sorry. I didn't mean to trespass. I was just-"

"What? WHAT could you possibly be doing here? You do know there is a highway less than two minutes away from here correct?" He was staring at me like I was no more than an animal that you'd find roaming here.

"Well, I'd tell you what I was doing if you would let me speak."

"You can't just ride on MY property, tear up MY land, disrupt MY peace and quiet and then act like you own the place. Who do you think you are?" He spat incredulously. I took off my helmet and sunglasses to look him in the eyes.

"Now listen," I leaned over so I was a little closer to the man, "I know that you're upset, but you have no reason to yell at me the way that you are. This is all just a big misunderstanding and I feel like calming down would be the most reasonable thing to do right now." I blinked once before the entire left side of my face exploded in pain.

He slapped me.

The smell of alcohol washed over me in one big wave as he pulled his hand back. It was the kind of slap that stings for more than just a few minutes. I held my face and looked back at the man shocked more than anything else.

"I-I.... I didn't mean.... I was just...," he said. His voice fell at the sound of my bike engine. I looked back at him as soon as I had put at least 40 feet between us. He looked at me with so much sadness in his eyes that I almost stopped. I almost did.... but I didn't. I will never stop riding because clearly riding is the only way I can stay safe.

"Honey, *what* happened to you?!" My mother screamed from across the room. As soon as I walked through the front door she noticed the bruise on my face.

"Some crazy man slapped me.... but I'm fine, Mom." I tried to reassure her as I watched her grab a bag of ice from the freezer and put it, gently, on my face. I held it in place as she clipped my hair back and led me to the couch.

"A MAN? Gwen, WHO did this to you?!" She asked already dialing 9-1-1. I grabbed the phone from her and sat on it.

"Just don't worry about it, Mom. It doesn't matter. He said he was sorry.... I could smell the alcohol on him. I'm pretty sure he was drunk."

"Gwen, I can't just FORGET about it. A grown man SLAPPED my daughter. That is assault, Gwen! I could press charges. You must think very little of me if you'd think I'd just let this go. I'll be d-"

"Don't curse." I cut her off as soon as I saw the red creeping up her neck. "Mom, I'm fine. Honestly, I am."

If I'd held my breath for as long as the silence stayed between us I would've passed out. When it ended, she shook her head and walked up the stairs. I was surprised to say the least. She usually doesn't give up that easily, but nonetheless, it was only a matter of minutes before I heard her door slam. Moments later I heard her crying. I walked up the stairs and knocked on the door. She didn't lock it so I just walked in. I sat next to her on the bed and tapped her shoulder to let her know I was there. She made a noise that sounded a lot like a squirrel. Our laughter started when I said, "Squirrel much?" We sat there in silence, staring at each other. Eventually, we both smiled and came to an unspoken consensus. We would get this sorted out later.

"Jerry will be here soon so I better get ready," I said to my mom before she pulled me into a hug. I heard her breathe in sharply before pulling away and looking me straight in the eyes.

"I'm sorry, baby. I know that lately I've been distracted and not really paying attention to you or how you've been doing. I want you to know that I love you and that if anything is ever wrong, I want you to come and talk to me about it." I nodded before my mother continued. "I got a call today from school saying that you've been getting picked on. Is that true, Gwen?" she asked.

I didn't answer.

"Darn it, Gwen, IS THAT TRUE?" I jumped at the sound of her shrill voice. I nodded, scared that she would continue to yell if I didn't.

"Gwen, you need to tell me these things. I would've never known! You're doing great in school.... I would've never suspected anything!" My mother's eyes searched mine as I tried to stay calm.

"And what can you do, Mom?! There's virtually nothing you can do. They're teenagers! They don't care! I'm fine, honestly I am. If anything, they are making me stronger. They are teaching me how to stick up for myself."

"But you are pushing everyone away. They're making you distance yourself from everyone. What ever happened to Lily? Weren't you two like two peas in a pod?"

I chuckled at the sound of that analogy and welcomed the distraction.

"That was until she told everyone lies about me." I laughed at how immature that sounded. Even to this day, I don't understand how anyone could believe her.

"Oh honey...." My mother's voice trailed off as the doorbell rang.

"It's Jerry, right?" I confirmed, standing up to go get the door.

"I rescheduled. So, I'm not sure who it is," my mother informed me, heading to the door to get it herself. I followed closely behind her.

She put her hand on the door and opened it slowly.

3 WELL THAT'S A SHAME

"People will usually hurt you in attempt to heal themselves."

It was just the mailman, but I was excited to see him because he was delivering my new helmet. Considering everything that has been going on in my life with the kids at school, I definitely needed a pick-me-up.

My mother handed me the box and walked into the family room.

"I'm going to watch *The Fault in Our Stars*. Would you like to watch it with me?" my mother asked, not looking at me turning on the TV.

"How about I pick up lunch? I can watch whatever is remaining when I get back," I suggested, trying to get out of seeing the movie. Don't get me wrong, I loved it, but I have to be in the mood to cry, if that makes any sense.

"Okay," she said with a tinge of disappointment. I smiled sadly at the back of her head and hugged her from behind the couch. She wrapped her arms around me awkwardly and nudged me towards the door.

"I'll be back.... 30 minutes tops." I walked towards the door and picked up my leather jacket, gloves, backpack, and sunglasses. My combat boots were already on my feet.

"Please use your new helmet instead of the old one," my mom requested from the couch.

"Of course."

I locked the door and decided that I'd get Chipotle. I don't love Chipotle, but I felt like that would be the closest and fastest option. I hopped on my bike, fastened my helmet and blasted my radio. I only use the sound system when I'm not on the highway. It's really hard to hear it when you're going so fast. That's also probably the reason why the bike didn't come with it and why I had to pay extra to get it added on. I know, I'm particular.

I pulled into the parking lot at 12:10. The line, luckily, was short so I got in and out quickly. I ordered Mom a burrito with all of her veggies, and I decided on a burrito with steak.

The cashier had taken so long to take my order that I thought I'd turn 70 before I got my food. He was flirting with the girl in front of me. From the look on her face I knew he wouldn't be getting anywhere on his own. I took matters into my own hands and decided to help him out.

I read his tag -"Jackson."

"Jackson, I just wanted to say thank you for helping

me save my boyfriend's little cousin from the trash truck the other day. The fact that you jumped into oncoming traffic for that little boy blew me away. You just never know what toddlers are going to get into. You literally saved my relationship with him." I fake laughed as the girl finally looked up from her phone and into his eyes. She smiled, one adoringly, and gave him her number. He waved her goodbye and rang me up.

You're welcome Jackson.

"Do I know you?" Jackson asked as if I didn't just help him land a date with Malibu Barbie.

"I'm the girl who just helped you get a date for this Friday." I reminded him of my chivalrous act from moments ago. He scratched the back of his neck and mumbled a 'thank you'.

"No problem, Jackson," I said pointing to his name tag. I took the receipt from the machine and picked up my food from the counter. I walked out and gave him a little wave goodbye, feeling great satisfaction from the look on his face. What can I say.... I like to make life interesting for people and he looked like a nice guy.

I secured the food to my bike and positioned my sunglasses underneath my helmet.

"Nice bike." I turned around to see none other than Jay Allen a.k.a football captain a.k.a quarter back a.k.a pain in the butt.

"Thanks," I said as monotonously as possible.

He scoffed. "You know you don't always have to be so sassy. You could try being nice for once." I took off my helmet and sunglasses and spun around to face him.

"Look, Jay, I don't need stupid advice on how to be a nice person when you haven't exactly mastered the act

24

yourself." I looked him straight in the eyes, not backing down.

"What is that supposed to mean?" He asked as if I was speaking in a foreign language.

"It means you are an incompetent jerk, who shows no respect for anything or anyone else but himself." I crossed my arms and raised my eyebrow, waiting for his comeback.

"I haven't done anything to you Gwen," he said, sounding as though he believed it. I laughed sarcastically before taking one step toward him.

"That's the problem, Jay. You don't do anything. All those times *your* teammates threw things at me, vandalized my house, called me crude names. You. Never. Did. Anything." I looked into his blue-grey eyes and was surprised to see hurt flash through them, even if it was only for a second.

He opened his mouth to say something but I stuck my finger up.

"I don't want to hear it." I turned to my bike and hopped on. I made sure to give him one last glare that I knew he could feel. He couldn't see it because of my glasses but I knew that he could sense it. I turned out of the parking lot and never looked back, not even once.

"So, when did you reschedule? With Jerry, I mean?" I asked carrying our trash to the kitchen and then sitting next to her on the couch. After we ate, Mom wanted me to show her my latest collage. She's developed a habit of asking me for one every day. It's nice to know that at least one person enjoys my work.

I love photography so I usually take hundreds of

pictures and put them into collages so my mom can see all of them without having to manually flip through each one. I get amazing footage in the forest and I'm so lucky to have my bike to help me with that. I don't just take pictures of inanimate objects though. I love to do candid photos too. I feel like candid photos let the world know what the person or subject is truly thinking and feeling at that given moment. There aren't any walls or restraints around a person who thinks they are alone.

"I told him to come over on Thursday around 3, so we could have dinner as a family." She didn't look over to me, but I knew that she felt me tense up.

"He's not my family, Mom," I snapped. I don't even know why I did though. I mean, I like him, she likes him, and he likes us so there really shouldn't be any issues. I really wouldn't mind seeing Jerry more often, but the word *family* struck something within me.

"I know, honey, I didn't mean it like that." She looked at me, sorrow and regret visible in her hazel eyes. I smiled to reassure her and stood.

"I'm going to bed. I can take the bike to school in the morning."

"You don't want me to drive you?" She asked, probably shocked at my sudden change of mind.

"No, I'm okay." I walked up the stairs and shut my door, trying to fight back the voice in my head saying that my plan was a horrible one. I knew it was, but I never give up a chance to prove a point.

I woke up to the sound of techno pop. I'm not sure about you, but sometimes my alarm finds its way into my dream and the sound gets inserted into it. It's pretty funny to me how easily our brain picks up on sound. It's definitely interesting to wake up to.

"Breakfast is ready!" My mother yelled from downstairs. I could already smell the bacon.

"Okay.... I'm coming!" I yelled back. I get a good feeling that rushes through me when I realize my morning routine is off to a good start. I have a system for my morning and it almost always improves when Mom cooks. It gives me an extra 20 minutes of procrastination time.

I had to plan an outfit that shows people I don't care what they say about me. I already knew I was whipping out the old leather jacket but I needed to figure out the rest.

A few thoughtful minutes in the shower led me to the perfect, 'I don't give two craps' kind of outfit. A maroon crop top with high waisted black jeans and my leather jacket. For the shoes, I was thinking my black combat boots.

"Someone looks happy this morning." My mother pointed out my mood before I even said a word. I looked at her and smiled. I get to ride my motorcycle to school!

"Thanks for the food, Mom!" I enjoyed my bagel and bacon while I sat at the kitchen table and played Crossy Road on my phone.

"No problem, dear," she said, cleaning up the pan she had used to cook. "I'm going out to dinner with Jerry today so I may be a little late coming home. Please don't wait up and don't ride past 9.... okay? Gwen.... GWEN?" My mother yelled to get my attention.

"Umm, yeah. Okay.... have fun," I replied, getting an eye roll out of her. I laughed at the sight of her rolling her eyes.

"I see someone is picking up on her daughter's ways," I commented.

"Just eat your breakfast," my mother jokingly spat. "Have a good day at school today and be careful."

"It's not the first day of school, Mom, I'll be fine."

"I thought you said that the rumors were getting really bad lately."

"Well, yeah but they always are. It just so happens that mine are the worst right now. It'll blow over." I'm fine whether she believes it or not. I can handle myself. I stood up and gave her a quick hug before putting on my gold chain necklace and gold cuff bracelet. It's time to show the kids at school that I care more about the size of ants than them. I waved to my mom who was leaning against the wall drinking her daily cup of coffee.

Hopping on my bike was the one thing that gave me joy during the day. The engine roared to life as I secured my helmet (safety first, kids) and put on my sunglasses. Rodger Wells High, are you ready?

I pulled into the parking lot and immediately got unwanted second glances. I parked in my spot and cut the engine. Hopping off and removing my headgear, I could hear the heels that were heading for me. Before I turned I already knew who it was. Amber Wood.

"You have a lot of nerve showing up here on that *thing*," she says in her prissy, popular school girl tone. Every school has them. A school wouldn't be the same without one.

"And you have a lot of nerve to purposefully shove your body into clothes that are 4 sizes too small, and yet, no one is saying anything now are they?" It feels good to see the shock on her face. She recovers as soon as she notices that her discomfort is visible. Good catch, Amber.

"You better watch your back," Amber barks. I open my mouth to reply but am interrupted by a low, seemingly masculine voice.

"Or what?" I turn around to see Jay standing a little too close to me. He's standing up for me? I say that as a question because it just sounds so weird. I look him in the eyes and can just tell he wants me to look back to Amber. I do, but I will never listen to him again.

"Jay, baby, *what* are you doing?" She asks through clenched teeth. He doesn't answer and that's when I start.... laughing. I know it's pretty out of the blue but standing here and watching these two is truly just classic.

"I'm going to walk away and pretend like I never talked to my stalker and pretend bodyguard. Have a good day."

I walked away still chuckling about Mr. and Mrs. Dramatic.

I grabbed my books from my locker and made my way to first period. I walked in and loved that I was the first one. This allowed me to have the first choice for a seat. Mr. Wells has this rule about not letting you sit in the same spot two days in a row. Surprisingly, we have figured out a way to almost completely avoid changing seats. All we have to do is sit in the one directly next to the seat we were originally in, and alternate between those two. Technically, we aren't sitting in the same seat so, therefore, we are obeying his rules. Every time I walk into this class I internally scream LOOPHOLE and smile.

"Glad to see someone's in a good mood today, Ms. Brady," Mr. Wells said from behind his desk. I looked up and continued to smile.

"Yes. I believe I am." The few students who walked in just in time to hear our conversation snickered while I smiled along with them. Honestly, being able to ride my bike is enough to bring up my spirits. As a way to pass the limited amount of time I have between bells, I take out the folder full of my pictures and sort through them. I sort them by date and picture type. For example, all of the candid pictures starting from last year get put in the very back of the right side of the folder. I know it sounds confusing, but trust me, I know what I'm doing.

A tall, broad shadow appears above me and I instinctively look up to see Jay. When did he get put into this class?

He opens his mouth to ask if he could sit next to me, but when the bell rings, he just sits. Luckily for him, the girl who usually sits there isn't here today.

"Hello, Class. Today, we are going to discuss the concept of an atom and more importantly the fact that the mass number of an atom is equal to the sum of the number of protons and neutrons in its nucleus."

By the time lunch rolled around I was beat. I usually go outside and sit underneath one of the trees on the school property but today, Jay was there. I was walking toward it when I saw him so, I turned around and began to look for somewhere else to eat.

"Hey, Gwen wait!" He shouted, running toward me as soon as he saw my back towards him.

"What is it, Jay?" I asked, hopefully so he could tell I was annoyed.

"I wanted to ask you about what happened this morning."

"What about it, Jay? You were there, weren't you?" I set my tray down on the bench next to me so I could take off my leather jacket. I was hot and definitely not in the mood for sweat stains.

"Well, yeah.... I. Can you please put your stupid jacket back on? You're very distracting." I widened my eyes at his bluntness.

"Poor Jay. Did your team not teach you how to talk to girls?"

"Just.... uh.... okay yes, I was there I was just shocked at how you talked to me. I mean I was trying to be helpful." He kept his eyes locked on mine almost as if looking anywhere else would kill him. I laughed at how uncomfortable I made him and took one step closer to him.

"Like I said before, I don't need nor want help from a guy who wouldn't help me until I asked." He smirked for some odd reason. I scrunched my eyebrows together in confusion.

"So, you admit to asking me for help then?" he asked, following my lead and stepping closer to me.

"The day I ask for your help is the day that we are the last two people on Earth and I have nowhere to live," I said, smirking just like he did and picking up my tray. Just like that, I was on my way to my tree. I hid the smile I had on my face when I heard him say, "Then I

31

guess I'll have to wait for that day."

The bell rang, signaling the end to my daily 7-hour prison sentence. I pushed my way through the busy hallways and made my final stop at my locker. Briskly shoving my books into place, I heard a loud slam before I looked down to see my left hand covered in blood. It felt like every ounce of blood in me was rushing to my hand. I yelled out in pain and jumped back, holding my hand to my chest.

I could move every finger except my index finger. My hand started to swell right away. I looked to see Amber snickering with one of her friends on the opposite side of the hallway. "DO YOU KNOW WHAT YOU JUST DID?" I yelled.

"I protected everyone from your death machine!" Amber exclaimed loud enough for everyone around to hear her clearly. She knew I couldn't ride with an injured hand.

"What don't you get about the fact that I had NOTHING to do with what happened to Mason?" I was talking as tears filled my eyes. " It wasn't me and if it was, I would physically put myself in jail. I couldn't live with myself if I ever did something like that. Are you hearing me, Amber?" I turned at the sound of phones clicking to see the football team taking a video of the whole thing. Guess who was right in the middle?

Jay. I looked into his eyes and I swear my hand broke a little more just by doing so. He started shaking his head as if to say no to something but I decided that I was done playing nice. I went over to Amber and let the blood from the gash on my hand drip all over her $400 shirt. Neither of us moved as we both watched the blood soak into her magenta blouse. She was still from shock and I out of pure malice. I spit on her shoes and picked up my bag.

"Thanks for the towel," I said between gritted teeth. I was using every fiber in my body to prevent myself from crying in front of everyone. Glaring at Jay one last time, I walked out. People looked out the glass doors to watch what would happen next. I clenched my fists to see if I could ride my bike safely, but I couldn't so I put the kickstand up and pushed it down the street. Desperately needing to distance myself from the school, I awkwardly turned down the street.

It took 45 minutes to push my bike home.

4 I DON'T MIND

"People can say they care, but it means nothing until they prove it."

I don't really want to bore you with the details of everything that happened when I got home but my mother screamed for about an hour before taking me to the hospital. It was the basic hospital visit. The relentless questions about pain and the doctors who act like they alone fix everything when really, all they're doing is taking down notes and passing it along to someone else. While we were there, my mother "ran into" the police in the lobby and spoke to them about Mr. Grumps (the guy who slapped me the other day). Thankfully, I was there to let them know that everything was okay and that I really didn't want to press charges. The fact that he had been in the system previously made me a little uneasy until I learned that all he was in the system for was 4 speeding tickets, including two speed traps. The police blew off the charge when my mother told them we didn't want to do anything. My mother was pissed, obviously, but I played the "you promised" card which eventually made her drop it.

In an effort to disguise my cast, I got special gloves made that didn't look so ridiculous. My left hand was the one that was broken, but I wanted both of my hands to look the same. The left glove had extra cushioning to help my hand heal.

"Can we stop by Starbucks to get a drink?" I asked my mother politely. The only reason why I bothered her for the drink was because the shop was on the way back to our house. She nodded as she turned onto a side road.

We pulled into the parking lot and I offered to go in alone. She gave me her credit card and I headed inside. The guy behind the counter immediately said 'Welcome' the second I walked in. I smiled, waved and ordered a frappuccino. He put in my order as I handed him the debit card.

"Marissa huh?" He asked, looking at my mother's card, thinking it was mine. I just nodded and took the card from him, not wanting to embark on a long conversation. Then I sat down in one of the cracked red booths.

It was quite ironic how all of the customers, give or take 3, happened to be from my school. There were a few people who could pass as adults, but besides them, everyone looked 18 or younger. They all quietly watched me as I looked around. Amber walked in and immediately left when she noticed me. I scoffed at her immature behavior. If I remember correctly, she was the one who broke *my* hand. Not the other way around. The guy called my order, and I walked over to the counter to pick it up.

"Can I have a sip?" My mom asked as I buckled my seat belt. I didn't answer until after I heard the click of the buckle.

"Sure," I said, carefully handing her my special drink. What can I say? My coffee falls high on my list of priorities. We drove to the sound of the radio. Neither of us spoke a word the whole way home, but the silence was comfortable.

I went to my room and didn't come out until I needed water for my pills (Codeine for the pain). My mother stayed in her room as well so it was a pretty quiet night. My mother and I have been distant lately and I can't quite figure out why. I have this weird feeling that she is getting tired of all the stunts I've pulled lately. I'm afraid that I'm pushing my mother away and she isn't even trying to hold onto me anymore. She used to. But I don't think she is now.

I'm lying in my bed and staring at the decals all around my room, contemplating many thoughts I currently have. Pictures from almost every photo shoot decorate my walls. The decals are silhouettes of the candid pictures I have taken. They definitely give me inspiration. Sometimes I wonder why people, I'll never see again, offer more insight than people I interact with every day. Amber and Jay have no idea what I am going through. I don't even know if they care. Well, I know Amber doesn't but Jay.... he's just so confusing. One second he is giving me those stupid puppy dog eyes and the next he is ganging up on me with his ridiculous friends. It's not that I don't think I could take them though, because I know that I could. Along with being a photographer and motorcyclist, I kick-box. I compete in local kick-boxing tournaments which help me earn enough money to keep up my motorcycle. I have, well had, a tournament coming up this Friday but now, since I have a broken fist, I can't compete. This means that if my bike breaks I won't be able to fix it, and that means I won't be able to ride. Not being able to ride is like telling me to stop breathing.

My phone buzzes, and I jump. I know it's hard to believe but no one EVER calls me, texts me, or anything for that matter. I have virtually no friends, and I really don't want any. Therefore, my contact list consists of my mother, Darren, Jerry, and 9-1-1. I decided to let the voicemail get it.

Unknown: *Hello, my name is Caroline Knoll. My 18-year-old son, Ricky Doone, has a severe form of Cerebral Palsy. Cerebral Palsy is a permanent movement/muscle disorder that is usually found in early childhood. It affects his muscles and how they move on a daily basis. Usually it's just a few muscle spasms here and there but Ricky is paralyzed from the waist down. Your mother, Marissa, told me that you might be willing to look after my son on days that I work for some extra income. I hear that you love to ride motorcycles.... how exciting! Anyway, I am reaching out to you to see if you would like to accept my offer of $30 an hour, 4 days a week, from 4:00 pm to 9:00 pm. Please let me know what you decide, I would love for you to meet him. We're right next door so come on over!*

I guess Mom isn't pulling away from me completely. The only thing that confuses me is why, in all of the

years that we've lived here, haven't we ever seen them?
We live in a townhouse so our doors are only inches
away from each other. If I wanted to jump onto their
front door step I could.

"Mom," I said, gently knocking on her bedroom door
in an effort to preserve whatever there was left of my
hand. I pushed her door open slightly to hear her snoring
on her bed. She was curled up in her normal sleeping
position, and I could tell she needed the rest. I'm not
sure what has been going on with her lately but it's nice
to see her relax, even if it is only for a little while.

I smile as I quietly pull her blanket higher up around
her and close the door. I guess I'll just have to ask her
about Ricky's family later. Time waits for no one.

I slipped on my shoes and walked over to the
neighbor's house. After knocking, I only had to wait a
matter of seconds before a tall blonde-haired woman
answered the door. She was dressed in a fancy rose
colored pantsuit that stuck to her thin stature. I smiled
and held out my hand, trying hard not to pay too much
attention to her indisputably small hands.

"Gwen Brady. It's a pleasure to meet you, Ms. Knoll."
I smile as she shakes my hand. I flinch before I realize
that she's shaking my right hand, not my left.

"No, I do believe the pleasure is all mine. I admire
your eagerness to meet us. Your mother told me about
your injury so I thought, why not? Please come in. I
would love for you to meet Ricky," she says joyfully,
opening the door wider so I could step in.

I walk in and am welcomed by the smell of chocolate
chip cookies coming from the kitchen. I close my eyes
and savor the smell but quickly open them to take in the

house before me. The house, although small, had an ornate feel to it. The crystal chandelier hanging above me sparkled from the natural light that flooded almost every room. The light blue curtains complemented the navy tassels dangling from the white pillows. The natural flowers gave every room a scent that I thought was only obtainable in the largest of gardens. The staircase, tinted with a subtle beige, led to a beautiful upper level that looked to be just as well thought out as the first. I hear a pair of wheels roll up behind me as I silently drool over their house. I turn around to see a boy sitting in a wheelchair. He seems to be about my age. His deep green eyes were captivating and made you question the color of grass. I'm not going to lie and say he wasn't attractive, he was. No doubt about it. But sadly, there was this sarcastic, know-it-all, kind of vibe that I was getting from him. It was visible in the way his shoulders never slouched and the way his demeanor never changed. I'm not going to judge him before I even know him though. Too many people have done that to me.

I recover quickly and smile, sticking my hand out in the process. "Gwen. Nice to meet you."

He smirks and gives me a, frankly obvious, once over. He doesn't stick his hand out either. "Ricky. Interesting choice in gloves. You must have failed horribly at whatever it was you were trying to accomplish." I look down, almost forgetting that I broke my hand less than six hours ago. I guess that medicine really is working.

"Yeah, I got into this, *situation*. It didn't end well." I raise my left hand with the bulky black glove.

"Well, you clearly lost," he says in a way that made it sound like he was glad that I did. Giving me a combination of a smirk and a grimace, he wheeled over to his mother. She mouthed, "Be nice," and spun him around to face me.

"He-He didn't mean that," she stuttered, trying hard to reassure me.

"Oh, yes I did," he whispered. I acted like I didn't hear him even though we all knew I did.

"No, please don't worry about it, Ms. Knoll." I gave him the same smirk/grimace he gave me. He looked almost shocked that I didn't say more. Clearly, they had never met anyone who could let things go so easily. I smiled when Ms. Knoll clapped her hands.

"I think you are going to do great here! You got the job." She put her arm over my shoulder and started to lead me to the kitchen.

Many words came to mind as I watched Ms. Knoll but one definitely over-powered the others. Stability. She strived for it. Scratch that, she needed it. The way she carried herself as though she was above everything that was as unfortunate enough to cross her path. Every movement, every breath that she took, there was a purpose. An underlying message was being sent every time she simply looked in your general direction.

The medicine cabinet was labeled down to the sell date. The alphabetized bottles were so organized they made my doorway look messy. It was amusing to watch her move through the kitchen so, effortlessly, fluidly. It was something right out of a paranormal movie.

About an hour and a half later she finished explaining what I would need to do for Ricky whenever I came over. It was quite interesting actually. His medications were some I have never seen before, and I think they just introduced me to three new vitamins I didn't know people needed. I was excited when I recognized the name of one of the medications! He takes baby aspirin! I smiled when she showed it to me. She looked at me funny, but that's okay. He was also taking an anticholinergic, whatever that is. Basically, I needed to give it to him once every time I came over. I also needed to feed him a snack and dinner. Easy enough.

I walked back out to find Ricky shaking in his chair. A seizure.

I ran over to his side to see if he was okay, and do you know what he did? He started laughing. I had put my hand behind his neck in an attempt to get him onto the floor because I read somewhere to make sure, whenever someone is seizing, that they were flat on their left side. This helps keep their airways clear in case they were going to throw up. I pulled my hand back and thumped him on the back of his head, his dirty blonde hair bouncing at the sudden impact.

"Oh, Ricky cut it out. You'll scare her away!" Ms. Knoll exclaimed from the kitchen doorway. Ricky's scene reminded her to review emergency procedures with me.

"I'm just preparing her for what might happen. Never can be too prepared right, Gwen?" He held up a blue box with a brand name that every girl would know. This boy went in *my* bag and pulled out my tampons. I snatched my stuff from him and stuck up my middle finger at him. He did it right back. We lowered our hands and glared at one another. If a train could barrel through their front door and take Ricky with it, I would be grateful.

"Well it looks like you two are going to be just fine on your own. I'll be back in a little while. I took the cookies out of the oven so they should be on the counter," Ms. Knoll said from the front entryway. I turned toward her, shocked, to say the least.

"Wait! Ms. Knoll-" She interrupted me.

"You can call me Caroline, dear."

"Caroline, you are leaving me here.... alone.... with him?" I pointed to Ricky.

"Well, that is what a part time caregiver would do. Right, dear?" She asked, picking up her purse, not showing any indication that she was staying.

"Well, yes, but I didn't know I was starting.... like right now," I said worriedly, looking between the two of them in the process.

"Yup! Isn't it great? I'll be back soon," she said briskly. Shutting the door to end all of my possible objections. I slowly turned around to Ricky, who was still staring at me. For all Caroline knows, I could be a murderer. I could be some 30-year-old in disguise who doesn't actually live next door.

"I need water," Ricky informed me. I raised an eyebrow at his tone and squatted down so I was on his level. He looked me straight in the eye and I gave him a sweet smile.

"And I was told that you were intelligent. So, Ricky, you can go into the kitchen and get a glass of water out of the fridge that was customized to fit your needs." He didn't move. I guess we are having another staring competition.

What I meant by the fridge being customized was that

Caroline had the ice and water dispenser moved down so he could get drinks for himself.

About 5 minutes passed and I couldn't do it. I blinked and he smirked. I wanted to smack him but I didn't. I went into the kitchen and grabbed a glass and handed it to him.

"Please get your own water," I said to Ricky who had followed me into the kitchen. He took the glass and wheeled over to the fridge. I watched as the water trickled into his glass. He pushed a button, and seconds later, out came the cubes of ice, splashing the water he already had in his glass. He pulled his glass away and got an ice cube with his hand. He turned to face me and chucked it at my face. Thanks to my awesome reflexes I caught it. Oh, Ricky, you are so on.

Two gruesome hours later and I am locked in the bathroom closet. How he locked me in here, I have no idea, but none the less, here I am. Locked in a bathroom closet for, going on, half an hour. There were probably hundreds of towels all stacked neatly on the wire racks that reached the ceiling behind me. There was a small light that was on the ceiling, but of course, the switch was outside the closet so the only light source I had was from the small crack beneath the door.

Since the light in here was limited, I couldn't tell you what color the towels were. All I knew was that they were soft, similar to the feel of silk. I wouldn't be surprised if they were. Caroline seems to have a lot of money even though they live in a townhouse. She seems like the kind of person who spends it on exotic trips and expensive household items like the silk towels.

"Enjoying yourself, Gwen?" Ricky asked from the other side of the door. He was laughing so hard I wouldn't be surprised to see tears coming out of his eyes. I'm not going to lie, his laugh had a nice gentleness to it. That definitely helped me remain calm.

"Actually, I am. I found a wallet in here!" The second he opened the door I threw the towels right in his face and ran out. I bolted down the stairs to hear the front door being unlocked. Oh, thank God! Ms. Knoll!

"Oh, hi honey how was your-" I cut her off by giving her a gigantic hug. She awkwardly patted my back in response.

"I can't take the job," I told her, looking around to make sure Ricky wasn't there. I looked back to her eyes and saw that she was.... crying? I blinked, and yes, she was definitely crying.

"Are you alright?" I asked, unsure if I'd done something wrong.

"I-It's just that.... I ca-can never keep anyone a-around because of that boy. He dr-drives everyone away!" she exclaims sadly, throwing up her hands in defeat. I looked at her and then at the stains on my fingers from the paint Ricky and I ended up throwing at each other earlier. I smiled at the thought of getting some in his perfect dirty blonde hair.

"I'll stay," I said, trying to convince myself that I wasn't putting my life in danger.

"Are you sure you don't mind dealing with his.... unique personality?" She said that in a way to try and convince herself that her son wasn't a psychotic miscreant. I smiled at the challenge.

"No, I don't mind." I pointed to the tray of cookies.

What? I wanted something for all of my troubles. She laughed and gave me the entire tray.

Walking home I kept replaying one question in my mind, what have I gotten myself into?

5 DAY ONE

"Responsibility is the price of freedom."
– Elbert Hubbard

My mom had to drive me to school today, and it was *great*. That was sarcasm, by the way.

Not riding has probably been the hardest thing for me. Not even 24 hours have passed since Amber broke my hand, and she hasn't spoken a word to me. We've seen each other in the hallway and in class but she hasn't said a thing. I kept replaying what happened at my locker in my mind and the only thing that I could think of that would encourage her to do that would be the car crash.

Two years ago, Mason Doe, Amber's 3-year-old cousin, died in a horrible car accident. I believe it was a Saturday and it could've easily been the worst day of my life. I was there for the accident and to this day, Amber blames me for his death. It wasn't my fault, for the record. I had gotten into an argument with my father so I went for a ride. I was riding my motorcycle and all of a sudden, this little strawberry blonde boy comes running out onto the street. I expertly dodged him but ended up braking too fast and flying into a nearby tree. I looked down at my hands and all I had was a splinter and dislocated thumb, but when I turned to the road.... the sight almost made me faint.

The guy behind me was in this huge pickup truck and didn't see Mason. It really wasn't his fault. That was until he drove away. He kept driving like nothing happened and he left me there with this dead toddler. Of course, it looked like I did it. I was flung up into a tree and my hair and clothing were all disheveled. The cops came, and I didn't have it in me to leave. I knew it would probably get me in even more trouble if I did, so I stayed. I told the police my version of what happened and they were actually starting to believe me. That was until Amber came running out and made up this ridiculous story. She started making up this version of what happened that made me look terrible. I tried to tell the officers that she wasn't outside when it happened but it didn't help anything. Of course, they believed the rich girl.

I got taken down to the station and I honestly thought that was it. I thought they would charge me with vehicular homicide and then close the case. Thank God for Amber's neighbors though. They had recently installed security cameras because their packages were being stolen. The cameras proved that I wasn't the cause of the accident. The cameras caught the license plate of the truck, but the man was never identified. It's sad that Mason still hasn't gotten justice, but at least everyone knows it wasn't me. Well, everyone except Amber and whoever was stupid enough to believe her. Since the video only involved Mason's immediate family, Amber didn't see it. To this day, she's always believed that I was the one who killed Mason Doe.

Long story short, she has me on her death wish list. I'm just lucky she didn't slam my head in the locker. Standing there again made me cringe. Everything except for the noticeable dent in the locker door looked normal. When I looked up, the devil incarnate was standing there. I tried hard to ignore her and fight down the uneasiness that was settling over me. Rolling my eyes, I turned to face her.

"What do you possibly want from me now, Amber? You've gotten what you wanted haven't you?"

She was standing there looking as shocked as ever. I waved my hand in her face to get her to snap out of it. Amber blinked and finally opened her mouth to speak.

"That's all you have to say? I did all of that stuff to you and you are doing NOTHING?" She asked so quickly and quietly that I had to re-run what she said in my head. She looked like she was yelling but it came out as a whisper.

I took a deep breath and answered honestly. "I've decided that I'm tired. I'm a 17 going on 18-year-old girl who is tired of fighting. I don't care about any of the people in this godforsaken place and honestly, I can't wait to leave. I'm sick of getting you back for things that you can't help. Nothing that I do is ever going to change the fact that you are a wicked human being who doesn't care about anyone else but herself." I slammed my locker and winced. The sound alone was enough to scare me. It reminded me of the pain that came when she slammed the door yesterday. It was the kind of pain that you can hear. The kind that you hear and look around to see whom was inflicted upon until you realize that it was you who'd gotten hurt.

I turned to walk away when I noticed the same crowd from yesterday. I didn't look at anyone, just the door to my first period class. I could feel Jay's eyes but decided every time I needed his help, he was never there. He needs to stop trying so hard to save someone who needed his help years ago. The infamous popular boy falling in love with the outcast just couldn't happen here. So, at this point, I was counting down the days until graduation.

The bell sounded signaling my freedom. I was given a note today to go to the principal's office after class so I headed there. I passed many people but no one said anything to me. In case you haven't noticed, that is very unusual especially when I pass the football team. I usually got something from them. From the outside looking in, it would look as if Jay was trying to keep the team's attention off of me. In my opinion, he wants attention from people in the hallway because he hasn't been getting any from me. It must be tiring to be him. He's lived, practically bathed, in attention since he was 6. He probably doesn't know any other life.

"Come on in, Gwen. It's so nice to see you again," Principal Sims said happily, ushering me into a chair he had in his office. I smiled awkwardly while taking my seat. I've literally never been in here so, naturally, I was a little worried and confused as to why he said it was nice to see me *again*. Shifting in my seat, I took in his unwelcoming office. It was a classic office that revolved around the glossy, copper brown desk sitting in the middle of the room. Every piece of furniture centered around the desk that ultimately belonged to our esteemed principal. You could tell, just by looking at the cheesy inspirational quotes hanging on the walls, that he needed other people and things to make him feel good about himself. The self-confidence wasn't there all on its own.

"Yeah, so Gwen. Do you know why you are here?" He asked, looking at me as if I was a one million-piece puzzle. I nervously shook my head and adjusted the cushion that was under my butt. It was easily the hardest cushion I have ever sat on. Could it be a brick?

"Well, I have called you in here to ask about your parking spot outside. I haven't seen you on your motorcycle lately so I was wondering if you still needed it? I have this *friend* that is planning on visiting me every-" I interrupted him.

"Wait. So, you called me in here to ask me about my parking spot outside? You don't have anything to say about, I don't know, Amber or me or AMBER?" I asked incredulously. I cannot believe this is the conversation we're having.

"Oh yeah. How are you doing with that? I watched the security video and laughed hysterically when you ruined her shirt. That was priceless. By far my favorite part of the entire thing." I sat there and stared at him. I stared at him for some time, trying to determine if he was being serious. Do you ever look at someone and silently wonder who you are looking at? Well that's exactly what's happening to me. Who are you, and what have you done with Principal Sims?

"Have a great day Mr. Sims," I said quietly as I stood to leave.

"Oh, you too Gwen. And just let me know what you decide about your parking space." He waved to me as I turned and left. I walked all the way home, skipping the bus I was scheduled to take. I'm not in the mood to deal with people today so avoiding the bus was mandatory.

I'm not sure if this has ever been something you've thought of, but more often than not I try to understand why people make life so hard for others. I get the whole *'I'm insecure and I need attention'* thing but isn't there some other way they can get it? "What do we live for, if it is not to make life less difficult for each other?" George Eliot wrote that. I actually put that as my wallpaper on my phone. Sometimes, I just look at it and wonder why people can't listen to him? Why can't people want to make life better? Why don't they want to make other's smile?

"Oh, honey how was school today? Weren't you supposed to take the bus?" I walked through my front door to find Jerry and my mother in the front foyer. I gave Jerry a fake smile and shrugged as the answer to my mom's question.

"Oh, dear, don't forget that today is your first scheduled day with Ricky. Caroline asked that you be there at 3:50 today just because it's your first day. I hope you don't mind me saying something to Caroline about you? I thought you would be great for the job and I know you'd appreciate the money while you're out of commission," my mother said, smiling at me I imagine. I have my back to her but I'd bet a lot of money she was smiling. She always does when Jerry comes over.

"Okay Mom." I ran up the stairs and went straight for the safe underneath my bed. The money I have in my bank account are my savings that I do not want to touch. I can touch this money though. I opened the safe and found $255.32 in it. Great.

The upgrade I want to give my motorcycle is closer to $1,000. Yes, Mom, I am grateful for the job.

I shoved the box back underneath my bed and put on my earphones, blasting the music in my ears as I did my homework. I try to laugh at the pointlessness of my homework, but I can't. They, being the teachers, act like we can't remember this stuff from 3 hours ago and it drives me crazy. I usually get it all done at school but today was my adjustment day. I had to figure out how to function with one working hand.

I looked to my clock and found that it read 3:45. How is that even possible?

Oh yeah. I walked home from school.

I closed my homework folder and put on a black romper and my black shades. I needed to look as unapproachable as possible. Hopefully, this way, Ricky would give me a break.

My determination was radiating off of me as I made my way over to Caroline's house. I gave the door a single knock and within seconds there she appeared. Her blonde hair was tied into a tight bun to keep it off the shoulders of her (very tight) pencil dress.

"Hello Ms. Knoll!" I said happily, genuinely excited to see her. There was something so pleasant about seeing Caroline Knoll.

"Why hello, dear. Come on in, Ricky should be coming down the elevator any moment now. I'm going to head out, and as I texted you, I shall be back around 9." She gave me a little pat on the shoulder before leaving the house. As I waited for him I pulled out my folder full of pictures I took of people around town. These people will never know that I took pictures of them and I think that that's why I love the photos so much. The people are real, but I've already said that, haven't I?

"Did you take those?" I jumped and dropped all of my pictures at the sound of a low silky voice coming from behind me. I turned around, blinking furiously to see Ricky sitting in his wheelchair right behind the couch. I wanted to slap him. I really did, but I didn't.

"What the heck, dude?" I asked, giving him one of my iconic grimaces as I bent down to pick them up. I picked up the pictures and put them back in my folder, angry at the fact that they were now out of order.

"I was just wondering if you took those?" He said as he changed his voice from curious to unenthusiastic, almost like he forgot that he was supposed to be repulsive and arrogant in the first place. I turned to face him. He was extremely close to me because he was leaning over to look at the pictures. That's when I noticed something.

His disability prevents him from exercising his lower body but his upper body was great. Considering everything he's gone through he looked amazing. His blonde hair looked healthy. He looked everything but pale. And I'm not going to lie, he could definitely pull off a tight fitted shirt.

He raised one of his eyebrows at my obvious staring. I looked into his eyes and immediately regretted every decision I had made in the last 30 seconds. He clearly knew what I was thinking, and he clearly liked it. I rolled my eyes at him and stood up. I know it's mean to use my ability to stand against him, but hey, a girl has got to do what a girl has got to do.

"Yes. I did. And I would appreciate it if you didn't make me drop them ever again," I said trying to sound as calm and composed as possible. There are three things in this world that I do not allow to be messed with. My mom. My motorcycle. My photos.

He put his hands up in surrender. "It was just a question. They're not horrible." He smirked and wheeled over to the TV. The funny thing was that he thought his comment was an insult. I chose to take it as a compliment.

"That might be the nicest thing you've said to me. I actually took these a-" He cut me off, quite rudely might I point out.

"Yeah I don't care. All I said was that they weren't terrible. There are definitely things you could work on. The depth of some of the pictures is questionable and your focus is a little off. It's almost as if you are pointing the camera at the people but the camera is only focused on parts of their body."

"Well yeah that is kind of the point. If you notice, the parts that the camera are focused on, their faces and their hands, are the most.... wait. You know about photography?" I asked dumbfounded.

"Everyone *knows* about photography, genius. I just have a more intricate understanding of it," he said shrugging and pointing to the remote that was sitting inconveniently on top of the TV. I crossed my arms and waited for him to ask me politely for it. If he thinks that I was just going to go wherever he pointed to then he had another thing coming.

"May I PLEASE have the remote?" he asked. He was clearly annoyed and do you know what I've decided? I like it.

"Sure." I handed him the remote and sat on the couch farthest away from him, a satisfied smile plastered on my face. I watched as he scrolled to the channel that 'American Ninja Warrior' was on.

"You like this show?" I asked, still not understanding why he watched something that revolved around the two body parts he couldn't move.

"I love this show," he said with conviction.

"But...." My voice trailed off as I tried to put my thoughts to words. I don't know how to ask him without hurting his feelings.

"You're wondering why a cripple watches a show that he could never compete on," he said as more of a statement than a question.

"Well I wouldn't call you a crip-"

"But you were thinking it. It's okay Gwen. I didn't expect you to be different than everyone else. I love watching it because it gives me good ideas. I have great upper body strength so I do shorter obstacle courses that don't require use of my legs." He turned to look at me, and I saw nothing. His eyes weren't filled with anything. The normal edge that was normally there, was gone. The mischievousness, was gone. The judgement, that was gone too. He looked empty. Seeing him like that made me realize just how uncomfortable that made me. I didn't like it at all. I didn't like it because a normal person would be sad to admit that they were "a cripple". They would be sad if they thought I thought they were incapable of one of their childhood dreams. He, though, looked unfazed. He looked as if it didn't hurt him in the slightest.

"Okay then, Ricky, show me how strong you are." I crossed my arms, challenging him.

"Excuse me?" His eyes finally came back. That's exactly what I'm looking for. He looked amused and perplexed. How lovely.

"You have cerebral palsy. You're not deaf. Show me what you've got. Unless you don't think you can." I smirked and looked at my nails, acting as if there was no part of me that thought he was strong. That's when I heard his wheels begin to roll.

I followed him into this downsized exercise room that was filled with upper body equipment. It took me a minute to realize that he was in the middle of the room tying his legs together.

"Yeah, what are you doing?" I asked utterly shocked.

"Showing you what I've got." He got himself onto a bench press and strapped himself onto it. Tightening his hands around the bar he proceeded to lift 300lbs! My jaw must've hit the floor because when put the weight back on its stand he smiled at me. I watched as he wiped his hands on his sweatpants acting as if that was nothing.

"You.... I just.... but...." I finally gave up trying to describe what I just saw and put my face in my hands. After a few seconds, I smiled sadly as I realized just how much I underestimated him.

"I know it's a lot to comprehend especially for someone as incompetent as you. It's okay really," he said cockily.

"I'm going to pretend like I didn't hear that and just say wow!"

Shrugging, he got his legs untied and back into his wheelchair. I left him in the exercise room to go get his medications from the kitchen cabinet.

I, ultimately, had to read the letter Ms. Knoll left for me again because I couldn't remember exactly how many pills he was supposed to take.

I handed him 8 pills and a glass of water along with his dinner. He ate breakfast food for almost every meal. Once in a while he would have mac and cheese but that was only when he was, and I quote, 'feeling it'.

He gave me a sorry excuse for a thank you and wheeled over to his spot in front of the TV. We, yet again, were watching American Ninja Warrior.

"Could we watch another show?" I asked politely, deciding that I should try to 'kill him with kindness'.

"I thought you were being paid to make sure I don't try and kill myself again, forget to eat, or forget my medications. Am I or am I not correct with that assumption?"

I almost did a spit-take when I heard the first thing he said. I didn't know that he tried to kill himself. You know, one would think that the mother of the teenage boy I am watching would tell me that her son tried to KILL himself BEFORE I took the job.

"By the look on your face, I'm guessing she didn't tell you," he said as more of a statement than a question. I'm noticing that he does that a lot.

"She forgot to mention it, yes," I said trying to stay calm and not freak out at the fact that I am watching a suicidal teenage boy. He pulled back the sleeve he had covering his left arm to show me a 5-inch scar running from the base of his wrist to the middle of his forearm. I almost choked on the Cherry Coke I was drinking.

"Yeah well, anyway, I thought that was all you were hired for."

"Yeah, I guess you're right.... I'm sorry." I stood up and left for the loft. I read while I waited for him to finish his food and meds. I was a little hurt at how he talked to me, but now that I think about it, I couldn't imagine being him. Stuck in a wheelchair forever. That is some fate.

About an hour passed when I decided that I would go check on him. His plate was empty and his pills were gone so I took his dishes away. I brought him back a fresh glass of water and took away the old one. As I was leaving I could've sworn that I heard him mumble '*thank you*'. I smiled at the thought as I left the room.

Before I knew it, Caroline was walking through the door. I said my hellos and goodbyes and made my way home. Hopefully tomorrow will go better. Who knows, maybe I could find a way to make Ricky smile.

6 SURPRISINGLY ENOUGH

"It takes one person to forgive. It takes two people to reunite." – Lewis B. Smedes

I woke up with a smile on my face. My hand wasn't hurting. I got paid $150 last night. I was in a great place. Briskly putting on a navy-blue dress, I grabbed a pair of black socks and put on a choker. With my teeth already brushed I grabbed a cup of coffee from my mother's machine. I'm not a huge coffee drinker but sometimes I just feel like something warm. Now if there was hot chocolate.... that would be a game changer.

"Someone looks happy this morning," my mother said, smiling at her realization. I looked at her from the kitchen table, got up, and gave her a big hug.

"I'm sorry Mom," I said into my mother's hair. She hugged me a little tighter before pulling back.

"For what, honey?" She asked, brushing some of my hair behind my ear.

"I feel like I haven't been talking to you enough

lately, and I'm sorry. I don't want you to feel like I am forgetting you or anything. I love you Mom." She smiles sadly before speaking again.

"I never thought that Gwen. I know you do and I love you too." We both smiled at each other and sat down at the kitchen table. I grabbed my waffles from the toaster and put them on a plate. I lazily poured a small amount of syrup on them while I grabbed an apple. My mother usually doesn't eat until she drops me off, so we sat there with the gentle sound of the radio playing in the background as I ate.

I hopped into my mom's car, and for once, I was glad that she was driving me. I didn't feel embarrassed. I was calm for once. I was calm, and I liked it.

Walking into school, with a big smile plastered on my face, I decided that I was going to have a good day. I got to my locker and got my science textbooks out before making my way to 1st period.

Another boring and uneventful morning passed, and it was time for lunch. I made my way to my tree when I saw a boy sitting underneath it. As I got closer I realized exactly who it was.

"Trey?" I called, totally surprised to see him here. He was the boy I met at the pizza place on Saturday.

"Hey," he said, walking closer to me. I stopped walking towards him, a little unsettled to see him here.

"What are you doing here?" I asked him backing up slightly. He took a step towards me before stopping, realizing that I was uneasy. He put his hands up as if he was surrendering before he continued.

"I came to see you."

"How did you find me?"

"Come on Gwen, you know me." I stared at him trying to figure out who he could be. Oh my god. I used everything inside of me to keep the embarrassment of not recognizing him off of my face. Tyler Curtis. I smiled and walked up to him, giving him a hug as soon as I put my food down. The second we touched, though, I regretted it. I regretted it because the second we touched it reminded me of what he did, and more importantly, how he hurt me.

"Ty! Why didn't you tell me it was you at the pizza place?" I asked, surprised that he hadn't mentioned it earlier. Ty was my only friend. He looked out for me and let me be his partner whenever we had classes together. He was always kind to me. He looked different back then though. He had big, chunky glasses and wore a lot more sweaters. Even his hair was different. He had curls and let's just say he hadn't exactly gotten the memo about Proactiv. He never came to school his senior year, so I haven't seen him in a while. He had this dream that he would become a male model, and honestly, I could believe it. I knew there was something familiar about him.

"Well, I didn't exactly recognize you at first, but when I did, I tried to tell you. You rode away!" He said chuckling, as he remembered our encounter at the pizza place. I blushed as I realized how flirtatious I was being with him.

"Yeah, that was funny. But wait. You asked me about my bike. I thought you knew I rode? And that name? What's that all about?" I said, confused by all of the changes.

"I remember you practicing on Jett's bike. This one is different. Or at least, it looks it. And the name.... My manager told me that I should have a stage name if you will. They switched the letters in Tyler, used my middle name as my last, and randomly threw in III to make it sound more sophisticated," he said, shamefully, leaning back on the tree I have eaten lunch at for three years now.

"Well, I'm sorry about the new name you were given. On the bright side whatever job you have seems to be making you a lot of money! I've been kick-boxing to make money. I actually used the money I made to buy a new bike and upgrade a few things, including the color," I said, picking up my lunch and taking a sip of my drink.

"Well, it looks great! So, do you! I'm loving the new hair style," he says brushing some of my hair behind me ear. I smiled at his compliment, remembering how he use to do that to me when he was here. "And kick-boxing? Wow!"

I guess he's surprised.

"Yeah, it's sort of a pastime. I always have had this fear of surprise attacks, so I thought it would be good to learn self-defense. I eventually just said, hey, why not learn self-defense and make money at the same time?" I explained. "But enough about me, what about you? Did you get into the modeling industry like you always wanted to?" I asked, genuinely curious at his progress since the last time I saw him.

"Yeah, I did actually," he said, smiling and rubbing the back of his neck. I laughed and playfully punched him in the arm.

"Look at you becoming all famous and stuff. I'm so

happy for you, really Ty! That's great!" I said, smiling a very big one I can only imagine. He smiled back and we just stood there for a few minutes, smiling at each other.

"It really isn't that big a deal. I've done a few shoots for Vogue, People Magazine, and Michael Kors but you know it's whatever...." He shrugged as if that wasn't a big deal. I jumped into a hug when I heard about all of his accomplishments.

"What are you talking about? That's AMAZING?! Dude you're famous! Do you NOT get that?" I asked him, totally not understanding how he could be so nonchalant about this. He is a rising male model.

"I don't know Gwen. My dad still doesn't understand why I haven't come to work for him." Ty's dad has always tried to get him to take over his company but Ty doesn't want that. His mother died when he was 14 and ever since then his father has turned into this control freak who thinks of Ty as more of a little robot than anything else. You don't even know how happy I am for him that he escaped his father, well at least somewhat escaped. The only thing is that, in the process of him escaping his dad, he also left me behind. I have mixed emotions about the whole thing.

"You know what I think, Ty? He is just jealous about how far you've come and nothing you do can change that. You need to focus on continuing to grow and planning your next moves in the modeling industry. I have every faith in you that you will make it to the top. I wouldn't be surprised if you make it to Armani, Ty." He smiled at me before giving me one more hug.

"I've missed you, Gwen. I'll come back and visit, okay? Oh, and put your number in." He handed me his phone, and I handed him mine. We exchanged numbers and he headed for his car. I hadn't noticed the sleek, black Porsche sitting on the side of the road waiting for him. Ty gave me a final wave before hopping into his car. I'm proud and upset all at the same time. The familiarity of Ty leaving brings back a lot of memories.

I watched as his car turned down the street and eventually out of view. However, that didn't stop him from texting me.

Ty: *Hey Gwen, I was thinking that we could meet up at the pizza place and talk some more ;) It would be great to catch up!*

Reading his text, I noticed the last time we spoke was two years and ten days ago. The day I found out he had left. That was also the day I deleted his phone number and threw out the keepsake box he had given me.

Maybe tying loose ends would be good. I still have a lot to get off of my chest and I'm sure he does too.

Me: *Sure. How does Sunday sound?*

I waited a few seconds before I heard the ring once again.

Ty: *6, It's a date!*

Me: *Cool.*

I threw out my lunch. I didn't have enough time to eat it. Heading back in the building, I couldn't fight back the feeling that maybe I was making the wrong decision by agreeing to meet up with him. Two years can change a person and that would go both ways.

When I finished my homework I still had half an hour before I had to go over to Ricky's so I decided to watch an episode of Tom and Jerry. Yes, I am a 17-year-old girl who likes Tom and Jerry. Don't judge.

When the commercials came on, I muted the TV in my room and took out my folder full of photos. I was studying a picture I took of the homeless woman in our town square. She really is the sweetest thing. I try to give her some money every week after my tournaments. It's only $15 but I feel the need to give her something.

As I placed the photo in the back of the pile I spotted a picture of a fox in the woods. I didn't even remember taking that shot. Searching for a date, I turned it over and discovered big black letters that read:

This is how your camera should focus. ~ Ricky Wondering when Ricky slipped the fox picture into my folder, I smiled at the thought of him going into the woods to take this for me. That is, unless he just got it off of Google Images. I shrugged it off as I put the photos away and turned off Tom and Jerry.

Slipping on a pair of Converse, I made my way over to Ricky's. Caroline explained there was no need to ring the doorbell, so I always give a quick knock and walk inside. Ricky was sitting right there. I jumped, not expecting someone to be staring at me when I came in.

"You're late," he says monotonously.

"It's 4:01, Ricky," I say, pointing to the clock on the wall.

"And what time are you supposed to get here?"

"I mean, 4, but that is literally only a 60 second difference. I reall-"

"So, you're late," he says, refusing to back down as he folded his arms across his chest. I crossed my arms and rolled my eyes, making the wise decision to ignore his inability to say anything nice. I walked into the kitchen and opened the refrigerator door. Caroline had asked me if there was something I liked to drink. I told her Cherry Coke, of course.

I took a sip and totally forgot about what Ricky was saying. It's just so good. It is the soda of soda. It is...

"Are you the reason why my mother has like 10 cases of that stuff now?" He asks, completely interrupting my thoughtful moment. I let out a sigh of frustration and shrug.

"Maybe, maybe not. All I know is that I love it, and if she says I can drink it then I am going to drink it!" I put my finger up to stop him from talking. I knew exactly what he was going to say. "And if you say I can't drink it anymore then I will duct tape your mouth shut whenever I come over here. I will stop at 7-11 every day if I have to. I love it. Don't question it." I spun on my heels and went into the family room. I waited to hear the sound of his wheels before I mentioned the photo.

"You know, I saw the picture of the fox. That was very sweet of you," I said, smirking at his obvious discomfort.

"I was just trying to show you how it's done," he says, trying hard to sound tough. I walk over to him and poke him in the shoulder.

"You know what I think? I believe you like my company and enjoy every second I'm here. I would even go as far as to say that you like me."

"You couldn't be more wrong. You are literally the epitome of annoyance. Every night I hear your shrill voice ringing in my ears before I go to sleep," he says cockily. That makes my smirk grow even wider.

"So, what you're saying is that you think about me

before you go to sleep? Wow, Ricky, I don't know what to say. I never knew you cared so much!" I exclaimed, joyfully throwing my hands together. He whipped his head around and rolled as fast as possible to the exercise room. He looked pissed, so I thought it'd be best if I just let him be for a while.

Thirty minutes later I quietly walked in to find Ricky exercising while wearing his earphones. What a perfect opportunity to show him just how amazing my candid pictures are! I grabbed my camera. Determined to show him how wrong he was about my focus, I hid behind the couch and used the glass French doors to my advantage. Some pictures included the French doors and others only revealed Ricky. I was really proud of everything I shot and thrilled that he had no idea I was taking pictures. These photos will create an amazing collage!

I walked away and put the camera back underneath my leather jacket on the side table. Turning on the television, I sat down on the couch and scrolled through channels till I found NBCSN. This channel was the one that showed motorcycle racing so I watched it a lot. I always love to watch the professionals ride because it gives me ideas for tricks and skills I could try to learn. I taught myself a lot of what I know. Besides YouTube, I really haven't had any other guidance on how to ride. Well, when I had my bike I didn't have any guidance. Before I got my bike, I got a lot of inspiration from my brother, Jett. He was an amazing rider and an even better teacher. He could do all of these tricks and he reached speeds past 150mph! He was everything to me and then, one day, he never came home. We called the police and tried for almost a year to find him. I called him three times every day for a year and a half. The calls went straight to voicemail every time until one day it didn't go through at all. The police said that after a certain amount of time we just had to accept that he was, most likely, dead. I still think that is a load of garbage but they dropped the case. He disappeared two years ago, right after I got my bike.

For the longest time, I told myself that I wouldn't change a single thing about the bike because that bike was the one my brother picked out for me. He even stitched his signature into the side of the seat and helped me pay for it. But then I finally decided that my brother wouldn't want me to hold back from doing things just because he was gone. That was the day I cut my hair, changed the color of my bike, and upgraded the wheels. I got the seat raised slightly so I would sit higher and lean over more and that was that. I became one step closer to moving on.

"And here comes Wade Osborn down the turnpike. Look at that! A perfect drift! Yes, Carl, you know....," The TV practically screamed at me. I rolled my eyes at the sight of Wade when he got off of his motorcycle and took off his helmet. His whole presence just screams, "I think I'm the best so treat me better than everybody else!" I hate it. I'm not going to say he's not a good rider. He is, no doubt, but he doesn't deserve so much attention. He doesn't deserve it at all.

"Motorcycles, huh?" I jumped at the sound of Ricky next to me. I turned to him and punched him in the arm.

"What the HECK, dude?! I've told you not to sneak up on me." He laughed for five minutes straight before responding.

"And I've chosen not to listen. Sucks, doesn't it?" He raises an eyebrow at the screen when he notices what was playing. I'm not sure why, I think it's pretty self-explanatory. There are motorcycles, and a track, and two black and white checkered flags stationed at a red line. I'm not sure what doesn't scream RACING?

"What is it, Ricky?" I asked, hopefully in a way that made me sound annoyed.

"You never answered me the first time I asked. You're into motorcycles?"

"You haven't seen me riding around here? We live right next door! That metallic colored FZ-07 outside doesn't ring any bells?"

"Nope, not one," he says turning to face me.

"I know that's a lie because I've seen from standing by this window before," I say, crossing my arms. He must be blind or something because my parking space is in clear sight from Ricky's living room.

"I don't usually keep the blinds open, so I rarely see outside." I look at him with my eyebrows probably touching my hairline. He must be kidding.

"You can't be serious? You must've seen it when you've gone outside."

"I don't really go outside. I haven't gone outside much in probably three years. Well, except for when I go to my doctors' appointments and… when I took that picture of the fox." I started to choke when I heard what he said. That isn't living.

"Oh Ricky.... we are definitely going to fix that," I said, already starting to brainstorm ideas about how to get him outside.

What can I say? I love a challenge. I love a challenge

especially when it's for the purpose of helping someone as unique as Ricky. I know it's only been a few days but I have this feeling like I've known him my entire life. He reminds me of Jett. I've even found myself.... happier. Yeah, like smiling more which is totally not what I am used to doing. Everything in my life has been so scrambled and hectic, so for me to even feel like smiling lately is like one in a million, but Ricky has done it.

Surprisingly enough, Ricky Doone has made me smile more than I have in the last two years.

7 PLANNING

"A goal without a plan is just a wish."

Finishing this school day was at the top of my priority list because I needed to plan. Ricky told me yesterday that he's barely been outside in three years. That should be illegal in my opinion. I was shocked when he explained that he only recently went outside for about ten minutes to take the fox picture. I'm glad he got outside because of me but ten minutes is not enough. So, in order to fix this problem, I've been trying hard to figure out a way to get him on my bike. I can almost guarantee that he'll like the idea.

I look down at the math worksheet I've been working on and realize that I've finished it. I pass it in 20 minutes early, as usual, and have time to kill. Luckily, Mr. Rodgers is pretty laid back when it comes to free time so I pulled out my personal notebook and started planning the day trip for Ricky. People around me noticed how intent I was and decided to check out my project. Normally I would make a flip comment about how big their eyes were or how they must not have good control over their body parts, but today I was content just thinking about Ricky. He's taught me to value the things that I take for granted every day. I mean, I know that my family life has always been shaky, but at least I have my outlets. My bike being the main one. Ricky, though, he has it hard. He can't go anywhere without letting his mother know and all he's known is that little townhouse. He's made me realize that I may not have special spots underneath a tree or a room that I call safe, but I have my motorcycle. I have my photography too. He's made me realize that I have my own luxuries. He's never experienced anything that truly feels like his own, and I have promised myself that I would help change that for him.

The bell rang, and I quickly packed up everything. I was hurrying out the door when one of Amber's "puppets" tripped me. I dropped my notebook and all of the papers went flying. Luckily, it's Friday so everyone will forget about this by the time Monday rolls around, but right now, I feel like I'm on national television. I looked up and glared into McKenna Hoover's eyes. Awkwardly picking up my papers and shoving them into the folder, I noticed my notebook dangling from McKenna's newly polished claws.

"Give it back," I bark.

"Who's Ricky? He your boyfriend?" Only a millisecond passes before she collects one of her thoughts that could only spawn in the gutters of New York City.

"Actually, you wouldn't have one so he's probably getting paid," she chuckles and gets others to chime in.

"I'm going to ask for it one more time. If I get to a third time I'll be walking away with *two* broken hands," I say, low and venomously. She rolls her eyes and throws the notebook at me. I catch it with ease and watch her, eyeing every move she makes carefully.

"So, Amber really did break your hand! Wow, you must be feeling pretty crappy right now!" she said smiling as if that realization was a joyous one.

" I'm surprised that she hasn't broken one of your bones yet, considering the fact that you cheated with her boyfriend," I said, shrugging as if everyone already knew that (I knew for a fact that they didn't.) I heard a few gasps and watched as she looked around worriedly.

"Oh, you did not just say that!" She said, raising her voice in disbelief.

"Oh, I think I did Mickey." I knew she hated that nickname so I was just waiting for her to pounce. I had learned over the years that the pain that hurts the most is the pain that comes unexpectedly. For a while, I have been channeling all of the arguments and confrontations I have with people down one path; the path that leaves the other person seething exactly when I want them to. That way I was expecting whatever was coming for me.

I counted to three before she charged at me. I moved to the left by a number of inches and watched as she jumped right into the beige lockers behind me. I smiled at everyone as I left the building, the sound of her angry screams echoing off the walls as I walked away.

Every Friday, Darren picks me up, so I sit on the bench outside to wait for him. Pulling out my phone and opening Scrabble I hear heels start clacking behind me. I guess this is the second defense line.

"Amber, what is it?" I asked, bored already of her company.

"I saw what you did to McKenna. I don't think it's nice of you to take out your anger towards me on her," she said crossing her legs and arms simultaneously. I rolled my eyes at how stupid and naïve Amber sounded.

"I know that this is hard for you to comprehend, but not everything is about you. I was actually in a very good mood today until she purposefully tripped me and took my notebook away. I don't stand for crap like that, Amber. I wasn't taking anything out on anyone. I was standing up for myself." I looked her straight in the eyes before turning back to the road, wishing that Darren was here already.

"Well, I didn't know that," she said as if that would make anything in this situation better. She jumped to conclusions, just like she normally does. I didn't answer her. I just looked down to my phone and waited for *GamerLion5437* to finish his turn. I heard her take a deep breath before continuing.

"I'm sorry, okay. I've been going through some crap right now and I just-" This is where I cut her off.

"You know, you had me there for a second. I almost believed that you were apologizing. Man, that's funny," I said, smiling sarcastically.

"I was," she said angrily.

"No, you weren't, Amber. You were trying to get me to feel badly for you. Instead of just dropping it at, *I'm sorry*, you had to continue on about all of your problems. I'm sorry you're going through crap right now, but the reality is, we all are. You broke my hand. I don't think what you're going through can measure up to what I am. My hand won't stop shaking and I'm worried that I won't be able to take pictures the same ever again. My motorcycle connects me to my brother, one of the few people I could count on. My way of making money involves both of my hands, and do you know what? I don't have them because of you. And then, when I go to sleep to try and escape it all, I worry about waking up because it's hard for me to even get ready in the morning." I took a deep breath before continuing, "Amber, I think you should go back to your puppets and football players. You're better at talking to people who don't have any trace of a conscience." Tears threatened to fill my eyes, but I willed them to stay back. I was not going to cry in front of this.... this.... this thing. I refuse to. She looked at me, almost as if she was hurt, but walked away in the end. I turned to see Darren pulling into the parking lot. I ran to his car and jumped in, slamming the door behind me, ready to shut her out of my life forever. Right now, Ricky was all I wanted to be thinking about. Darren could tell I wasn't in the mood to talk. He smiled reassuringly as we listened to Trina in the backseat.

"Thanks, Ren!" I waved to Trina in the backseat as I nodded to Darren. It's nice to have people in your life who understand that, sometimes, you just aren't in the mood to talk.

"Bye, Gwenny!" Trina yelled from her car seat. I smiled at her and opened the back door, leaning over to give her a hug. She laughed as I tickled her.

It always makes me feel good to see the two of them.

My mother wasn't home when Darren dropped me off so I blasted the radio. She's never been one to understand why I like music so loud. My taste in music doesn't appeal to her either so I try to keep the loud music to a minimum. If she only knew how therapeutic music was for me.

I glanced at my phone ~ 30 minutes until I needed to head to Ricky's. I wrote down an idea for a schedule. I'm hoping that my hand will be strong enough to ride safely in the very near future. I could ride right now if I really wanted to but the majority of the time I would be riding one handed. That is my mother's worst nightmare.

It only took fifteen minutes to plan out an entire day! A feeling of accomplishment came when I finished. I felt so excited and proud that I decided to go over to Ricky's house early. Nothing would've prepared me for what I walked in on.

8 RICKY'S REALITY

"Nothing destroys a relationship quicker than our fears of inadequacy and loss." – Bill Crawford

She's unexplainable. That's the only word I can use to describe her. After she left, my mother and I had a discussion about whether or not she would be good for the job. Of course, I said she was great! She's terrific except for the times when she makes me *feel* things I've never felt before.

The purpose of Gwen's first visit was primarily to meet with my mother, but she ended up staying for close to four hours. Let's just say those were the best four hours of my life. She talks to me as if I wasn't in a wheelchair. She doesn't underestimate me and doesn't degrade me. I love how she makes me feel like a regular guy and not some pathetic boy in a wheelchair. I've only known her for four hours but she is making me see things differently. I'll tell you one thing. I'm loving it. When I went to sleep, for once, I wasn't thinking about my legs and all of the things I can't do.

Two days have passed, and I miss her. Gwen shakes
up my life a bit. Makes it more bearable. I keep
replaying the four hours we spent together and I realized
that I actually laughed. After I threw that ice cube at her
we kept doing things to annoy each other. I waited
awhile to bug Gwen again just to give her a break. One
second I'm watching *American Ninja Warrior*, and the
next a large cup of ice is being poured down the back of
my shirt. I was definitely not expecting that. Following
her lead, I didn't react instantly. I waited probably thirty
minutes before I ripped out the old blue and red paint
and threw it at her in little water balloons. Somehow, she
managed to get blue paint in my hair. Then I pulled the
"I can't reach it" card" in retaliation, and she fell for it.
When she tried to grab the towel, I bumped my
wheelchair into her and slammed the door to the
bathroom closet. She was probably in there for a good
twenty-five minutes. That was until she said she found
the wallet I had been looking for for almost a year. It had
a picture inside of it that meant a lot to me. Anyway, it
was fun. It was nice to be myself for a day. Not the
Ricky who was in a wheelchair, just Ricky.

"Ricky, Gwen will be here in half an hour!" My
mother yelled to me from the kitchen. Oh yeah, it's
Wednesday, her first real day on the job! Thinking about
what I should wear, I wheeled over to the elevator and
went up to my room. I hated how long it took me to
change into jeans so I decided to put on a flannel shirt
and keep the sweat pants. At least I would look a little
more put together without the under shirt on.

"Hello, Ms. Knoll!" I heard Gwen's voice downstairs
and smiled. I really like her smile and the way her eyes

seem to light up whenever she does.

When I made my way downstairs I wheeled behind the couch to see Gwen flipping through a folder of photos that looked like her own. They were amazing! She really has a lot of talent to be taking photos like that, especially the candid ones. They're great! The way the light plays off of the people's faces makes it look like runway lights are in the background. She takes pictures of the most thoughtful people. I think that makes them so particularly appealing. Whoever looks at the pictures knows as much as the photographer about the personal life of the subject.... nothing. In one word: amazing.

But, she can't know that I think that.

"Did you take those?" I asked trying to sound like I didn't care. She jumped as soon as I spoke and I couldn't help but chuckle.

"What the heck, dude?!" She asked angrily as she bent down to pick up the photos. If I wasn't in this bloody chair I would've helped her, really, I would've.

"I was just wondering if you took those?" Every time I speak it's as if I'm in a movie acting as someone else. I sounded so unenthusiastic at the moment, and I hated how disappointed it seemed to make her. I didn't want her to realize that I actually think her photography is great. That would ruin the entire image I have going here, and besides, she's not going to stick around.

I was looking at her pictures when I realized she was looking at me. I hate it when she does that. It makes me feel like I'm on trial or something.

"Yes. I did. And I would appreciate it if you didn't make me drop them ever again," she said sounding very annoyed.

"It was just a question. They're not horrible." I smirked and wheeled over to the TV.

"That might be the nicest thing you've said to me. I actually took these a-" I cut her off. A part of me hurt when I noticed how sad that made her. Why is it so hard to treat her just like every other person who walks through that door?

"Yeah I don't care. All I said was that they weren't terrible. Besides, the depth of some of the pictures is questionable and your focus is a little off. It's almost as if you are pointing the camera at the people but the camera is only focused on parts of their bodies." I had to make up almost every flaw that I just stated. The truth was that I loved how she took her pictures. They make you focus on the things that are important on the human body. It's amazing, really, to see how her photos reflect what she finds interesting and they're worth a second glance.

"Well, yeah that's kind of the point. If you notice, the parts that the camera are focused on are their faces and their hands because those are the best.... wait. You know about photography?" She asked as if being a photographer was the craziest thing she'd ever heard of.

"Everyone *knows* about photography, genius. I just have a more intricate understanding of it," I said shrugging and pointing to the remote that was sitting inconveniently on top of the TV. I crossed my arms and waited for her to get it for me. I was going for the bratty wheelchair kid approach. She didn't move and that's when I realized this was going to be harder than I thought.

"May I PLEASE have the remote?" I responded trying to sound annoyed that she made me ask politely.

80

Honestly, if my mother was there, she would have expected nothing less from me.

"Sure." She smiled as she handed the remote to me. As I scrolled to *American Ninja Warrior* I realized something. I have tried so hard to get rid of every single caretaker, so being rude has always been second nature. It has been something that comes naturally because I have felt less than human for such a long time.... but Gwen, she doesn't ask me if watching TV is bad for my health. She doesn't ask me if drinking more than three glasses of water will drown me on the inside because of my disability. She treats me like I have feelings. It's funny because I almost forgot that I did.

"You like this show?" she asked. Now I wish I didn't have so many feelings.

"I love this show," I answered with conviction. Why can't I like this show? I mean, just because I'll never compete like that doesn't mean I can't watch it. I know for a fact that plenty of fat people watch the show. How am I any different from them?

"But....," her voice trailed off as she obviously tried to find a way to ask me the inevitable politely. That's when I knew I had to show her how naïve her doubts were. I don't mean to brag, but I am basically hulk in a wheelchair.

I woke up on Friday thinking about how, in the few days that I'd spent with Gwen, I'd actually gotten to know her a little bit. She didn't learn as much about me because I wouldn't let her. Either way, I still had fun. I had a fantastic time which means that this has to stop.

Sitting in my bed, I came to the realization that I

could never be good enough for Gwen. She has all this ambition and persistence while I can barely walk. I'm stuck with a life in my wheelchair. I am nothing compared to her, and I feel like it is selfish to distract her from all of the stuff she could be doing with her life. I can tell that Gwen will never be able to settle for anything less than what she wants. She explains everything that she loves to do as if she's known all along that those would be her passions. There is no uncertainty whatsoever. I have talked to many people in my life, believe it or not, and only a select few talk with the confidence that she does.

I got dressed at 6 am. My personal tutor wouldn't be coming until 10:00 but I felt like getting ready early. Maybe, it would distract me. Maybe I could get out of this "funk" as my mother calls it.

After my session was over I still felt the same way as I did earlier this morning. That means I was right earlier. I took my medications and soon after knew exactly what I had to do as her friend. I feel like if I were out of the picture it would give Gwen the nudge she needs to explore jobs outside of our small town. Hopefully my actions will prevent Gwen from doing what most kids in this town do ~ settle and never leave….

9 WHO GAVE YOU THAT IDEA

"Uncertainty is the most stressful feeling."

I rushed over to Ricky and slapped the pills and alcohol out of his hands. I picked up the bottle of Codeine and the glass of rum and put them both on the kitchen counter. I walked back over to stand in front of Ricky. Was that my prescription?

"WHAT ARE YOU DOING?!" My voice came out as an angry yell instead of a worried one. He looked up at me with tired eyes. I bent down so he wouldn't have to.

"Ricky, where is Caroline? I'm early today so she should still be here," I said, praying to God that she was still in this house. His hands were shaking so I took them in my own.

"I'm sorry Gwen," he said in a sad whisper. I kept shaking my head back and forth trying to come up with a better explanation as to what he was doing.

"Wh-what were you doing?" I asked, quietly-shakily.

"I was trying to free everyone," he said, even quieter

than the last time he spoke. I stood up and started to pace. I would've walked in on him dead if I hadn't come early. I realize slowly that I would've had to make the call and explain to the paramedics why his eyes wouldn't open.

"What are you talking about? Free everyone? Ricky!?" I yelled angrily. He jerked back at the sudden change in tone. I didn't mean to scare him but rather warn him that the next thing that came out of his mouth better be realistic and/or understandable.

"Everyone who has ever helped me has treated me like I was some robot. They shove pills at me without even telling me what they are giving me. They wheel me around without telling me where we are going. Some of them act like I am two years old. But you," He wheeled a little closer to me, "You treat me like I'm a human. You treat me right, and I don't deserve it." Tears were coming out of my eyes by this point. The sound of him being completely honest and believing what he just told me broke me inside. "I was trying to free you from me, Gwen. You don't deserve how I've been treating you." I shake my head violently as I try to physically shake the idea of him killing himself. I can't believe that this is what he thinks. He couldn't be more wrong.

"Ricky, I've loved working with you and to tell you the truth, thinking about coming here has made me smile even at school. You've made my life better, if anything. So, I don't want you to ever think like that again. Don't ever pull something like that Ricky," I said the last part as a demand to hopefully get the point across that I never want to walk in on him doing anything even remotely close to what he just did.

"But I don't treat you right," he said, shaking his head in confusion.

"And who told you that?"

"Well, no one, but I kno-" I cut him off.

"I've never thought that. Honestly, I was really starting to like getting to know you." I pulled out my notebook and opened to the page I had used to plan our little adventure. "This is the trip I was starting to plan for us to take. I was going to try and figure out a way that you could ride my motorcycle with me. I thought that would be something you could look forward to. It's just a rough plan so you can take everything with a grain of salt." I smiled, awkwardly fixing my hair as I watched him read over my plan.

He finished reading and looked up at me. I wasn't sure what he was thinking, but all I knew, was that it was scaring me.

"Ricky?" I asked, taking a step towards him.

"Thank you, Gwen. But, I can't accept this."

"What do you mean 'you can't accept it?'" I used air quotes to emphasize how stupid his words sounded.

"I don't deserve you or this trip," he said, breaking eye contact with me. I had stood up before but now I am practically at his feet, demanding that his eyes land on mine.

"And you don't get to decide what you deserve when it comes to me. Come into the kitchen with me." I made him follow me to the kitchen table. I opened the notebook to the planning page and pulled out the collage I made for him. I used the candid pictures that I had taken of him just the other day.

"I was going to show it to you when I was done, but

clearly you need a pick-me-up," I said chuckling at how bad the collage looked. "I know it's bad, and I know you don't love my work but I thought that-" he cut me off.

"See that's why I'm upset, Gwen. I put these horrible ideas in your head, and I feel terrible." I blinked at the sound of his voice.

"What do you mean horrible ideas? I love candid pictures, and if I'm being honest, you look great," I said, truthfully. I searched his face for any sign of an emotion that could make me feel better but I found nothing.

"No not the idea about the type of pictures. The idea that I don't love them. I've been telling you everything that I would've told my old care takers but you're different." I smiled at how sad he was at the thought of hurting my feelings. At least that means he cares.

"Then tell me the truth, Ricky. You can be nice to me, I give you permission." I jokingly add the last part as if I am granting him powers. He turns his head to look at me.

"I'm not sure I know how to do that," he said. Finally telling me what I've been suspecting this whole time. I smiled sadly at his confession.

"Then let me teach you." He smiled at my offer. "You can start by telling me what you think of my pictures," I said handing him the collage that he had put down. He took it from my hands and looked at it once more.

"The truth?" he asked raising an eyebrow. I nodded nervously, scared to find out what he actually thought of them.

"You're an amazing photographer. Your composition and focusing ability are strengths. It's really interesting how you capture your subjects' personalities by zooming in on different body parts when you take your candid pictures. My favorite was the close up of the old lady's eye. I find it extremely interesting how you focus specifically on what you find important on the human body. The angles you used in the pictures you took of me are amazing, but the setting needs to be better. Your landscape photos are a little bright. The lighting in the fox picture I gave you worked well because I took it in the early evening. You should try to take some at night. The trees look like they're glowing when you take them at just the right time. Overall, I think they're great!" he concluded with not even the slightest hint of doubt in his voice. I liked how Ricky's compliments sounded so factual. He seemed very sincere when he said he thought my pictures were great.

I clapped my hands together before telling Ricky what I thought of his attempt at telling me the truth. "See, that was terrific! Now all I ask is that you try to make more eye contact when you talk to me. Your critique was helpful, and it seemed honest. When you look right at the person you are talking to the conversation usually goes more smoothly. When you are talking to people you have to soften how you critique them though. Like, when you tell them something negative you need to say it in a way that makes it sound positive even though it isn't. When you're talking to me, you can just give it to me straight I can handle it. But with other people you need to be gentle." He furrowed his eyebrows as if he was confused but I know he was following my idea. I giggled at the face he made. I'm just now noticing that he must have missed one of his barber shop visits recently. I can tell by the way his bangs are starting to hang in his eyes.

"So, was I being too hard when I gave it to you straight?" Ricky gently inquired.

"You did a super job of saying things nicely. Whenever you talk to someone and you're criticizing them, that's what you need to do. Just kind of hint at the criticism, you know?" Ricky nodded, looking like he understood what I was saying.

"So, I shouldn't be so direct?" he questioned.

"Direct is good like you were with me, but remember to be gentle whenever you can. It's important to use kind words. Sometimes that's difficult."

"I think I get it. That doesn't sound too hard," Ricky said.

"You see, society has grown soft. Many people nowadays can't handle the truth, and therefore, they come up with ways to get around the truth and make reality sound better than it actually is," I said laughing hysterically at how crazy that sounded.

"So, what you're saying is that people are ninnies and can't handle criticism," Ricky chimed in with a big grin, already confident that he was correct. I nodded and turned my attention to the notebook. Next on the list of things to be truthful about is my plan. I push the notebook to Ricky and give him a questioning look.

"I think that taking me along would be a real pain in the-" I cut him off.

"Ricky," I warned crossing my arms.

"It would be too difficult to take me along. Maybe you should try and take someone with you that is more, let's just say, mobile." He looks at me, and again, I believe that he is telling me the truth.

"You see this title here? It specifically says *Ricky's Day Trip* because I plan on taking you with me," I explain while pointing at the page. He chuckles at my exaggerated movements.

"How are you going to fit my wheelchair on your bike?"

"Well, I'm planning on taking you for a short ride without the wheelchair if it's okay with your mom, I have a driver's license for both cars and motorcycles you know? I just chose to get a motorcycle instead of a car," I said pointing to the first slot in the schedule. I was excited about the notes I had jotted in the first column of the notebook. Ricky smiled right away, but his cheerful expression faded in seconds.

"I don't know how this is going to work. I'd hate for you to get your hopes up..." he said to me, turning his wheelchair slightly. We were sitting side by side so it was hard to look at each other.

"If anyone should get their hopes up it's you," I interject. Ricky shakes his head as if to say no. "Well you must've gotten your hopes up in the past. Making progress during physical therapy would get anyone's hopes up," I said decisively. I couldn't imagine going through physical therapy and treatments for years and then to hear one day, "Oh sorry, it looks like you're never going to get better." I mean that just sucks!

"I haven't done physical therapy, Gwen. Who told you that I did?" My eyes almost popped out of their sockets when I heard what he said. I thought for a few seconds before I asked for clarification.

"You mean you *have* done physical therapy," I state firmly, hoping, wishing, praying that he had done some physical therapy program to try and get his legs working again. Many people with serious injuries or disabilities have gotten some strength back in their legs through intense exercise programs. I stood there feeling exasperated and confused about how it could be possible that Ricky never had physical therapy.

"Gwen," he reaches over to touch my shaking hand but I pull back, "I haven't done anything because my mother has never put me in any programs. I really don't think anything is going to work. Most people with cerebral palsy don't have it as badly as I do. You know that, Gwen." I look at him and his face starts to blur as my eyes fill with tears.

"Gwen? What is wrong? A-ar-are you crying? Hey, Gwen," he says pushing a piece of my hair behind my ear. He pulls me to him and sits me in his lap. I don't lean into him because I'm afraid that I might never get up.

The reason why I'm so upset is because everyone knows it's best to do treatment as a child. Early intervention is always most effective. His mother made his chances 10 times worse by choosing this path for him. I wipe the tears from my eyes as I look at Ricky.

"You have to see how wrong that was of your mother. You know that, don't you?" I ask hoping that he realizes her serious mistake. No matter what the reason, she should have given him an opportunity. The possibility may have been slim but there still could have been a chance. As his mother, she should want to try and help her son. He's in a wheelchair for crying out loud. She should want to do everything in her power to get him out of it. It doesn't seem fair. He wipes one of the tears that had slipped down the side of my face and smiles sadly.

"I'm sure she had a good reason not to. I trust her. She's been there for me through everything, and I don't have any problems with it."

"You can't be serious, Ricky! What if you could've gotten out of this chair years ago!"

"But I don't live for 'what if's' and 'what could've been'~ Those excuses make life a heck of a lot worse."

"Well, I am going to look into a physical therapy class with or without your mother's help!" I crossed my arms and stood, determined to at least get him able to stand for a few seconds on his own. He pulls on my shirt to get my attention.

"Like I've said before, I don't want you to get your hopes up, Gwen." I smile sadly at his comment and push some of his hair out of his face. His eyes are amazing and definitely should be seen.

"Never." I wheel him back into the family room and turn on American Ninja Warrior. Handing him his pills and water glass I get a glimpse of the scar he had shown me before. I cringe at the sight of it but choose not to let him know that I saw it. I can tell he isn't proud of it and I would hate to make him feel even more uncomfortable than I know he already does.

Sadly, walking back into the kitchen, I step on a plastic cap from one of my Cherry Coke bottles. I smile when I realize that I'm not the only one who's been enjoying them.

"You have NO right to keep him from physical therapy!" I whisper-yell at Caroline right outside of her house. I told Ricky that I saw her pull up outside so I thought it'd be okay if I just left. I said goodbye to him and promised that I would see him on Monday. I really had just wanted to go outside to talk to Caroline alone.

"Gwen, I can understand how this would look from your perspective but I really would appreciate it if you tried to understand it from mine. Ricky was diagnosed with cerebral palsy when he was about 18 months old. I cried myself to sleep for almost two years after that when I finally decided that I needed to get my act together and just accept that he was who he was. His father left me a week after he found out and said that he wouldn't have a son who was, and I quote, 'incapable of being a man'. I brought Lewis, his father, to court and I eventually got $4,000 out of him. I was happy that I finally got justice for what he had said, but I still had Ricky. My beautiful boy." Tears were streaming down her face by the time she got to the part about Ricky's father, "I went all over creation looking for special doctors and got second and third and fourth opinions about his condition. They all said that there was no cure but only therapies that could improve his condition. Either way he would never be able to fully walk again. There was a slim to no chance of that happening and I just couldn't bare taking him to classes that made us both hope for something that had almost a 0% chance of happening. I decided to just accept who he was and leave it alone. In my opinion he's turned out alright."

I looked at her to make sure she had stopped talking. I know it is impolite to interrupt adults. I know I still have to be respectful.

"Ms. Knoll, I am sorry to have to break this to you, but that is selfish. Ricky is an amazing person and has more determination than half of the people I have met in my entire life. He is funny, intelligent, and he feels things. For you to be withholding the chance for him to improve tells me that you are prioritizing yourself over him. I can't even imagine what you were feeling when you heard his diagnosis, but to not even give him the chance to try and get better.... that just sickens me. It's selfish of you to put your feelings before his. He has a chance, even if it is slim, and as his mother, you should be doing everything humanly possible to give it to him. You need to forget about your feelings and focus on his if you want him to be happy."

I looked at her and all I saw was red. Her face was red and puffy from crying the entire time I talked. She was crying because we both knew I was right.

I know I probably over stepped. I know I probably just crossed like 30 boundaries. But, if given the chance to redo this day, I wouldn't have changed a thing. I would tell her what a therapist, a doctor, even what one of her co-workers should have told her years ago. Ricky should always come first.

Ricky should've been put first from the start.

10 BIG NEWS

"They've promised that dreams can come true – but forgot to mention that nightmares are dreams too."

"AHHHHHHH!" The screams. I heard them before I realized they were coming from me. I walked into Ricky's house to find blood gushing out of the scar on his left wrist. I grabbed a towel hanging by the door and flew over to him, tightly wrapping it around his reopened wound to stop the bleeding. The blood instantly soaked the whole towel. I almost threw up seeing so much blood as it began dripping onto the floor. When I finished wrapping his wrist, I looked at Ricky's face. His complexion was so pale and he felt cold. I ran around the house screaming out Caroline's name, "CAROLINE!" "CAROLINE!"

She was nowhere to be found.

When I went back downstairs there she was, sitting silently on the couch, staring at her dying boy. I shook her knees yelling, "Caroline, he is dying do something!" She didn't move. She didn't even flinch. I slapped her face, finally gaining her attention.

"Isn't it amazing how fast someone can die?" She asks, almost whimsically staring straight ahead.

"You're sick! You're a sick human being who never cared about him. You NEVER cared about him!" I was screeching now. Continuously, yelling over and over how she never cared about him. She eventually shot up

and grabbed me by the shoulders.

"He's dead! He's dead and do you know whose fault it is? It's yours!" I jumped back at her accusation. How is it my fault I thought?

"What in GOD'S name are you talking about? I have done nothing but-" She cut me off as we were screaming at each other.

"You have done nothing but make him see how good life would be if he could walk! HE'S NEVER GOING TO, GWEN! Just get that in your mind! Understand that you are the reason why he's gone. YOU are the reason his body is going to be buried in a few days. It's YOU! It's always been YOU!" Her voice echoed as I heard something along the lines of techno pop play through my mind.

I jolted out of bed and wiped the beads of sweat that decorated my hairline. It was a nightmare. Realizing that what just happened wasn't real I looked over at my clock. It read: Sat 4:59 a.m. I rolled my eyes and dropped my head back on the pillow. I couldn't possibly sleep now. This may or may not happen to you, but once I sit up and see any light at all I can't fall back to sleep. At least not right away. I hate it when that happens especially when I make the mistake of sitting up.

Still shaky from my nightmare, I stood up and walked into the bathroom. I jumped at the sight of my face. I had worn a little mascara yesterday and forgot to take it off. Now it was smudged all over my eyes. Curse you cheap makeup.

Some time passed before I finally got the last bit of makeup off my face. It just kept smudging! I glanced at the clock in my bathroom and saw that it was 5:30 a.m. Deciding that I would never get back to sleep at this point, I hopped into the shower. The water trickled down my face as I thought about what Ricky's mother said to me last night. I tried to decipher Caroline's conversation from her terrible statements in the nightmare. Recalling her actual words, it seemed that Caroline believed that her excuses about why she didn't take Ricky to physical therapy were valid. Just thinking about it made me lose the respect I had for her. Don't get me wrong, I couldn't imagine having a child, being so excited about his future, and then one day hear he would be in a wheelchair, most likely for the rest of his life. Almost no chance of him ever walking again.

I turned the shower head off and grabbed the towel that hung from the rack. I hopped out and stood in front of the mirror. The extra-long, hot shower helped me relax. Looking at my hair in the mirror, I realized just how mean I look with it styled this way. I used to have long, dark red (going on burgundy) colored hair, with side-swept bangs. And do you know what? I think I'm ready to go back to that. Instead of re-doing my highlights I threw the dye into the trash can. As I brushed my hair my thoughts returned to what Caroline had said in my nightmare. My head was spinning.

"Honey, do you know where my car keys are?" my mother asked coming down the stairs in a rush.

"In the cabinet by the front door. Where are you off to?" I asked standing up from my comfortable spot on the couch. Mom turned and looked at me almost as if she wasn't expecting me to be in the family room.

"I need to buy a fancy dress for tonight's concert. Jerry's taking me. We're going on a date," she shared looking worried of all things. I blinked to make sure I interpreted her facial expression correctly.

"Mom, why do you look so concerned? It's just a date...." My voice trails off as I realize how long they've been dating. "You don't think this is *the* date...." Hesitating, I step toward her. She nods nervously, clearly on the same page. Only one word could possibly be swirling around in her mind.

Marriage.

"I do," she says quietly. I run over to give her a gigantic hug!

"Mom, this is great! You should be so excited!" I squeal keeping her locked in my arms. I hear her gulp before she speaks.

"I'm so scared. What if *he* causes problems for Jerry and me, Gwen?" my mother asks worriedly. She lowered her voice to a whisper.

"I won't let anything come between you and Jerry," I smiled trying to lighten the situation. She shakes her head as if to rid the notion of him altogether. I don't blame her. My mother was referring to my dad. I don't talk about him much because I usually try to keep thoughts of him out of my mind.

My father was a strange man. He lived his life very structurally. He had a reason for *everything* he did. There was a purpose for *everything* he bought. He worked in an office exactly 20 miles from our house and came home *every* day at exactly 5:42. He never stayed up past 9:00 and the earliest he got up was 7. He didn't bend the rules for anyone, not even his wife (my mother). I never understood why she married him, but she insisted that she knew what she was getting herself into. I guess looking back, I could see how he would be a reassuring person to have around because he didn't let anything deter him from what he was trying to accomplish.

Dad was very detached from his kids, and he never approved of Jett. Everything Jett did was wrong. Mistakes ranged from things as ridiculous as bringing home a girlfriend with blonde hair to eating an extra piece of cake at a party. My mother tried to make up for Dad being so harsh by secretly giving us what we wanted, but I never felt right about that. Jett was always fascinated by motorcycles. My father couldn't deal with the thought of him owning one though. Jett was ecstatic when he turned 16 and was able to buy his first bike (with my mother's help, of course). That was the day my dad officially announced that he hated all of us. Claiming that my mother, and I quote, *"should be admitted to a mental institution,"* he left. Several weeks later he returned, and my mother, being the loving person that she is, let him back into our lives. Everything was starting to improve until Jett left. I don't like to think about what happened after that because it's truly awful.

"Would you like to help me look for a dress, dear?" my mother asked, slipping on her sandals and sunglasses. I grinned, grabbing my bag by the door.

"Let's find you such a pretty dress that Jerry is going to want to marry you on the spot!" We both giggle as we make our way to my mother's Lexus. As I watch her drive, the perfect dress idea begins to swirl around in my mind. My mother has beautiful brown hair and hazel eyes. I'm thinking that a red dress would look amazing.

We walk out of the store with a $500, sunset red, A-line dress that makes my mother look 20 years younger. We also found silver jewelry to complement the outfit. I smile at her as she happily places the dress in the trunk. As soon as she sits down I turn to her.

"Celebratory ice-cream?" I ask, already knowing what she's going to say.

"Of course!"

I knew it. I can only imagine that Mom is thinking about Jerry as she pulls out of the parking lot with a big smile on her face.

The taste of cookie dough ice cream is still lingering in my mouth as I watch my mother come down the stairs. Jerry is supposed to be here in fifteen minutes, so naturally my mother is stressing about everything.

"Are you sure it looks okay? I mean, my butt isn't too big? Oh, you're not saying anything, I knew I looked like a slut! I should go change into a little black dress and sandals and just call it a night -" I interrupted her ridiculous rant and put a hand on her shoulder, stopping her from turning around and walking back up to her room.

"Mom, you look amazing! I'm sure the second Jerry sees you he is going to say -" I'm interrupted by a masculine voice coming from the front foyer. I jump and go into total defense mode when I realize it's just Jerry. Oh, Jerry! I almost forgot that she gave him a house key.

"Wow, you look.... stunning." It takes him a second to come up with the right word for how pretty Mom looks. I smile and feel a sense of accomplishment when I see how nicely the dress I picked out complements her. Everyone was speechless. Jerry and I were speechless because Mom looked amazing. My mother was speechless because Jerry had never looked so handsome. I backed up to let the two of them have their moment before I ushered them out the door. Shutting the door behind the two love birds I realized something. My mother has a better social life AND love life than I do.

I turned on the TV and clicked on Netflix. One of the show descriptions reminded me of Caroline. I tried hard not to think anything of it, but I couldn't shake the feeling of disappointment I felt whenever I thought about her. The way that she handled everything just surprises me. I mean, I know that she was put in a hard position but the choice just seems so obvious to me. Put Ricky first. I always thought that mothers had that innate feeling even before their babies were born.

I reached over and grabbed the remote to mute the TV. Whenever I can't get something out of my head I either go out and take pictures or ride. Seeming that I can't safely ride my motorcycle I guess I will be taking pictures. I know that my hand is shaky but there are plenty of one-handed photographers. I at least need to try because I can't handle being deprived of riding and taking pictures at the same time. It's just too much of my life taken away from me at once.

I grabbed my camera and threw on a black hoodie

along with my yoga pants. My camera was strapped across my body as I snatched my leather backpack from the front hall. I've noticed that wearing all black makes animals in the woods less likely to notice me right away. They eventually smell me or sense that I'm there, but yeah, the black helps.

Walking into the woods, I realize that I'm missing my phone. I believe I left it charging on the counter, but when I get home I'll have to check. I follow a short path and sit on a rock that is in the center of a circle of trees. Pointing my camera directly above my head, I take a picture of the trees making a nearly perfect circle around me. The stars are just starting to peek out from behind the horizon, and eventually they act as a beautiful night light. Spotting constellations has never been a strength, but the Little Dipper is completely visible tonight.

Describing this photo shoot in one word would be a challenge, but I would have to say: *perfect*. I guess Ricky was right. Nighttime pictures are truly phenomenal. Ricky's advice was still playing in my mind when I noticed a Red-tailed Hawk land on a huge oak tree. Risking everything, I crept closer to the tree and snapped a picture. The hawk heard the click and flew away but not before I got the shot. I was smiling like crazy because I've never taken a better picture of an animal! Its feathers, despite the lack of light, were well defined and could be easily seen. Its beak was lined up perfectly with a bright star so its head lit up and appeared to be glowing.

I backed up while admiring my pictures. I had taken a total of fifty-five pictures in thirty minutes. I was ecstatic! They turned out great ~ I could almost guarantee Ricky would like every one of them. Even though we've only known each other for a week I'm noticing how his feelings are impacting me. When he's happy, I'm happy. When he's sad, I'm sad. The scary thing is though that I've never felt like this before about anyone except for my mom and Jett. Not even Ty. There was always this sense of competition between him and me, and it drove me crazy. Constantly we would try and one-up each other, and it just made every conversation difficult and frustrating. When Ty was still in school, people never picked on him. I'm not sure if it was the fact that he wasn't afraid to fight or the fact that he started a lot of them, but he was never a target. I know it sounds mean, but I have always blamed Ty for not protecting me more than he did.

Don't get me wrong, asking me to sit next to him and being his partner was nice and all, but that only helps so much. When Ty wasn't around people would throw things at me and harass me. I didn't expect him to shield me from everything, but he barely protected me from any of it. Jett was the one who intervened during most of the bullying. It makes me feel sad when I think about the few times that Ty should've stepped up, and he didn't.

I didn't realize that Ty was gone until school started. Jett left the second week of school that same year. I lost my friend the first day of school and my protector on the seventh day. When it finally sunk in that they were never coming back, I threw out whatever hope I had left. I lost it. I went completely crazy.

I trained like never before and completely threw out my entire wardrobe. I adopted an entire new persona. Ty left a few months before Jett did so I lost the only two people who remotely cared about me at school. Ty and Jett were both heading into their senior year. I was starting my sophomore year, and it was supposed to be great. It was supposed to be the last year we would all be together, and it was *supposed* to be our year to say goodbye....

Of course, that never happened because life never does what you think it should or is supposed to. Life figures out what you think is supposed to happen and does the exact opposite, crushing whatever idea you had about the future in the process.

Ricky has taught me a lot in a short amount of time. I have this feeling that he is going to show me way more than Ty ever could. Previewing my pictures and thinking about Ricky, I feel confident about where our friendship is going. He's already shown me so much about life in a short amount of time and there's still more to learn. It's going to be great, and it's going to be huge.

I made my way home not even trying to hide the smile that took over my face. Anticipating good news about Mom's special date, I started to unlock the front door. Not even one foot in the door my mother came running toward me. Before I knew what was happening I was engulfed in my mother's strong arms.

"He proposed! He proposed!" She squealed jumping up and down still holding me in her arms. One word. Painful.

"And?" I asked as I nearly choked in her grip.

"I said YES, of course!" She screamed, nearly waking up the entire neighborhood in the process. I honestly wouldn't be surprised if Caroline ran over asking if there was a problem. In an effort to see her face, I tilted my head up with a broad grin. Mom loosened her grip slightly when she felt me move. She looked down and smiled right back, her snow-white teeth glistening in the light bouncing off the street light outside.

"That's great, Mom!" I exclaimed the second she dropped her arms. She truly loves Jerry. I can tell. I feel like it will be great to have him around. Who knows? He may even help her heal emotionally from the years of pain caused by my father.

"Jerry and I were getting dessert at the local bakery, and the ring was sitting on top of this beautiful cake! The frilly little banner said; Will you marry me? Look, isn't it beautiful?" She pulled out her phone revealing the picture of the special cake. Mom swiped her screen again to reveal a picture of the happy couple beaming and holding hands. I couldn't help but light up at the sight of the two of them. They looked truly happy, and to be honest, I can't remember the last time she looked like this. Then I saw the ring! Let's just say this guy has some serious cash because it was *gorgeous*. The ring was silver with tiny diamonds running down each side. The large oval diamond in the center is what caught my attention. The ring was so sparkly and looked magnificent on Mom's hand.

"Did you get to eat the cake?" I asked, receiving a laugh from her. The funny part here is that I was serious. I'd never joke about a delicious dessert.

"Yes, I did and it.... wait! Where were you tonight, young lady? I texted seven or eight times and when I got home you were nowhere to be found. You left your phone here so I couldn't reach you," she asked trying hard to sound angry. It wasn't working.

"I just went down to the park to take some pictures." I didn't want her to worry that I wasn't safe because of my hand and my lack of quick transportation.

"Did you go into the woods?" She crossed her arms while inquiring. We both already knew the answer to that question.

"Yes," I said, giving up on trying to make my outing sound as safe as possible.

"I'm guessing you walked," she assumed.

"Of course." I walked around her in an effort to enter the house but she stopped me.

"What were you thinking, Gwen? I wasn't home. You have an injured hand and no fast way to get out of a bad situation. You didn't even have a phone...." Her voice quiets to nothing in a way that I'm only guessing is her telling me she wants me to explain myself.

I let out a frustrated sigh before setting my case down. "Mom, I was safe. There was nobody around and I could practically see the trail from where I was sitting. I had my camera and the stars as flashlights. I was fine, Mom, really I was." She shook her head firmly. I'm not sure what that was for, though, because I didn't ask her a question. I knew she was getting ready to lay down the law.

"No, you weren't safe, Gwen. *Practically* seeing a trail and seeing a trail are two very different things. From now on you can't take pictures at night without somebody else with you." I almost choked when I heard what she said. I turned my head to look her straight in the eyes but I could tell she was serious.

"Mom! You can't take this away from me too! I came home before curfew like I was supposed to! I promise that I'll bring my phone next time. It was an honest mistake. By the time I realized I had left the phone I was already there. It took me some time to walk to the park." I was begging her by this point because I didn't think I could handle no photography, no bike, and no kick-boxing. That would just be basically everything I have.

"Fine, but only if you promise to be my maid of honor." I laughed and nodded. Well, that was until I realized something.

"Wait, were you being serious about the whole photography thing?"

"Well, of course I want you to be safe but I wouldn't stop you from going out to take pictures. You love doing that sweetheart. I just needed you to look at me." She laughed while I stood there dumbfounded.

"I mean, I'd love to be your maid of honor but making me beg was really unnecessary. You couldn't have just asked me to turn around?" My eyes must've shown how confused I was because she laughed even harder. This was a situation where you know for a fact that the person in front of you is not laughing with you but at you.

"My way was a lot more fun." Patting me on the shoulder, she walked into the house and sat next to someone on the couch. I didn't even realize that Jerry had been sitting there for the entire conversation.

Welcome to the family, Jerry!

11 TIME GIVES GOOD ADVICE

You know how advice is. You only want it if it agrees with what you wanted to do anyway."
– John Steinbeck

I woke up already knowing that today was Sunday. The day that you spend stressing about school on Monday. The day I would normally ride for close to three hours without stopping. But this particular Sunday is the day I go on my date with Ty.

I have mixed emotions about the whole thing. Part of me is saying, "Go and just have fun and forget that he left without saying a word to you." The cautious half is saying, "Don't go and continue to blame him for leaving." It's telling me to remember that feeling of disappointment I got when I saw him. That feeling that he left me for his own personal benefit.

It's hypocritical of me to think that though. I already said that he barely protected me from all of the hate so maybe it was best that he left. I'm probably just blaming him for what Jett did to me. Jett was the one who made me cry every night. His disappearance made me wonder if it was something that I had done. I'm never going to know, and I know that, but I can't help thinking about it every day. Maybe Ty returning is a sign that people can come back. Maybe he can help me forget about the pain for a little while. Even if it isn't forever.

"Would you pass me the butter, honey?" We were eating breakfast with Jerry because he apparently "fell asleep" next to my mom on the couch. I passed Mom the butter as we enjoyed the homemade waffles I made. Celebrating their engagement with a congratulating breakfast seemed like a nice idea. I was feeling creative this morning so I Googled a recipe for waffles. They actually turned out pretty well. Mine were a little burnt but that was due to the fact that our waffle iron acts more like a volcano than a toaster.

My mother smiled and handed the butter to Jerry who was heading to the refrigerator to get the syrup I neglected to put on the table. Studying the two of them as we sat there I decided that I am okay with it. I mean, I already told my mom that I was, but I really hadn't decided for myself. I'm not sure if your parents have ever dated, but when they come to you with the infamous, "Do you like him?" question, what can you say? I couldn't tell her no when she literally cried because she was so happy about him. I just couldn't do it. I would understand if he was abusive physically or emotionally, but he wasn't. He seemed nice so I told her that I was okay.

Now that I've finally had time to sit down and have a real conversation with him, for more than 20 minutes, inside my house with my mother, I've decided that he actually is a great guy for her and I wouldn't want anyone else sitting across from me. I've been to movies with Mom and Jerry, but the mood is different when you're socializing inside your own house.

"So, do you have any plans for today, Gwen?" Jerry asks me after soaking his waffles in liters of syrup.

"Well, I actually have a date tonight. Mom, you remember Tyler Curtis." I aimed the last part of my sentence at my mother who nodded while chewing her food. I looked back to Jerry and smiled awaiting his comment on my evening plans.

"Oh, that sounds great. I hope you have fun, and I'm sure we can hang out some other time." I looked at him questioningly.

"Oh, were you wanting to take my mom and me out today?" He shook his head at my assumption.

"No, actually, I was thinking that the two of us could go to a photography museum. I know how much you love to take pictures, and I was thinking that we could go together." That does sound amazing! I've always wanted to go but my mother has never had enough time or money to take me to a really nice one. I was already thinking of different museums we could go to that wouldn't be crazy expensive.

"That sounds fantastic, Jerry! Thank you. I know a few museums close to here," I said looking down at my untouched waffles.

"I was thinking that we could go to the Roundel Museum." I stopped cutting my waffles and looked up at him, completely shocked. That museum had like a $400 entrance fee. Let alone parking and everything else. That would be incredible.

"Are you serious?" I asked in disbelief. That brought a huge grin from my mother.

"100%," he said smiling at me. It took everything in me not to plow him over with a big hug. I've always wanted to go.

"You have no idea how excited I am!" I clapped my hands together. He laughed and looked at my mother who was glowing at the sight of us bonding. I guess it would be a mother's dream for her daughter and fiancé to get along.

"Well, good. Now all we have to do is figure out a time."

"Oh, I mean, I could cancel today-" He interrupted my attempt at a compromise.

"No, no. You don't need to do that. Besides, you wouldn't want to hurt the young man's feelings." He shook his hand in front of him to say no.

"Believe me, he's hurt mine plenty," I mumbled, barely audible over the radio that was playing in the background. It turns out Jerry likes music as much as my mother and I do.

"What was that, Gwen?" He questioned my sudden change of spirit. I guess he heard my comment. There is a lot more pain that comes whenever I think about Ty. In my opinion, a lot more than necessary.

"Oh nothing. I was just saying how I'm sure Ty could cope with rescheduling."

"No, I don't think that's necessary, and I'm pretty sure there is some sort of discount when you go on Tuesdays." He looked at both of us waiting for a response.

"Yeah, okay that sounds good. I guess we would go

after school? Maybe around 4 or 5?" He nodded and popped a strawberry into his mouth. I had cut some strawberries to go with the waffles. My mother couldn't stop smiling.

That breakfast wasn't horrible. By the time the wedding comes around I'm sure that we will be more comfortable with each other in and out of the house. I'm going to have to get used to this, and I'm happy to do so if it equates to my mother's happiness.

"Well don't you look nice!" My mother was standing at the bottom of the stairs, getting ready to head up. I was getting dressed for my date with Ty and came to the conclusion that dressing up for a date that was bound to go downhill was just stupid and unnecessary.

"Why, thank you. I really didn't put that much effort into it, but you know." I shrugged and headed for the front foyer slipping on the green high-tops I got for Christmas last year.

"What do you mean you didn't put much effort into looking nice? Don't you like Tyler?" I sighed and looked at my mother who was standing behind me. She watched me with confusion in her eyes.

"Not for two years." I gave her a sad smile and opened the door. We had decided that instead of walking there he should come pick me up. I probably would've had to leave an hour early. I'm a pretty slow walker so maybe even earlier than that, but who knows?

"You look terrific," Ty said from the driver's side of the car. I gave him a small smile and closed my door.

"Thanks." He looked at me confused, but brushed it off quickly. His attention went back to the road as he decided to drop it.

"Music?" He asked hovering his hand over the power button. I nodded as he turned it on. It landed on Prince and he didn't change it.

"Could you please change it?" I gulped. He looked at me, weirdly, before switching it. I let out a sigh of relief before turning my attention back to the world outside of the car.

My eyes kept going to the trees we passed. Viewing them through a glass window made me feel so far away from them. I've always loved how close I get to the trees when I'm on my motorcycle. I always felt like I was moving through the wind with them.

"What can I get you two today?" Carly smiled at me. We made it to the pizza shop in almost complete silence. I was happy at that because I wanted to be able to see his entire face when I talked to him. He needed to be able to see mine as well. As soon as we sat in a booth Carly had grabbed some napkins and her notepad.

Carly has been working here for a year now, and when she was hired, I can remember hitting it off with her right away. She's extremely laid back and one of those people who you can always count on to be in the same mood. She never changes and there is something reassuring about that.

"Two root beers," Ty answers for me. I almost vomit when I hear him say that.

"Actually, I'll just take a lemon water." I smiled at Carly who already knew what I wanted. When she walked away I turned 100% of my attention to him. He did the same.

"You sure have changed a lot since the last time I saw you." I shrugged at his obvious observation.

"Well, a lot can happen in two years," I spat coldly. He jerked back at my sharpness.

"Okay, like what?" He crossed his arms and sat back. There was practically no one in the restaurant except for the occasional walk-in's so we got a huge booth.

"Too much that can't be changed." I followed his lead crossing my arms and leaning back. He sat up to get closer to me.

"What is up with you, Gwen? I know there is something you want to say to me so just say it." I was surprised that he caught on to that. I thought I was covering the fact that I wanted to ask him a few questions pretty well.

"I'm sorry that it's hard for me to be excited that you're back. You're not even addressing the fact that you left without saying anything." He looked at me shocked for some reason as if my being upset was surprising. Is it surprising to you?

"Well, that's why I wanted to get together. So, we could talk. I've been trying to be considerate, but you go and change up on me. You don't want to listen to your favorite singer anymore, you don't want to drink your favorite soda when I order it, what is up with that?" I'm debating whether or not I should tell him about Jett. Jett was the one who introduced me to Prince and I completely fell in love with his music. He also hooked me on a few sodas including root beer. I loved that too.

I'm not sure that I want to come out and tell Ty everything that has happened in my life because the point is he was the one who left. He left without saying a word and I can't just let him back in with open arms. I'm not making the same mistake as my mother. I already promised her that years ago and I don't plan on breaking it anytime soon.

"I'm not ready to get into all of the details of my life right now. We can go there as soon as you tell me why you left without a word. We've gone to movies together. We've sat next to each other in class. We used to text often. We were science lab partners, and I even went over to your house to study with you. You were pretty good friends with my brother too. Does any of that ring a bell?" My voice sounded quiet but deathly serious. You'd think we were talking about a top-secret FBI case or something.

"Yes, it's all very familiar and upsetting you was exactly what I was trying to avoid. I didn't want you to be angry and feel like I was leaving you." He took a sip of his drink that had just been placed on the table. I put my index finger up as if to say one minute to Carly. She nodded and left quickly.

"Well here we are, Ty. We are having the discussion that would've never happened if you had just told me you were leaving." We were both staring at each other. I was hanging on his every word and he on mine.

"Of course, we would've had this conversation before. That's the kind of person you are, Gwen. Just face it, you hang onto things and care so much that it just suffocates whoever is on the receiving end of it." I wanted to hurl my water at him. I wanted to get a sledgehammer and completely wreck his Porsche outside. I wanted to pull a Carrie Underwood.

"Well then you clearly don't know me, Ty. I've let go

of a lot of things over the past few years." He shook his head obnoxiously disagreeing with whatever it was that I was saying.

"See, I don't think you have."

"I would've told you to go, Ty. I would've said go follow your dreams and get out of here. I would've said that you deserve this and that I have every faith that you will make it to the top. I also would've said don't worry about the people here and just try and forget them. Clearly you've done that all on your own." I saw hurt flash in his eyes. It remained the entire time we sat staring at each other. I knew we both were thinking the same thing. What has happened to the person sitting across from me?

"I didn't forget you, or Jett. I thought a lot about you guys while I was gone." I rolled my eyes at his comment. It doesn't matter now.

"I highly doubt that. Besides, Jett doesn't even know you're gone." It slipped. I wasn't going to tell him about Jett until things got better between us. I didn't want him to pull the pity card. I don't need his pity. I don't need any of it.

"I'm surprised. I thought the three of us were pretty close and-" I interrupted him. Obviously, he isn't getting that Jett doesn't know because Jett left the second week of school. No one except me knew for sure that Ty had left. Everyone thought that he was still on vacation weeks after school started.

"He's gone, Ty. He left a few weeks after you did and never came back. So, to answer your unspoken question, yes, I have changed and it's because of the two of you. Mostly him, but you too." He gazed at me stunned. If you were to look at his face you'd think I was growing a second head.

"I'm so s-" I cut him off here too. "Don't say sorry."

"I don't want to hear it. I know it's sad but we aren't here to talk about him. We are here to talk about you. All I want you to do is accept the fact that you left me, without a word, and hurt me a lot. I just want you to admit that. Can you do that for me?"

"Yes, I know I did. I accept it and I feel awful for doing that to you," he said with a small smile. I gave him a small insincere one in return. He doesn't deserve my smile, in my opinion.

"Okay, good. Now I can explain what happened with Jett. So, my brother vanished. It was the second Tuesday of the school year when he picked up his bike and left. Luckily, I didn't find out until school was over that day. I would've been a total wreck if I found out any earlier than I did. I got home and my father was yelling at my mom. Of course, it was about Jett, but the thing that surprised me was how Dad sounded sad that he was gone. My father had never liked Jett so I always thought that the day he moved out would be the happiest day of his life. It wasn't apparently."

"My mom was crying uncontrollably and my father was screaming. He went outside and my mom followed him. Dad smacked her and drove off. The police helped us search for Jett for about two months. After that they said that the likelihood that Jett was dead was high if he was kidnapped. If he wasn't then, since he is technically an adult, there was nothing that they could do. They said that there was also the possibility that he could have disappeared willingly. I know Jett and he would never do that! I wanted to kill them, Ty." Tears filled my eyes but I didn't let them fall. Ty doesn't get to come back and play the knight in shining armor.

"I wanted to take the motorcycle Jett helped me pick out and run them over. Instead of hurting them though, I took it out on myself and the people around me. I cut my hair, changed my bike completely, and started standing up for myself at school. Granted, I have no friends because of it but I couldn't care less. The only people who really have been giving me problems are the football team and Amber. Well, Amber and Co." Ty looked worried when I mentioned the football team so I elaborated.

"Don't worry about the football team. I stick up for myself and they eventually clean up whatever mess they make. Usually they bother stuff at my house, so luckily my attention doesn't have to be taken away from my school work." I shrug and swirl the ice in my lemon water. Carly knows how much I like lemons so she added three. I smiled at the thought.

"I don't know what to say." Ty finally spoke and it actually startled me. I hadn't heard him talk for the past 5 minutes.

"There is nothing to say. It's really not your problem. What I wanted you to get out of that little depressing life story is that crap happens, but being honest is always the best way to go." I cracked a small smile to let him know I was alright.

"Okay, and I'm sorry I wasn't honest with you. You want to talk about me for a while?" I nodded at his suggestion and blinked the remaining tears away. I haven't cried about Jett in a long time because I have never been forced to talk about him. Obviously, no one forced me to talk about him now, but how could I leave Jett out of the conversation when he is the main reason I am the way I am now? He introduced me to Prince and root beer. I think that makes him the best older brother ever.

"So," Ty went on about his life but I tuned it out. After Carly took our order I zoned out and just thought about how good it felt to talk about Jett, even if it wasn't for very long. In my opinion Jett deserves to be remembered every day.

As soon as she placed my pizza down I started to eat. I didn't bother with any formalities. I was hungry. Period. End of story. I heard Ty chuckle as he watched me completely pig out. I really don't see what's so funny about a girl being hungry.

After I wiped off the sauce that was obviously all over my face, I laughed along with him. It felt great to be distracted, and I'm not going to lie, it's nice to have that feeling of closure with Ty. I don't see anything past this pizza night, but it helps to know that he admitted what he did and we can both move on.

Time truly does give good advice.

12 THE LOCAL TARGET

"Life begins at the end of your comfort zone."
– Neale Donald Walsch

The date was a good goodbye. It provided closure that was long overdue. I told Ty straight up that where his life was going and where mine was going were in completely opposite directions. He looked sad, but ultimately, he understood. I have this feeling that he knew it was coming. I'm glad he did because I don't think I could handle seeing him anymore. Ricky and my mother's wedding was enough for me right now. Not to mention, my hand is still healing and I swear, the second it does, I am taking Ricky for a ride. I know he is bound to love it.

"Could you tell me Newton's three laws of motion?" I was sitting in 1st period listening to Mr. Wells go on and on about Newton's incredible discoveries. My heart skipped a beat when I thought he was pointing to me. Luckily, he was calling on Janessa. It's not that I don't know the answer, because I do. It's just that I don't like being caught off guard.

"His first was something like, every object stays at rest or in its straight line of motion unless another force changes it. His second was, force is equal to the change in momentum and something about mass equals mass times acceleration. His third was easy, for every action there is an equal and opposite reaction." She nodded, proud of reciting the basic idea of Newton's laws. She wasn't exactly spot on but she was close. I'll give her that.

"Good job, Janessa. I am going to write the exact laws on the board so everyone can review them." She smiled at his compliment. I looked at her and realized how little she talks during class. Amber isn't in this class so Janessa is easily the prettiest girl here. She has long blonde hair that looks natural, imagine that. She has big, dark brown eyes and considerably long eyelashes. I'm surprised she doesn't have more friends in here. At this school, it seems that many kids try to become friends with the prettiest people around. I guess that is their idea of a smart plan to become popular. I would call that popularity by association.

Before I knew it, the bell was ringing and it was time for my last class. Nothing interesting happens while I am at school so that's why I normally don't talk about it. We only have a few more months to go, and I think everyone is just pushing through each day to get to our final one. It's amazing how we, unintentionally, agree on certain things. The students here say that they don't get along, but I've noticed that they can agree on certain topics.

I'll be walking in the hallways and when the popular students aren't around their friends they actually have real conversations with the "outcasts," as they call them. They say things like, "Yeah, I cannot wait until school is out," and "Can you believe there are 40 more days left?" It's funny how these exact same conversations take place between the bully and the poor student who gets bullied.

Those same conversations happen to kids like me. They make you believe, even if it's only for a second, that they might actually leave you alone. That is until their friends come around and throw the piece of gum you gave them in your hair and call you some crude name that they think describes you best. It's stupid, I know, but it happens. Immature is one of the best ways to describe them.

I sat down in my usual spot by the wall near the window. There were two desks in front of me and two behind. I liked my spot because I was out of the way, but I wasn't looking for trouble in the back. I also liked that I could look outside. Nature makes me calm, and it's the closest thing to my motorcycle that I have in school.

Many kids came sauntering in at once but there was one I didn't recognize. He caught me staring at him so I immediately whipped my head to the front. Ignoring me, he walked toward the teacher, giving me a chance to stare at him again. I eavesdrop a lot so I was able to learn that he's a foreign exchange student by the end of his conversation with Mr. Rodgers. I believe he said that he was from Australia but don't take my word for it.

Of course, the only open seat was the one directly in front of me. Funny how destiny works.

Mr. Rodgers pointed to it, and the mystery boy walked over. He gave me a genuine smile before taking his seat. I watched as Mr. Rodgers handed out the quiz results from last week.

"Nice." He was staring at the 100% scribbled at the

top of my paper. Just by that comment I could tell he was Australian. I'm not going to lie, he wasn't hard on the eyes. He had dark brown hair and brown eyes to match. I decided that I was going to give him a chance. Besides, I haven't talked to anyone in class for a while.

"Thanks. You are?" I looked him in the eyes and could tell he was kind. He wouldn't stay that way if he fell into the wrong group though. He's exactly the kind of person who would get himself tangled up in Jay's mess.

"Carter Jones. It's nice to meet you." He stuck his hand out, and I shook it. It's refreshing to know some of us have manners. I smiled.

"Gwen Brady. Likewise." He smiled at me before turning back to his paper. I'd say that introduction went pretty well. Considering the fact that most teens don't even state their name, I'd say that was a success.

"Class, you need to have this page done by the time the bell rings. If not, it's 10 points off and you have to do it for homework." I looked up to see Mr. Rodgers behind his desk. He was taking a sip of coffee out of the mug I bought him last semester. I smiled at the thought before turning my attention back to my worksheet.

"But isn't the entire worksheet 10 points?" some boy yelled out receiving laughs and chuckles from the friends seated around him. I recognized him as one of the boys from the soccer team. They were usually the ones interrupting.

"Well, I'm sure you can do the math, Mr. Fowler. If the worksheet is worth 10 points, and I said that you lose 10 if you don't complete it by the bell, then that would mean the worksheet would be worth 0 points if you don't finish it. Correct Mr. Fowler?" He was speaking to the soccer player in his designated "teacher" voice which made it even more entertaining.

"I guess that's my point, Mr. Rodgers. Why didn't you just say that you would take *all* the points away in the beginning?" the soccer boy asked. His friends next to him were dying of laughter as the athlete copied the same perplexed look on our teacher's face.

"Well, I thought that seniors would be able to figure it out without having to take 11 minutes away from my class. I'm sorry that I overestimated your ability to do 2nd grade math, Mr. Fowler." His tone had grown more agitated, and for a moment, I stopped breathing. A mad Mr. Rodgers is not a good one.

"I actually learned that in 1st grade, Mr. Rodgers." Fowler crossed his arms and proceeded to press Mr. Rodgers about the topic. By this point, I really just wanted both of them to shut up so I could finish the work.

"Well, clearly that class didn't leave much of an impression on you." That resulted in a few more chuckles from the class.

"How would you know about 1st grade though, sir. You probably can't even remember since it was so long ago." Fowler scratched his head as if to act confused. I find it interesting how I still don't know the kid's first name.

"Nico," There it is, "I would watch it if I were you. Enough of this. Class get to work, and Mr. Fowler, I will be seeing you tomorrow at lunch."

"Don't you think that would be moving a little too fast in our relationship Mr. Rodgers?" That got the entire class to start laughing. Thinking about Nico dating anyone is hilarious but to throw our teacher into the mix, that's comedy gold.

"Nico." Mr. Rodgers' voice had a ring to it that made it sound a lot like the guy from Alvin and the chipmunks. Nico was quiet after that, but his silence didn't hide the smile that was playing on his lips. I rolled my eyes at the entire situation and finally returned to my work. If I don't finish this in time I will be blaming Nico.

I handed in my paper five minutes before the bell rang. Due to the "unscheduled interruption," Mr. Rodgers stated that we had the first ten minutes of class tomorrow to finish it. I had already handed it in but I thought that was very nice of him.

Packing up my stuff I felt a tap on my shoulder. I looked up to see Carter standing in front of me with his things already organized to leave.

"Yes?" I continued to gather my belongings but looked at him the second I got it all in my bag.

"Do things like that always go on here?" I chuckled at how confused he looked.

"Not usually for that long, but yes. Why? Do things like that not happen where you're from?"

"They do, but usually the teacher would've stopped it from taking nearly 20 minutes out of the class." I laughed again at his facial expression. He really doesn't understand Mr. Rodgers' tactics.

"Mr. Rodgers has interesting ways of dealing with obnoxious students." I gave him a little pat on the shoulder before passing him and walking out the door. He smiled at me as I walked by.

"You're early." Ricky was sitting in his wheelchair watching his TV show when I walked in his house. I decided that coming over early for the next few weeks would be a good idea, considering what happened just last week.

"I thought we came to the agreement that you would work on being nice?" I crossed my arms and shut the door behind me. I was walking in as Caroline was leaving so I said goodbye to her outside. We decided that my schedule would be every Monday, Wednesday, Thursday, and Friday.

Her plan worked for me because that meant I would be earning $600 a week. That's amazing!

"Yeah, we said I would be *trying* to work on it. That doesn't mean I am going to be nice 24/7."

"Is that so?"

He looked at me while muting the TV.

"Yup."

I walked over to him slowly and put each one of my hands on the armrest of his chair. Looking him straight in the eye, I heard him clear his throat.

"You see, Ricky. I think long and hard about what I promise to do when I make deals with people. I think long and hard because there is always some way that the deal could come and bite me in the butt. However, it can only do that if the person I made the deal with doesn't follow through. Do you understand what position that puts me in?" He didn't say anything. It's funny how uncomfortable I was making him.

"How about we try again?" I backed up a few feet and took my hands off of his wheelchair. He let out a breath that I was surprised he'd been holding. He finally calmed down and I couldn't help but laugh.

"Are you scared of me, Ricky?" I asked between gasps. I was laughing so hard that tears were coming down my face.

"That was the most uncomfortable I have ever seen you, man. You sure are one interesting guy." As my laughter died I headed into the kitchen to grab my drink. I almost passed out when I opened the fridge and saw nothing but water sitting on the shelves. Ricky rolled in and answered the question I was going to ask within seconds.

"Mom didn't go to the store this week yet so we don't have any Coke." I closed the fridge gently trying to stay calm. I turned to Ricky who broke out laughing at the sight of my face. I am not a happy camper when I don't have my drink.

"Then we are going." I kicked his brake back and wheeled him toward the door to their one-car garage. He started to squirm in his seat when I spun him around to face me.

"I don't care what your excuses are. Whether it is the fact that you are older than I am or the fact that you don't feel like it. I really don't care! I need my drink and you are coming with me either willingly or by force." He started to object when I stopped him with one finger.

"I will carry you," I warned. He quickly shut his mouth, clearly understanding that I wasn't joking. I took the handles on his wheelchair and pushed him down the few cement stairs that led to the garage. Unlocking the car door, I pressed a button on the keys and watched as the small ramp lowered so I could roll him in. I strapped him in since he was being difficult and gave him one more pep talk.

"I know this probably isn't what you want to be doing, but the priority right now is refilling that refrigerator! This is code *no more Cherry Coke* and I repeat, this is not a drill." Patting him on the shoulder I headed around to the driver's side. I locked the doors just in case Ricky tried to pull something during the few seconds I was outside of the vehicle. As I said, there is no more Cherry Coke. That's equivalent to a country wide lockdown, urgent and incontrovertible. Hopping into the driver's seat I closed the door and put the key in the ignition. There was a small black button on the ceiling of the car that controlled the garage door so I pressed it and watched out the rear-view mirror as it opened.

"I hope you're good back there, Rick." I gave him a nickname just for the heck of it.

"I really don't want to go in there, Gwen." We had pulled into the parking lot of Target when he started to go on and on about how he didn't want to go into the store. I kept rolling my eyes but he clearly wasn't getting that I didn't care.

"Why? This is a great time for you to practice your honesty. Why is it so traumatizing for you to go into a Target?"

"I just don't like people staring at me. They do that thing where they look at you and then feel badly the second they realize you noticed them staring. It's like, if they were staring at a regular person it wouldn't be considered rude but at me they feel like they can't." I laughed at the thought of him being fazed by other people.

"Would you like the attention to be on someone else?" I asked, turning around in the front seat. The car was parked we just hadn't gotten out yet.

"And how would you manage that?" A mischievous smile played along my lips as I thought up a perfect plan to get the attention onto me and not Ricky.

So, I was going to be playing the part of a drunk teenage girl who just came from a club that she wasn't supposed to be at. Ricky and I are going to act like we don't know each other so while he is getting the soda I will be acting. I think it is the perfect plan except for the high probability of someone posting it on YouTube and getting the footage back to my school. But hey, anything for friends am I right?

I put on my sunglasses, put my hair into two pigtails and took off my shirt. Don't worry I was wearing this crop top bra thing that looked like a scandalous shirt so, I was technically clothed.

I walked around to his side of the car and pulled open the van door. He was staring at me, but what did I already tell you, I love my drink and if this is what I have to do to get it then, so be it.

"Let's go." I got him out of the car and let him wheel in first. This way, no one would think we were together. I would be staying pretty close to his general area, though, so the people around him would be looking at me and not at him.

I watched as he made it to the sliding doors. It's go

time.

I sauntered in and immediately thought up the most outrageous story I could be blabbering on about.

"Has anyone seen GLORIA?" I waited until I got everyone's attention. I watched as Ricky made his way to the Cherry Coke. Perfect.

"I bought GLORIA for $1000 yesterday and now, poof, she's gone. I need help finding her." I made my legs wobble as I walked towards the cash register that Ricky was at. I was close enough so everyone around him could hear me and easily watch but not close enough that you would tie the two of us together.

"She is about 80 feet long and lives in this GIGANTIC," I swung my arms out to represent how big the container was, "Water bowl. She's a blue whale." I tried to mimic a drunk giggle, and from the looks of the people around me, I pulled it off quite nicely. Ricky was making his way towards the sliding doors so I decided to just take it home.

"OH! Do you HEAR that?! It's GLORIA! She's CALLING me! I'm coming BABY!" I ran for the door, and just for the heck of it, pretended to run into the sliding one. I heard a few people laugh but mostly they were quiet. In most situations, the performer would be sad, but in this particular instance, that's a great sign. That means they truly thought I was crazy.

I hopped in the car that Ricky had already found shelter in. I looked to him questioningly until he held up the cans of heaven. Awesome.

"Could you hand me my shirt?" I beckoned towards my pile of clothes in the backseat. When he didn't answer, I turned around to see his face. I exploded into a fit of laughter at the sight of his face. He looked shocked to say the least.

"Why.... why would you do that?" He asked very cautiously. He probably was referring to my very nonchalant-like state. I thought about the answer to his question as I untied my pigtails and put my leather jacket on.

"Well, you said that you felt uncomfortable with everyone in there staring at you and so I fixed it. Aren't I being paid to help you with all of your personal needs?" I jokingly asked as I reapplied the makeup I had smudged for the full affect. I really did look like a drunk.

"But the job doesn't say you need to publicly humiliate yourself like you just did," he said incredulously. I looked at him through the rear-view mirror, completely enjoying the mix of facial expressions I was receiving from him. At this point I knew my performance was worth it.

"But it doesn't say that I don't need to either." I winked at him before pulling out of the parking lot simultaneously taking a sip from my soda.

I definitely did not go through all of that just to wait longer for my drink.

I let the taste of the drink consume every cell in my body as I drove. He kept shaking his head back and forth as if he couldn't believe I did all of that for Cherry Coke.

He'd be surprised at how far I'd go to get myself this heaven-in-a-can right here. I'd go to Mount Everest and back.

13 PARTNER IN CRIME

"Let's do some 'We shouldn't be doing this' things."

"Are you happy now?" Ricky said, while wheeling into the family room. We had gotten back about an hour or so ago but I was beat. It's a lot of work pretending to be drunk, and especially so when you have never been drunk before.

"Never been better." I smiled and raised my can as if to say cheers. He chuckled in a way that made me think he thought I was crazy. I dismissed his rude notion as I took another sip.

"Can I ask what happened to your hand?" I was wondering when he was going to ask.

"It's really ridiculous...."

"I still would like to know."

"This girl slammed it in my locker as I was getting my stuff out of it."

"Ouch."

"Yeah." I shrugged and looked down at my cast imagining how ugly my hand most likely looks.

"Have you found out when you can get that glove off and start riding again?" I turned to him and found him closer to me than I had expected.

"Doctor Lucero said that I could see how it feels in about a month. He doesn't think it will fully heal for about six weeks from now though." My spirits lowered ever-so-slightly at the thought of not riding for close to two months. I'm guessing Ricky sensed that because he put a hand on my shoulder.

"Thanks, Rick. I hope you don't mind waiting several more weeks to ride with me."

"No, I don't mind. It's probably better that way anyway because we still have to figure out the mechanics of it all." Ricky wheeled away and came back with a binder filled with notebook paper and folders.

"What's this?" I took the binder from his hands and opened it. I discovered a blueprint for a seat we can attach to my bike. I analyze it more closely and realize just how smart Ricky is. He even has the calculations for how the speed and wind will affect the restraints on his seat.

"Where did you learn all of this?" He scoffed at my question. I know in my head that he is 18, but sometimes he seems much older.

"I have a talented tutor and my obstacle courses provide great practice in engineering." He took the book back and set it on the kitchen table. That oak table has become our planning place.

"Are you coming?" He nodded his head toward the table. Delighted by Ricky's initiative I hurried to the kitchen. We sat down, well I did, and he started to explain the plan.

By the end of our designing session we had a rough draft of the seat on paper. It was great because not only did it fit Ricky's needs, but it also looked terrific. I'm not a fan of super bright colors, if you couldn't already tell, so the fact that Ricky suggested using the same metallic color as my bike was appealing.

"What are you doing?" he asked when I stuck my fist out for a fist bump. He didn't make a move to fist bump me back.

"We're fist bumping. Oh, come on! Please tell me you know how to fist bump!" I was actually a little irritated that he left me hanging for so long. I probably held my fist up for two minutes.

"Oh, I do. I just like it when you get mad." I glared at him and blinked. Ricky spun his chair around and wheeled away, leaving me there pissed off. If I could slap him, I promise you, I would.

I really would.

"Plot twist! The giant drops Inigo and Vizzini." We had settled on watching "The Princess Bride." I thought it would make the movie less awkward if we played plot twist throughout it. I love playing, especially through movies I've already seen five or six times.

"Plot twist! The sword Inigo is using turns to jelly."

"Plot twist! Westley slips on the rocks he is running on and gets a concussion."

"Plot twist! Buttercup sprouts wings and flies away from the king."

"Plot twist! The poison that Westley got was the wrong one and it ends up killing both of them."

"Plot twist! The rats in the forest follow Buttercup into the quicksand and eat her while she's down there."

The movie ended with Ricky making the last statement. "Buttercup catches a cold, faints, and falls off the horses they were riding into the sunset." I laughed hysterically at his comment because his face was completely serious. There was no trace of a joke in his voice.

"You like that one?" he asked as if my laughter wasn't enough confirmation for him. I wiped away the (happy) tears that had been accumulating throughout the entire movie. I was the one who laughed at a lot of the plot twist jokes but he chuckled at a few. It's really fun to see him relax for once. Even though Ricky never goes anywhere he's always tense. It's ironic really. You'd think he would be the most relaxed person in the world.

"Yes, I did. I liked it a lot!" I responded. He smirked and put the disc back into its case. When I looked up I noticed Ricky's face masked in an emotion I couldn't decipher. I went over to him and sat in his lap. This action seems to make him uncomfortable so I tend to do it whenever I want to get something out of him.

As soon as I sat down his eyes shot out and immediately went to mine. I couldn't help but laugh.

"What's wrong?" I asked using a sing-song voice. He shrugged slightly.

"Not about me sitting here. I was talking about before. You looked upset. What was that about?" I could tell what I said clicked. His eyes changed a little as he gave me a sad smile and shook his head.

"Yeah, see, I'm not accepting that Rick. What's

wrong?" I asked a little quieter.

"You can't fix everything, Gwen! It's not your problem!" I was taken aback by his sudden change in tone. I hopped off his lap, hurrying to get away when I felt his hand reach out and grab my wrist.

"No, you're right. Your problems aren't mine, and I don't even know why I care." I tugged my hand back and he let go. I knew that, if he wanted to, he could've kept it. His eyes made him look like he was sorry but I didn't stay long enough to find out if he truly was. It was time for me to get his medications anyway, so that helped me escape. I ignored the sound of Ricky behind me and continued to organize his pills on the plate. The plain white plate looked expensive so I was always particularly careful with it.

"Gwen?" he called me very quietly, but I chose to ignore him. He was right. I butt into his life too much, and I need to back off. I can't fix everything, I get that.

"Gwen." He wheeled in front of me when I turned around. I kept my eyes on the plate with the 8 pills on it. I counted them over and over again to make sure I had all of them.

1, 2, 3, 4, 5, 6, 7, 8

1, 2, 3, 4, -

"Gwen!" He took the plate from me and placed it on the counter. "Please talk to me," he pleaded. I finally looked into his eyes. The degree of sadness I saw in Ricky's eyes made a piece of my heart break. I tried to suppress my feelings though, because he's not the one who's supposed to be sad.

"It's okay, Ricky, I get it. I need to learn to mind my own business."

"Please don't, Gwen." I looked at him shocked. He told me, less than five minutes ago that he wanted me to stay out of his business and now he's telling me to jump into it?

"What?"

"You're the only one who cares about me, Gwen. So, please, don't stop."

"Then why did you-"

"I was thinking about what would happen when you leave. I'm going to be stuck here in this wretched chair, alone." I shook my head at his comment and that confused him. He hadn't caught onto the fact that I wasn't going to let him be all alone in a wheelchair. Clearly, he wasn't aware of the promise I made to myself to help guarantee that he would improve physically and emotionally.

"I made you an appointment with a physical therapist next Monday."

"A-are you serious?" he asked excitedly. I was glad, no, ecstatic that he was excited about the idea of visiting a physical therapist. At this point, he can only get better. Since Ricky has no control over his legs there really isn't anything bad that can come from this.

I nodded with a huge smile. Assisting Ricky in remaining happy and confident for long periods of time is hard, but I have this feeling that it isn't impossible.

"I don't know what to say."

"How about thank you?" I laughed at how obvious the response should be.

"How?"

"Well, you open your mouth and say-"

"No, I mean how did you arrange the appointment?"

"I called the physical therapy office at the hospital and explained that my friend needed some help."

"Friend, huh?" I blinked at his question. What's wrong with *friend*?

"What? You would've preferred that I said, 'Client? Patient? Customer?" I laughed when he shrugged at all of my suggestions. I turned around and grabbed the plate he had taken from me. Setting the pills on his tray, I waved him over.

He wheeled behind the tray and took the pills. I've only known Ricky for a short time but we've never talked about what we do on a regular day. I mean, I know he's here but besides the obstacle courses I don't know that much about him. It's hard to get him to open up. He's the typical, closed off, yet mysterious 18-year-old boy. I am making the executive decision to change that.

"Ask me." He rolls his eyes as he demands me to ask him the question that was obviously displayed on my face.

"What do you do?"

"Excuse me?" I gave him my iconic 'you can't be serious' look. The way that he usually asks for confirmation about the questions I ask him makes me think that I am speaking in another language. He makes me feel incompetent 95% of the time.

"On a regular day, what do you do?" I crossed my arms and sat down on the arm of the couch. I remember when I was little and my mom would get so mad when I did this. She claimed I would put a dent in the arm.

"I get up and wheel around to the TV. I stay there for probably five hours or so before I take what I've learned from 'American Ninja Warrior' and build a new obstacle course. I try out the course and train for the remainder of the evening. Bedtime is by 10:00 or so. What about you?"

"Oh, so the infamous Ricky Doone wants to hear about *my* life?" Similarly, to the way he feels, I find it funny when he gets agitated.

"I suggest you start talking, Gwen, before I change my mind." I put my hands up in surrender and laugh. Reveling in his utter annoyance could become my full-time hobby.

"You're going to have to specify what you want to hear. Unlike you, I don't have the luxury of having such a simple life. My life is pretty involved. There are many different facets/aspects, so many ins and outs…." I cross my arms, awaiting his response as usual.

He rolled his eyes. "What did you do yesterday?"

"Well," I brushed my hands together, acting as if my story was complicated. "I woke up and was shocked to see my mom's fiancé, Jerry, sitting at the kitchen table. I made everyone waffles with the toaster that burns every single thing you put in it. I put on some crappy clothes for the crappy date that I went on last night. I was really upset because I had to reschedule with Jer-"

"Y-you went on a *date*?" My eyes darted to Ricky's. His eyes locked onto a spot directly above my right shoulder, so I couldn't see everything that he was feeling through his eyes. Eye contact with Ricky is crucial if you want to have even a chance of finding out what he's thinking.

"Yes. Is there a problem here?" I laughed, very curious about Ricky's next line. He looked surprised of all things.

"No." He didn't look convincing at all.

"Is there something you want to say to me, Ricky?"

"Nope." I still wasn't buying it, but he looked completely uncomfortable so I decided to drop it.

"Well, then, if you don't mind, I'll finish the account of my day. Basically, my date was the reason why I had to miss out on going to this expensive museum with Jerry. The evening served as a helpful closure date, but it started off with us whisper-yelling at each other. He was apologizing but for most of the conversation it sounded the exact opposite of an apology." I scoffed at the mere memory of my conversation with Ty.

"What was he apologizing for?" I raised an eyebrow at how nosy Ricky was being today. He awkwardly chuckled and rubbed the back of his neck.

"Well, if you must know, he left two years ago without saying anything and didn't come back until just a few weeks ago. He left me, just like my brother Jett did." I wiped away the tear that came whenever I said Jett's name. I looked down to see Ricky's hand covering mine. It's nice to know that Ricky can tell when he shouldn't ask particular questions about my family. This was one of those times. I smiled at him before moving a piece of his blonde hair out of his eyes. That's better.

"You loved him?" At the sound of that word I thumped him on the back of his head. Where in God's name did he get that idea?

"Heck no!"

"Sorry, I was just asking. You seemed so sad that he left you. I guess I understand why, with him being your boyfriend and all-" I thumped him again, a little harder this time.

"You are just jumping to conclusions left and right today, aren't you?" He rubbed the spot on his head that I just smacked. I laughed at the thought of Ty and I together. Gwen and Ty, what a funny thought.

I walked around Ricky and jumped onto the couch. His appointment wasn't until next week so, until then, we are stuck in this house. Well, unless I change that.

"Why are you looking at me like that?" he asked watching me smiling at him mischievously.

"Are you up for a little adventure?" I could feel the twinkle in my eyes getting larger. I've always wanted someone to help me with this little, shall we call it, project.

He sighed making a smart decision to stop fighting the battle he could never win. "Okay, where are we going this time?"

I wanted to do something with spray paint. I've always had this dream of making a spray paint angel. It's like a snow angel but with spray paint and I've always wanted to do it. I'm pretty sure I got the inspiration when I took a picture and saw how amazing the silhouette of the girl was. You could see everything down to the finest strand of her hair. I know the spray paint won't be that accurate but it ties into the candid picture I took of a local artist. It's going to be colorful and will have components of a shadow. It's one of my many peculiar dreams.

"Is this it?" An older gentleman with a long beard asked us from behind the counter. He was a friendly cashier and I honestly felt badly for him. We ended up setting down a 70-square inch white canvas along with fifteen different colors of spray paint. Not to mention the paper towels we needed to protect the furniture in their house and the brushes we got in case the paint landed inside the outline.

"Yes, sir." I smiled at the sight of his dimples. He seemed like a really nice guy who was happy to help us. I find it reassuring when cashiers are genuinely pleased to help. It makes me feel like there are still a few good things left in this world.

"It comes to $83.91," the cashier announced looking from the computer screen to me. I handed him my credit card and signed the receipt. My signature wasn't anything fancy but it was always an accomplishment if I could write it similarly to how I first drew it in the beginning. I waved goodbye to the bearded man and placed the bags that contained our supplies in Ricky's lap. I took the large canvas in my arms and unlocked the car from inside the store. Our purchases were heavier than I expected so I needed to be able to set them down quickly. Unlike Ricky, I don't have superhuman strength.

When we got to the car I threw everything in the trunk. It took me a few minutes to get everything to fit, but Ricky seemed to find enjoyment in my struggling, so I guess that was a positive. Brushing my hands together I walked over to Ricky and put my hands on my hips. An accomplished smile tugging at my lips.

"Ready finally?" He grinned at the messy state of my hair. I looked completely disheveled, but I couldn't care less. I was so happy to finally be attempting the project I'd wanted to complete for years now.

"You could've helped me more at the car. I do believe that it's your legs that don't work, not your arms or upper body." I waited a second, pretending to get a last-minute thought. "Oh, but I guess I forgot, your brain seems to be getting slower by the minute." I smiled sweetly and gave his chair a forceful shove into the van. He chuckled at my aggravation. You know, it's pretty funny how this whole "relationship" is working out. One second we're telling each other our darkest secrets and the next we're chucking whatever object is within reach at each other.

"Where would the fun be in helping more?"

"Forget fun, there would be this sense of honor that comes with helping a woman."

"Oh, so you're a woman now? If I do recall, your birthday is still two months and six days away," he shot back smugly. Once again, he didn't realize how caring he sounded. He literally remembered my birthday. The fact that he even thought about me was enough to let me know that he cared. I smiled at the thought.

His birthday isn't until November, in case you were wondering.

"You remembered my birthday, Rick? I never knew you cared *this* much. I knew you cared, but to actually remember my birthday, now that's saying something." I smiled at him through the rear-view mirror. His face vividly showed how mad he was. He slipped up. Sometimes he tries so hard to insult me that he ends up sounding kindhearted.

"Whatever," he mumbles and looks out the window while I laugh hysterically in the front seat. He looks so pissed right now, you'd think I just told him that I'd been using his toothbrush for the past month.

When we finally got everything set up, I stood with my back up against the canvas.

"So, basically, you're going to spray the edges of my body with whatever colors you want ~ just make sure there are at least 4 different ones visible. I want it to look like a unicorn threw up on me, tripped on a rainbow, and then got into a fight with the color spectrum." He laughed at my analogy and picked up the first can of spray paint.

Guess what color it was?

14 BLACK ISN'T A COLOR

"Opinion is the medium between knowledge and ignorance." – Plato

He chose black.

It's funny how his mind works. Ricky explained how the canvas, in order to look like a true silhouette, needed to be mainly black. The cool part about that was that he was going to copy my candid picture ideas. Instead of using black for my head and hands he would use different colors. So, basically, your eyes would catch my head and hands before the rest of it. I honestly didn't know what to think. We were both just experimenting.

"Okay, you need to close your eyes." Ricky was sitting in his wheelchair above me, holding a black spray can. We decided that laying me on top of the canvas would be the most logical way to get this done.

"I'm so excited!" I exclaimed happily. He was laughing the way he does to make you feel like you're crazy. I knew I would need to ignore all of his snarky comments today and focus on enjoying my wish that was about to come true.

"That's great and all, but unless you want xylene in your eyes, I need you to close them." I sighed and followed his directions. When he said "that's great" he didn't sound like he meant it. In fact, he sounded as though he wanted to say "you're crazy." That's a good example of one of the comments I'm going to ignore.

I could hear the small metal ball rattling against the inside of the spray can. A few seconds later I felt the cold paint on the edge of my shoulder. It was extremely cold but I promised myself that I wouldn't flinch. Flinching would ruin the look of the outline, and believe me, I was definitely not going to do that.

It probably took a little longer since Ricky was seated in a wheelchair, but I wouldn't have wanted anyone else to do this with me. He told me to remain still for a few extra minutes just so I wouldn't smudge the entire thing when I stood up. Time ticked slowly as we waited anxiously for the paint to dry. Finally, I used the arms on Ricky's wheelchair to help me stand.

Backing away from the canvas, I gasped when I saw how cool it looked. Clearly, Ricky has dealt with spray paint before because nothing was smudged. Everything was perfectly in line and the places where he used colorful spray paint really stood out. Just like I thought it would.

"I'm not sure how I did it but I think it looks *pretty* good," Ricky commented tilting his head. I wanted to smack him for saying that. The canvas looks fantastic and the fact that he can't see that really makes me wonder if he's blind.

"You have to be kidding! It looks AMAZING!" I jumped on his lap and gave him a huge hug. I purposefully got colorful paint from my hands in his hair. He hates it when his hair gets messy. I started laughing when he practically threw me off his lap to check on his hair in the mirror. As Ricky worked hard to remove the red-green-yellow combination, I caught his eye in the mirror. I could tell from the look on his face that he wanted to throw something at me. If his eyes could throw daggers I would've been impaled by a hundred.

After a quick recovery we sat there side by side admiring our success. I believe Ricky was as happy as I was. He even snuck in a little compliment.

"Not only did the artist design a creative project, she also managed to keep as still as a statue on the canvas," he stated trying not to smile *too* much. Yes, that was a compliment, and I'll gladly accept it!

"Now stop worrying about your hair and help me clean this up," I said with a grin. His compliment meant a lot to me, but it was time to get back to business. I had Ricky hold the trash bag open for all of the empty spray cans and dirty paper towels. It was difficult to navigate around our mess in his wheelchair, so I thought the most efficient way for Ricky to help clean up would be to have him do something where he could stay still. I leaned the canvas on the wall and admired it again as soon as we finished cleaning. The fact that you can see all of my fingers probably made me the happiest. I was worried that my fingers would look webbed or something, but each one is visible. I looked from Ricky to the canvas, smiling widely. He laughed after using his phone to determine that I'd been standing there for nearly 10 minutes. The idea that my dream came true was amazing. I finally have a real-life silhouette! And what a unique one it is.

"So, what do we do now?" Ricky snapped me out of my trance. I looked at the clock and realized that we only had 45 minutes until Caroline would return. That's enough time to take candid pictures of Ricky secretly. This day just keeps getting better and better.

"I'd like to go out back. Please come with me." I put my hands together begging him to join me. Well, that and to pray he wouldn't catch my ulterior motive.

"Fine." Perfect.

I followed Ricky outside and watched as he went straight for the oak tree they had. I watched as he looked up. I followed his gaze to a small bird's nest that had settled itself into a crook in the tree. I smiled at the thought of how perfect this picture would be. The bird's nest could be seen from where I was standing so the viewer, if observant, could spot the nest and know what Ricky was looking at. I also had the option to make it a mystery by moving five steps to the left. If I moved to the left you could only see Ricky and the tree because branches hide the nest from this angle. Secretly, whipping out my camera, I took a picture. I had my silent camera today so he didn't hear the clicks that usually came when I pressed down to take the shot. I had hidden it underneath my coat when we walked out here.

I stayed on the outskirts of the yard as I watched him. His back was tense and he frequently looked for people who could possibly be watching him. He knew I was, but that was not what was worrying him. He's the kind of person who doesn't like a lot of attention and likes to keep everything he does under the radar. Constantly, he watches every moving thing that could possibly have an opinion about him. Unlike me, he cares about what other people think. If only he knew how he looked on a day to day basis. If only he knew how many people in town admire him and think he's a true inspiration. I wish that I could tell him how strong and confident he looks when he relaxes and stops worrying. Every time he worries it's obvious in the depths of his eyes and the way his body tenses. His hands grip the arms of his wheelchair so tightly that, sometimes, his knuckles turn white. His body language changes depending on who's in the picture. When I first met him, the confidence radiated off of him like it was his job. The next second though, he'll be cowering behind the wheels of his wheelchair as though there was a hitman coming for him. It's a shame to watch how much others affect him.

He's the kind of guy who secretly worries about you but immediately regrets it the second he finds out you've realized. It's funny how Ricky works. He'll only openly worry about you when you're too upset to realize he is.

I click the button and take a picture of Ricky looking down at his wheels. The shadow that casts down the side of his face is perfect. It makes him look thoughtful and extremely mysterious. The funny part about it, is that it makes him look extraordinary. The one thing he tries to avoid.

"When did you get that camera?" I jumped at the sound of his voice so close to me. I was busy reveling in how good the pictures looked and didn't even notice Ricky coming towards me. He looked surprised that he hadn't figured it out earlier. The fact that it was dark out really helped me in this situation. I got a ton of pictures of him, and they all looked great. I can't wait until I finish the collage that I've started.

"Probably 20 minutes ago. Why?" I pretended to be confused. I really don't want him to get angry. He has a scary angry face.

"Let me see them." He sighed, deciding to give up on arguing with me. I smiled at his surrender and handed him the camera.

"What do you think?" I crossed my arms, anxious to hear what he thought of them.

"Honestly?"

Well, when you ask me like that, I'm not sure. "Of course."

"I'm not loving the shadows. The pictures with the stars in them are good but the shadows take away from my extremely handsome face." He subtly added that little ego-boosting comment just to piss me off. I laughed at the sound of him complimenting himself. That was also to hide the fact that I wouldn't disagree with that comment.... at all.

"Well, the shadows suit you. They symbolize the mystery that is Ricky Doone," I explained. He thought over what I said before handing me back the camera.

"So, I'm a mystery now?" He asked with a mischievous smirk.

"Oh, Ricky you've always been a mystery to me," I laughed and patted him on the shoulder. Honestly, what was he expecting? He's the one wheeling around and saying things that almost always have a double meaning.

I turned to head into the house when I heard him mumble, "You are an even bigger one." I acted as though I didn't hear him because I wasn't sure how to respond. I mean, how do you respond to something like that?

The second I opened the back door I heard the front door unlock. I rushed to get it and smiled when I saw Caroline. I've come to the conclusion that holding the past against her would only make things worse. At least, this way, we both can focus on what Ricky needs.

"Why hello dear. How was he today?" She asked, setting down the grocery bags that she'd been carrying. I picked up as many as I could and walked into the kitchen.

"He was great! He helped me create this beautiful piece of artwork that I've always wanted to make. It looks great! Oh, and don't worry. I made sure that nothing in your house got hurt." I wanted to reassure her because I could see the distress in her eyes. They filled with that emotion the second I said 'art'. She clearly couldn't wrap her mind around the idea of her house getting messed up.

"Oh good. I'm so glad that you could get him to help you. Do you need help carrying it over to your house?" I shook my head and turned to wave to Ricky.

"Okay, goodnight everyone. I had fun today!" I walked into the family room and picked up the canvas. The second I got out the door I had to set it down. It felt like it got heavier since we added the spray paint. I lifted it once again and got it into my house. I smiled when I saw Jerry immediately come over to help me carry it in. When we knocked into the stairs, I couldn't help but laugh.

"Oh, my honey! What is this?" My mother came around the corner and gasped at the sight of the giant canvas.

"I made a silhouette at Ricky's house! I absolutely love it." I turned it and let it rest on my shoulder so the two of them could step back and look at it together. They both smiled at the sight of it.

"It's great, Gwen!" My mom and Jerry said in unison. They laughed at how their voices sounded together, and I could tell this could turn into a lovey-dovey moment rather quickly.

"Well, thanks guys. I'm going to go put it in my room and get ready for bed." I smiled awkwardly at the two of them and made a quick break with the canvas for the stairs.

"Okay, but Gwen, we need to discuss the wedding plans sometime tomorrow." I heard my mother shout to me.

"Okay!" I let the stairs carry my voice to her. I bumped into a lot of things on the way up the stairs but the thing that almost made me cry was the motorcycle statue Jett got me along with my bike two years ago. I have this feeling that all of my gifts were, in a sense, goodbye gifts. The statue was of a silver motorcycle during a wheelie. My brother was obsessed with doing wheelies and he was the one who taught me how to do them. I took it a step further and started to stand up while doing them. My mother refuses to watch me doing tricks, but I can understand why. It's scary for me but probably even scarier for the people watching. I used to be in her position when I would watch Jett with all of his friends. He had this huge group of guys who would ride with him. They were as crazy as I was. When Jett left I even tried to join the group. They wouldn't let me though. They told me I reminded them too much of Jett.

Anyway, long story short, I love that statue and I had it right next to my bed on my nightstand. I was stupid and left it there while I was moving the canvas into my room. I knocked it over, and when I heard it crash I had a panic attack.

Setting the canvas against the wall, I turned to the floor. Luckily, the statue didn't break. I let out a breath that I'd been holding ever since I heard it fall. Shaking my head and putting the statue back on my nightstand, I looked around my room. Where am I going to put this thing?

The wall behind my bed looked like the perfect spot. I opened the drawer with my nails and hammer and held the canvas up so I could mark the center spot. I took a pencil and drew a small circle where I wanted the nail to go. Putting the canvas down and picking up my tools, I hammered the nail in the wall. After adjusting the canvas to hang properly I took a step back and.... wow! It looked even better than I thought it would. The white Christmas lights that hung on the end of my bed made the silhouette look that much cooler. I smiled at my handy work and turned to my closet to get ready for bed.

I climbed into bed and spent thirty minutes thinking about Ricky, and everything that he has changed in me. Now when I go to school I don't completely shut people down. I don't pretend to be content anymore. Ricky has been a great distraction from my hand and the fact that I can't kick-box. If anything, I've actually liked having my hand broken because it gives me more of a reason to keep taking care of Ricky. He's really sweet, when he wants to be, and he's been honest with me lately. I really do think that we are having a positive impact on each other.

Just the other day, Caroline came to me crying. She told me that she hasn't seen Ricky this happy since the day she took him to see "American Ninja Warrior" in person. I'm really glad that I'm having such a positive influence on him. He seems friendlier when we go out, and I really think that his social skills are improving. I've also been looking forward to seeing some of his obstacle courses. Ricky mentioned the other day that he wanted to show me one soon ~ I'm extremely excited about that! It's going to be great, I can just tell.

Don't get me wrong though. I'm a little worried about a few things. Thoughts of the day that I walked in on Ricky trying to end his life haunt me more than I'd like to admit. His mood swings and aggression come from all of the medications he's taking. Those random impulses that he acts on don't represent the amazing person that he is. The positives in our relationship definitely surpass the negatives but that's one of the reasons why I worry. What happens when I'm not around as much? What happens when I can only visit him once every month? That answer scares me. That's why I'm doing everything I can to get him to be more independent. I am praying with everything I have that this physical therapy will help decrease the number of medications he needs to take. Consequently, his emotional state will improve. Ricky deserves that.

It's hard for me to be honest with people. My history makes me seem weak, and I'm afraid that if I told Ricky about it he wouldn't see me the same way. I've built this fearless image for myself, but here I am crying over family that didn't care enough about me or my mother to let us know where they were going. I feel like it is my job to be strong for Ricky. His mother isn't exactly the greatest image of strength and his father clearly has his issues. I really want Ricky to be able to have (OR: It's important to me for Ricky to feel like he has at least one person in his life who he considers strong. I know that he's 18, but he hasn't had experiences that most 18-year-olds have had. Ricky hasn't done half of the things that people at my school have done. He hasn't experienced a high school football game. He hasn't been on a date. He hasn't talked back to a teacher. He hasn't missed a bus ride. He hasn't cheated on a test. He hasn't been nominated for valedictorian. He's never had the thrill of a cafeteria food fight or been invited to a high school party. He hasn't done any of it.

He hasn't lived like most young people out there, and the thought of that makes me sad. I've loved some of the dramatic things that have happened to me because they have taught me valuable lessons. The top lesson being never to mess with the popular girl's shoes.

The point of all of this is that I am trying to make a difference in Ricky's life. I want to show him things that his mother would never understand because he deserves to have a glimpse of a normal teenage boy's life. In my opinion, he is more together than most kids out there, but that doesn't change how he feels about himself. It's a shame to think about how Ricky perceives himself. The mirror that he chooses to look in is the one that you can find at carnivals. He needs to stop.

My eyes began to feel heavy as I thought of one last thing. Maybe I could take Ricky to school and expose him the "normal" teenage experience. Yeah, that's what I'll do! I can show Ricky what all of us go through and maybe that will make him feel better about his situation. He says that he accepts his disability and all, but I don't believe that. He has a lot of pent up anger that, one day, is going to get the best of him. He's going to explode and not know how to deal with it all. That's when I'll be there to help him. It's going to be like that time I stopped him from overdosing on purpose. Right there, just in time.

My eyes closed finally as I let the darkness consume me.

"That's the color you chose, Rick? Seriously?" I looked at his hands that were currently holding the black spray paint. "I thought I told you that I wanted it to be colorful?"

"Well," he said, "silhouettes aren't colorful. If you want it to look real you need to let me do it this way. I can make your head and hands colorful though. That'll make this canvas more representative of you." I nodded at his evaluation. I knew he was smarter than he let on.

He always tries to cover the fact that he has a deeper understanding of almost everything in this world. In my opinion, it's really impressive. He should embrace it more.

"Okay, just don't get that color anywhere that isn't necessary." I warned. He shook his head disagreeing with what I was saying. What is there to disagree about anyway?

"Gwen," I opened my eyes and looked into his at the sound of my name, "Black isn't a color."

See what I mean?

15 REPEATEDLY

"There is no harm in asking."

Rubbing the sleep from my eyes, I sat up to see my mother sitting at the end of my bed. Startled, I sat back abruptly and hit my back on the headboard. The sudden impact definitely didn't help with the headache I was sporting. When my thoughts get jumbled together with dreams I wake up with a massive headache the next morning. I went to a doctor to see if there was something wrong but he said I was okay.

I'm not sure that I trust that doctor.

"Oh, I'm sorry, Gwen. I didn't mean to frighten you. I just wanted to discuss the wedding." I looked at her shocked to say the least. She couldn't honestly want to talk to me about something this important on a Tuesday morning? I have school in less than an hour.

"Mom, it's Tuesday." She smiled and nodded at my comment, clearly missing the point. "I have school today." A few more seconds passed and I realized nothing seemed to get through to her.

"So, I wanted to ask you about the specific day. We have a choice between a Friday or a Saturday. Which one?" She stood up beside me.

"Because of school, I'd say a Saturday."

"But I'm pretty sure it's going to be during your summer break."

"Well I'd still say a Saturday because I feel like more people would be free on a Saturday than on a Friday." She smiled and clapped her hands together.

"Thank you, honey. Let me know when we should leave." She headed down the hallway toward her room.

That was weird.

I looked in the mirror and scared myself. My bed head really is a problem and should be diagnosed by a medical professional in my opinion. I brushed my hair before I even stepped into the bathroom. I can't brush my teeth and be forced to look at that abomination the entire time. That would be inhumane.

I hopped into my mother's car wearing a green romper and black leather jacket. If you haven't noticed, I am in love with my black leather jacket. Surprisingly nothing has happened to it so far.

"You look nice today, Gwen." Mom shared her compliment as she climbed in the car to join me.

"Thanks." I looked over at Ricky's house and got this urge to run over and drag him to school with me. I didn't though. After a few thoughtful moments, I realized how obnoxious and overly assertive that would be.

As the trees blurred together I suddenly felt homesick. Ricky really helped the last few days fly by, but today I'm seriously dragging. I didn't finish breakfast. My hand was twitching and my index finger went numb for a few seconds earlier this morning. It was one of those mornings when you really don't want to go to school, more than usual.

"Okay, honey. I'll see you after school." I smiled at my mother and hopped out of the car without a word. I really wasn't liking that plan because it involved me staying at school the entire day. As I glanced back I saw her car turn onto the main road toward our house. I was so tempted to run, jump onto the back of it, and let the car take me home, but I didn't do that either.

First period.

Second period.

Third period.

Fourth period.

Lunch.

Sixth period.

Seventh period.

Freedom. What a comforting word. I find it empowering. I made my way to my locker with a little pep in my step. After rearranging a few things that were too disorganized I quickly zipped up my backpack. I don't have OCD or anything, I just like other people to think I do. With that thought, I smiled and closed my locker with a little too much force. The people directly to my left and right subtly looked at me through the corners of their eyes. Of course I noticed and waved to both of them. They whipped their heads back toward their lockers as if smiling or showing me any form of kindness would've gotten them killed.

My mom waved the second she saw me. Luckily, she was in the car so only those who were looking specifically at her could see that. The look on her face would've made you think I just finished my first day of preschool.

"You look extremely happy," I commented. Mom nodded confidently at my observation as I closed the car door. What is going on with her? I don't understand why she's been so weird lately.

"I am!"

"And why is that? Did you get your tax returns?" She gets excited about those usually.

"No, Gwen, I'm.... pregnant!" she whispered in excitement. I looked at her stunned. She clearly didn't know how to handle my expression because she stepped on the gas and rambled on.

"Since this is the case, Jerry and I had to move the wedding to next month. I've already sent out most of the invitations but I wanted to check to see if there is anybody else you would like to invite."

Thinking about that snapped me out of my trance. I nodded as four names popped into my head. Darren, Trina, Ricky, and Caroline.

"Can I invite four people?" She nodded. "Okay then, I'd like to invite Darren, Trina, Ricky, and Caroline." My mom smiled at me and giggled when she saw the confusion on my face.

"I've already invited Darren and Trina. Trina is our

flower girl." I smiled happily at the thought of Trina throwing flowers down the aisle. She's going to look even more adorable than usual.

"Well then, just Ricky and Caroline."

"Not Ty?" Mom inquired gently. As we pulled in front of the house I tried to picture Ty being at the wedding. For some reason the first thought that came to mind was of a plane crashing into the side of a mountain; dangerous and extremely problematic.

"No. Not Ty." I don't want to see him there. I can't go through that for a second time.

I unlocked the door and waited for my mother to get inside. Closing the door, I heard the sound of Jerry's voice behind me. He was talking to my mother so I decided that I would go upstairs and leave them alone. Ignoring my mixed feelings about my mother being pregnant is the only way I can handle this. Besides, I really need to get my homework out of the way before my appointment this afternoon.

The doctor wants to take a look at my hand to see how it's healing. I already know what he is going to say so, honestly, I think this appointment is a little unnecessary. He'll explain that it is healing just fine but I need to keep the glove on for another six weeks or so. The thing is, I don't have six weeks.

I don't even know what college I want to go to and by the time my hand heals I will already have had to make a decision. Senior year is ending in about six weeks and I haven't received all of my acceptance letters yet. One thing that frustrates me when I think about college is the pressure of choosing a profession. Nothing that guarantees you a good future is interesting to me. I would love to be a professional photographer but I don't know how practical that is. My mother has always wanted me to go into some type of medical field. For example, she thinks I'd make a good surgeon or neurologist. The only thing I know about those two professions is that I don't want to do that. I like racing, taking pictures, and kickboxing. I'm not sure what profession could get me into doing anything that I love.

Don't worry. I've applied to colleges already, and I'm waiting for the responses. The few that have arrived all say I'm eligible for their scholarship programs. That's great, truly it is, but none of them let me ride, take pictures, or kickbox. My grandfather told me that loving your profession doesn't matter. As long as you can support yourself and your family then you are going to be fine. You don't work for pleasure, you work to survive.

I'm not sure if I can accept that. The thing that doesn't work about that in my life is the fact that I can't survive without the things that I have grown to love. I will only stop riding when I physically can't ride anymore. I will stop taking pictures when my hands can't click the capture button anymore. It's that simple. I've really been looking forward to getting a letter from the New York Institute of Photography. I've been trying to decide whether I should take the risky path and go after what I love or study for a profession that I hate.

You already know which path I'm going to take.

"Honey! We have to go!" Mom yelled up the stairs. From the sound of it, I'm pretty sure that Jerry was coming along. I wasn't particularly loving that idea because Jerry would be seeing me cry for the first time. The pain that I have felt from this hand is unbelievable. Whenever Dr. Lucero examines my hand it clenches up and ends up hurting for about two days. I've had two appointments since the locker incident and this is the last check up for about a month. If it isn't obvious, I'm extremely excited.

I hopped into the passenger seat and immediately regretted it. Jerry nodded like he thought I was trying to make a point or something. My mom looked at me with so much disappointment in her eyes that I couldn't handle looking at her for even a second.

"No, Jerry," I opened the door and got out, "I didn't mean to. I'm just so used to sitting in the front. Here." He smiled at my confession, obviously feeling better about where he stands in my life. He got in the passenger seat, and when he shut the door, I let out a sigh of relief. I would hate for him to feel like I didn't approve of him. Maybe, I should pull him aside one day and tell him how I really feel. I have a feeling that, until I do, many more awkward situations will arise.

"So," my mom was pulling out of our parking spot and turning down the radio when she started talking, "would now be a good time to talk about the wedding?" Jerry and I both nodded as she continued. "Okay, so we were thinking the 4th Saturday in June for the wedding. The venue is small but it is outdoors on an open field. It's going to showcase the stars and everything that is so beautiful about the nighttime. What do you think, Gwen? Jerry and I have already discussed it. I would like to know how you feel."

She's lucky that I am so flexible and understanding.

The average daughter would've been hurt that her mother already planned the venue without consulting her first. I do have to remember though that she did just ask for my input. That definitely counts for something.

"Yeah, that sounds beautiful. I really like the idea of an evening wedding. Is it going to have a normal color scheme or are you guys using crazy wedding colors?"

"No, we're planning a black and white color theme with the exception of the bridesmaids. It's going to be small, so we were thinking of only inviting close friends and family. Jerry's about fifteen people. I'm at about twelve and you're at two so everything should work out perfectly." I thought about how much fun it will be to have Ricky and Caroline come to the wedding. It will be great for Ricky to get out of the house for a festive occasion.

Jerry and my mom smiled at each other. It's one of those smiles that makes you want to jump out of the car. If only I had a giant spoon to use to gag myself. They truly don't understand that I am seventeen and still susceptible to emotional and visual scarring.

I fake coughed and started speaking quickly. "Oh, look! It's the office. You guys can just sit here. I can check myself in." I started to get out of the car the second she put it into park. "Come in whenever you're ready." I nodded at my own advice and ran for the office, grateful for my physical fitness.

I was greeted by the lovely receptionist. Have you ever met someone who is a lot older than you, but you just know that if they were your age they would be such a good friend to have around? Well that was Miss Mae. She is one of the sweetest people I have ever met. I've only seen her twice but she is always so friendly and charismatic. I would put her age at about thirty-five.

"Hello Miss Mae." I smiled at her and began entering my information at the check-in counter. I typed in my first and last name, my email, my mother's email, and phone number, and our address.

"Gwen! You know you can call me Mae, right?" I laughed at her reminder. She's told me about four times now.

"Hello, Mae." She looked so pleased at the sound of her name without the "Miss" in front of it. I'm not really sure why.

"Isn't it such a pretty day today? I purposefully left my house about twenty minutes early just so I could procrastinate outside for a little bit." I nodded in agreement. When Mae was excited her black curly hair bounced. It makes you want to go over to her and bounce one of her curls yourself. She has gorgeous caramel colored skin that complements her very dark brown eyes. They get a lot brighter whenever she's happy.

"Dr. Lucero should be out in just a moment, dear. We haven't been that busy today for some odd reason. A lot of patients canceled at the last second so our wait list became almost non-existent." She chuckled at how odd that sounded and turned her attention back to her computer screen. I grinned as I took my seat in the waiting area. The number of magazines this place had was incredible. Everything from parenting tips to the Kardashians was displayed on the front covers.

"Gwen Brady." I looked up to see Dr. Lucero standing in the doorway with a clipboard. Mom and

Jerry walked in just as I stood up. Waving to them, I followed Dr. Lucero into the room and sat down on that "bed thing" that doctors have in their patient rooms.

"So, how have you been, Gwen? I hear that you are helping out a boy with cerebral palsy in your neighborhood?" Dr. Lucero always starts every appointment by checking in and seeing how I am doing. He's an orthopedic doctor, but sometimes he acts like my therapist. It's nice, I guess. I just find it strange how he sounds like he cares so much. Once my hand heals I probably won't be seeing him again.

"Yeah, I have. I feel really good about it. Ricky is one of the smartest people I've met, so I've been learning a lot from him."

"And your hand.... it hasn't been getting in the way of anything?"

"No. I mean, I always feel it, but the only time it really hurts is when I lay down and when I wake up. Besides that, I'm just really anxious to ride my motorcycle again."

"Yes, your mother was telling me about all of your hobbies. It's a shame that you need both of your hands for everything you love to do."

"Tell me about it." I chuckled, softly, in annoyance. I hate it when people point out the obvious. He does that a lot.

"Well, let me take a look." He took my hand in his and gently pulled off the glove. I was as surprised as he was to see so many bruises on my hand. He made a clicking noise under his breath that I couldn't decipher. I'm not sure if it was a "Gwen, you're not doing this right" noise or a "This is going to take longer than I thought" noise. I searched his eyes frantically, looking for any sign of hope. I found nothing.

"Gwen, I know you wanted to stay in this glove, but I'm afraid we are going to have to switch you over to a more substantial cast." I was afraid he was going to say that so I had prepared myself for it. "We'll take a quick x-ray here in the office to confirm."

"Okay," I said quietly. I knew my mother and Jerry had been standing in the doorway the entire time so I wasn't surprised when I felt someone's hand on my shoulder. It was bigger than my mother's so I knew it was Jerry's. I was too upset to look at him though. My hands are extremely important to me so, of course, I'll do whatever Dr. Lucero recommends. I hate how casts look though. They look like you purposefully stuck your hand in a coffin to let mummies wrap it.

"So, I am going to give you a-"

"I'm sorry, excuse me doctor, but couldn't she use a splint in conjunction with her soft cast to stabilize the main break? I've heard a lot of great things about splints especially since her index finger only has a broken metacarpal. Maybe that would work better than the hard cast?" Jerry spoke up, and it made me feel really good. I take back what I said earlier. I'm glad Mom brought him. This is a good example of what fathers are supposed to do and he is receiving an 'A+' for it. I smiled up at him and nodded at his suggestion.

"Umm, yes. Okay, I guess that would work. It's going to cost you though." Dr. Lucero crossed his arms, and I immediately looked at my mother. She reached into her purse but was stopped by the sound of Jerry ripping a check from his checkbook. I smiled even wider at his reflexes. He knows exactly what he's doing and knows my mother is just eating it all up. Thankfully the x-ray sealed the deal! Dr. Lucero agreed that Jerry's suggestion was the best way to go about my recovery.

"Thanks. So, here is the splint you'll need to use. You'll probably have to wear it for another 5 weeks. Mae can get it for you and just let her know that you already paid for it." I hopped off the weird "bed thing" and walked out with Jerry and my mother. I looked at Jerry with the biggest smile on my face.

"Thank you, Jerry," my mother whispered to him. He put his hand in hers and gave her a little wink. They need to understand that PDA isn't just a code for kissing.

"How'd it go, Gwen? Does everything look alright?" Mae sat up in her seat just a little at the sight of us. I beamed as I walked up to her counter.

"Yeah. I need a splint though. Dr. Lucero said I could get it from you. We already paid him."

"Oh, yeah. I'll get it right away," she responded happily and spun in her rolling chair. She bent down and reached into a little white cabinet that was labeled "accessories." She handed it to me and smiled at all of us.

"I mean this in the nicest way possible, I hope I won't be seeing you for a while." She changed her voice slightly for the last part, and it made me laugh. We all waved to Mae and headed back to the car.

I let the two of them walk a little ahead of me so I could play my games and simultaneously ignore their unconcealed affection for each other.

When we got home I put on the splint and

immediately felt the difference. We had dinner relatively early so I could take more of my pain medications. They helped but didn't get rid of the feeling of discomfort that was always there. Oh well, at least I know it's healing correctly. Sometimes your fingers can deform and curl over each other if they heal incorrectly. The results from the x-ray helped me to relax.

Things could be worse. So, for now, this is good.

16 A SMALL GLIMPSE

"And sometimes, against all odds, against all logic, we still hope."

The week passed pretty quickly. I finally got into the swing of things and decided that every day Ricky and I were together we would do something fun. I got into the habit of surprising him with random trips all over town. I had to bribe him to go on a few, but after a while he started to accept the fact that staying cooped up in the house wasn't an option.

It was Monday and that meant today was Ricky's appointment. All day at school I had been antsy and desperate for the clock to read 2:30pm. Ricky's appointment wasn't until 5:45 so I would be the one taking him. The fact that Caroline didn't know about it probably added to my uneasiness, but I like to pretend that that's not the case.

I watched the second hand as it seemed to slow down every time I looked at it. We had five more minutes in this class, and I honestly thought I wouldn't be able to make it through. The thought of giving Ricky some measure of hope truly excited me. It made me feel that I really was having a positive impact on his life. It also helped me deal with my nightmares. Ever since the day I walked in on Ricky attempting to overdose I've had trouble sleeping. The thought of him even thinking like that scared me, but to actually see it with my own eyes, that's what traumatized me. I keep worrying that I might walk in one day, and it will be too late.

BING! BING! BING! The bell sounded making me jump up in excitement. The second I got out in the hallway I made a Beeline for my locker only to be stopped by none other than Carter. I hadn't had a lengthy conversation with him ever, so to say I was surprised, was an understatement.

"Hey," I greeted him, awkwardly. He smiled sincerely, getting me to calm down. I honestly don't know why he's talking to me. People usually don't do that.

"Hey, Gwen." He gave me a small wave before taking a deep breath. I blinked and checked to see if my ears were working right.

I smiled nervously before he took one step toward me.

"I was wondering if you would like to go out with me on Friday night?" He looked me in the eye to try and gauge my response. His stance made it look like I could make him fall back with a single blow. In reality, I wouldn't succeed because he was huge. Muscular I mean. Carter was muscular, and really, he would be the one who could knock me down with a single blow. He looked extremely uncomfortable though and, in a certain light, nervous.

I put both of my hands on the straps of my backpack to give me something to fiddle with while talking to him.

"That's very sweet of you, Carter, but I barely know you," I pointed out giving him a knowing look.

He nodded. "Yeah I get it. I'm sorry for even ask-"

"Now don't do that. I never said no." I crossed my arms, a bit frustrated that he couldn't man up and ask me with confidence and conviction.

"So, is that a yes?" He asked hopefully, the light I had briefly turned off sparking in his eyes once again.

I quickly considered my options. I could continue to avoid society as a whole. I could proceed to live my life that revolved around only about five people, or I could screw it. I could screw the feeling I got whenever people purposefully tried to make my life harder. Being so motivated to help Ricky has resulted in me doing a lot of crazy things, but this…. what I am about to say is probably the craziest.

"Sure. I'd love to go out with you." I couldn't help but notice the boyish grin he was now sporting. It was cute in a shy, bemused, kind of way. I'm not exactly sure what possessed me to say yes, but you know what? I'm going to pretend like I don't care that, for once in my life, I wasn't using my head.

"So, I'll pick you up at 8?" He squirmed as he asked. He really is an interesting guy. I've never seen someone act so uncomfortable while asking me out. That would cause a red flag to go up in any other girl's eyes, but in mine, I just found it amusing. The infamous, mysterious, new boy…. was…. scared of me? Is that what was happening here? I smiled at the thought.

I began to nod but quickly stopped when Ricky came into my mind.

"You're probably going to hate me for this, but would it be possible for you to pick me up at 9? I know that's not how dates usually work but I'm taking care of someone until then."

"Umm, yeah sure. I could make that work. We probably won't be back until late though. If that's alright?" He stepped out of the way of bustling students, sliding me over with him.

"Yeah, that's great. May I ask what we're doing?" I asked with a curious smile. I know curiosity killed the cat. Yeah, I get it, but I'd like to know exactly what he's planning. As I've said, I barely know him.

"It's a surprise."

"Okay," I said. Not convincing anyone that I was okay with that.

"May I ask exactly who you are taking care of on Friday?" He was trying to sound like he didn't care but something inside me thought he did. That bothered me just a little.

"His name is Ricky. He has a congenital disorder called cerebral palsy. I'm not sure if you've heard of it?"

He nodded his understanding. "How do you know him?"

"He's my neighbor. He and his mom have lived next to me for a while but just recently they contacted me and asked for my help.

"Well that's very sweet of you. Should I pick you up at their house instead of yours?"

"Well, I live in a townhouse so they are literally right next door, so either way you'll find me." I smiled and headed for my locker. I really need to get going. Ricky hates it when I'm late and his appointment is today. He finally would be getting a fair chance. The euphoric feeling I got thinking about his appointment today was exciting.

"You're late." Ricky crossed his arms with a very stern, annoyed look. I rolled my eyes and let out an agitated sigh. Every single day I come over he blames me for walking in at 4:01. I'm pretty sure there is something called a grace period.

"I'm going to start waiting outside and walking in at the exact time the clock strikes 4:00," I said sarcastically. He'd better not make me do that.

"I'm surprised you haven't been doing that already." The amount of annoyance that was swirling in his eyes made me wonder if he had separation issues. I'm pretty sure that is called autophobia.

I coughed "imbecile" into my arm. He feigned sadness, receiving an accomplished smirk from me. I rolled my eyes and decided, as I do on most days, to ignore his stupid unrealistic demands. I'll bet you a lot of money that he purposefully has his clocks run fast just so I always look late. I'll catch him one day though I promise I will.

I opened the fridge and helped myself to a Cherry Coke. It's gotten to the point where getting one out of the fridge is an instant reflex. Funny how controlling habits are.

"Hey Rick!" I called him from the kitchen, taking a seat on one of the two bar chairs next to the fridge.

"What?" he called back, his voice gradually getting

louder as he drew closer. I didn't turn around or begin to speak until I knew he was behind me. I tend to lose track of people when they're behind me. I've been stuck talking to myself before and let me tell you, it's embarrassing. I try my hardest to prevent that from happening.

"Are you excited about your appointment?" He shrugged in answer to my question. I tried my very best not to show how irritated I was, but by the look on his face I failed horribly.

"I'm going to ask again. Are you.... excited.... about your appointment?" I crossed my arms being careful not to spill the can I was holding.

"I don't really care." I wanted to strangle him. His comment was infuriating.

"You know, Ricky. I do A LOT for you and your family. I try my best to get you out and expose you to things you already should've been exposed. I try to explain things to you that most 18-year-olds learned many years ago. But, no. You have the audacity to sit there and-" He ran a hand through his hair, interrupting me with his incessant chuckling.

"I was joking, Gwen. I'm extremely excited about this appointment. Believe it or not, I have a lot of hope now. So, I guess, thanks." I lightened up at the sound of him thanking me. Deciding that now would be a good time to get him back, I harassed him about his inability to give a proper "thank you."

"What, I'm sorry, what was that? I couldn't quite hear the last word. You sort of mumbled it."

"Gwen," he growled. I cupped my ears dramatically, reveling in his discomfort about showing me appreciation. This guy was something else.

"I said thank you." He rolled his eyes and wheeled out of the kitchen quickly. I can only imagine that was an effort to shut me up. For his sake, that probably was the best option.

"You look nervous." I looked down to see Ricky hesitating to enter the therapist's door I was currently holding open for him.

We arrived at Dr. Knight's office 20 minutes early, so I wasn't pressing Ricky to go in. If we were running behind, however, I would've forced his brake back and wheeled him into the office myself. I like to be punctual. I think your punctuality reflects a lot about your character and makes a big first impression. Remember, there's never a second chance to make a first impression.

The car ride over was silent. It wasn't a comfortable silence, though. It was one that was filled with unanswered questions and insecurities. I felt like the closer we got to the office the wearier Ricky became. It was almost like his confidence was shot. Each mile away from the house was another one closer to his, seemingly, anxiety-producing destination.

I'm guessing the idea of having your legs move after eighteen years is scary. I'm not sure if he understands that this therapy is going to take time to work, if it even works at all.

"Nope. I'm just grand," he spoke monotonously. He was uncomfortable, and I could tell by how his eyes went back and forth between the two glass doors. The one to the right read **ENTER** while the one to the left read **EXIT**.

"See, I have this inkling that you're lying to me," I pointed out, trying my best to suppress the smile that was threatening to form on my face. His annoyance was amusing.

"Whatever. Let's just get this over with." He let out an agitated sigh and wheeled through the open door. I rolled my eyes due to his immaturity and followed him. For some odd reason, there were another set of doors that led to the actual office. I didn't have nearly as much trouble getting him through those.

The door creaked open, and I was happy to see that there was no one else in the waiting room. The receptionist smiled when she saw us and beckoned us over.

"Hello. Who's the patient?" I heard a small scoff come from Ricky but I was confident I was the only one who could hear it.

"Ricky Doone. 5:45 appointment," I told her happily. She smiled and typed in his name. A few more questions were asked and then she handed us the clipboard. I offered to complete the forms but Ricky said, and I quote, "It's my legs that don't work NOT my ability to think, read, and write."

I put my hands up in surrender and turned to the magazines. I was excited to see *Cycle World* thrown into the mix of magazines on the table. I grabbed it, almost greedily, and started flipping through the pages. Ricky was probably staring at me due to the fact that small gasps were leaving my mouth when I saw motorcycles like the Harley-Davidson Low Rider S model, the Kawasaki KX450F, and the Yamaha YZF-R1. My dreams in ink.

"So, you REALLY like motorcycles," Ricky pointed out. I jumped at the sound of his voice, forgetting that I was here with someone.

"No." I shook my head, disagreeing with his observation. He gave me a look of utter disbelief.

"I *love* them!" I gave him a serious look not faltering even slightly. He shook his head and scoffed again looking back down at the document he had completed for the physical therapy session. I shrugged and turned back to my magazine. His wheels spun before I heard him set the clipboard in front of the receptionist and looked up to see him give her a slight nod.

Then, we waited.

A little longer.

A little longer.

I was on page fifty of the motorcycle magazine when Dr. Knight walked in. She was dressed in long white scrubs. As she stepped toward us the light bounced off of her bright blue name tag and her long red hair that softly framed her face. I would place her in her mid 30's but I could be wrong. I was thankful for her cheery disposition.

I gave her a small smile and a wave before glancing at Ricky who was completely silent. He looked at her as if she just told him he had five minutes left to live.

"You must be Ricky! I'm Dr.-"

"Knight. I know. As crazy as it may seem the kid in the wheelchair actually knows what's going on." I gave him a hard glare before turning to Dr. Knight apologetically. I didn't bring him here to harass the professional who would be trying to help him.

"You can call me Ever." I raised my eyebrow at the sound of her friendly tone. I give her props for keeping her cool. When Ricky's involved, that can be a real challenge.

"What's that short for?" he asked inconsiderately. At this point, I was "throwing daggers" Ricky's way. He gave me one of those, "What?" shrugs as if he didn't know his behavior was absolutely ridiculous. I was surprised at his attitude especially considering Ricky was originally excited about the appointment.

"Now, Mr. Doone, I do not believe that information is required for my job as your physical therapist. It's also not my job to wonder why you have the inability to act your age. It's just not protocol. But showing you to your room, now that's my job so I can freely say that your room is just down that hallway on the left." It took everything in me not to get up from my seat and start clapping. It really did.

Thankfully Ricky kept his mouth shut. I stood up and walked behind Ricky's chair, seeing that he would obviously not be wheeling himself willingly into the room. I rolled my eyes at his immaturity as I pushed him through the doors that she held open for us. Dr. Knight walked next to me and I smiled at her fondly. Repaying the kind gesture, she walked ahead and led us into a spacious room. There was a lot of equipment that you would find in a regular gym. A few of the pieces though were unique and specially designed for patients. The equipment was scattered sporadically around the room. A chair was placed next to each piece of equipment that,

I'm guessing, is for the physical therapist to use to evaluate the patient.

"I'm Gwen." I stuck out my hand for the therapist to shake. She had a firm grip and didn't let go until after she whispered in my ear. "I'm sorry to have to ask this, but would you mind going back to the waiting room?"

"Yeah, no problem." I backed away from the therapist and left Ricky in the room with her.

Taking a seat in the same chair I was in only moments ago, I picked up my magazine. I smiled when I turned right to page fifty.

"Gwen." I snapped my head up to see Ricky and Dr. Knight standing five feet away from me. I was so engrossed in my magazine that I didn't even notice the two of them approaching me. I was reading about the Ducati Supersport S. I was probably drooling. The RPM rates were amazing and the torque was just right to make the possible HP in the 100's. To say that I was okay with those rates would probably be an understatement. I addressed Dr. Knight by putting the magazine down and standing up. Anxiously waiting for one of them to speak, I looked from one to the other.

As the seconds ticked by with no answer I began to grow antsy. I made myself believe that there was virtually no way for Ricky to get worse, in the walking department at least.

My heart skipped a beat when Dr. Knight opened her mouth.

"I believe that Ricky has a chance to regain some feeling in his legs. It will take time and hard work. There are no guarantees, but I think he has a very good chance." Although Ricky was silent I could see the hint of a sparkle in his eyes.

I couldn't hide the smile that exploded on my face when I heard the great news. We have a chance!

17 BUILDING

"Every true genius is bound to be naïve." – Friedrich Schiller

It's been four days since Ricky's physical therapy started and I have found myself practically skipping around town. Ricky doesn't seem nearly as excited as I am but I've decided to ignore his stubbornness and look at the silver lining of the whole situation. Dr. Knight really thinks he has a shot and is willing to see him four times a week, every day that I am with him. It works out perfectly, and so far, Caroline hasn't suspected a thing. It's going to be hard to keep this from her forever, but I'm going to try and prolong it for as long as possible.

"Ms. Brady?" I looked into the eyes of Mr. Rodgers, realizing that I was the last one still in class. I smiled and quickly packed up my things, blushing from the embarrassment of being caught in a daze.

"Gwen?" Mr. Rodgers was still standing in front of me when he called my name. I looked up, nervousness creeping its way into my system. Teachers usually don't talk to me.

"Yes?" I asked shakily, my voice coming out as almost a whisper.

"You've been a little.... out of it.... lately. Is everything alright?" Concern was visible on his face and something about that made me extremely happy. It was nice to think that my teacher cared.

"Yeah. I've just had a lot on my mind. I've been keeping this boy, Ricky, company. He has cerebral palsy so-" Mr. Rodgers cut me off.

"Oh really? My niece has cerebral palsy too. How has he been handling it?" Mr. Rodgers crossed his arms and took a seat on the arm of his rolling chair.

"Well, as good as any 18-year-old who has never had physical therapy would be." I shrugged and tried to keep all of the frustration and anger inside of me at bay.

"Wow! That surprises me. His parents haven't taken him yet?" I shook my head and waved goodbye to Mr. Rodgers, shutting the conversation down quickly. I was done talking about it. I had too many things on my mind to go into a full-blown conversation with Mr. Rodgers. He was one of those teachers who didn't understand the importance of, what I like to call, "time management."

I stepped probably two feet into the hallway before being accompanied by Carter. Oh yeah, our date is tonight.

"Are you excited?" he asked happily. The excitement beaming from his eyes and the way he was fiddling with the collar of his shirt caught my attention. I smiled and nodded.

"I'd like to know what I should wear, but yes." I raised my eyebrow, insinuating the idea that my attire was important. I wouldn't seem normal if I acted like I didn't care, but in reality, I couldn't care less. He chuckled and put his arm around my shoulders. I humored him and let his arm rest there, only until I got to my locker though. He'd have to do a lot more than ask me on a date to be able to touch me. A lot more in "my book".

"So, I'll see you at 9?" Carter confirmed. I nodded and gave him a genuine smile. His eyes brightened ever so slightly at the sight of my smile and I couldn't help but get this uneasiness in my stomach. He turned and walked out the front doors, not before giving me one last wink. I rolled my eyes at the thought of how his ego has grown.

"Honey, are you alright?" I looked up to see Jerry and my mother standing in the doorway of my room. My mother was the one who spoke but I couldn't help but look at Jerry for a moment longer. He has never seen me in one of my "homework" moods.

"They didn't even TEACH us this crap," I cried out in frustration. I hate it when teachers set you up. They say they don't want any of us to fail, but they make that really hard to believe.

"You could always google it," my mom suggested. I wanted to roll my eyes at the sound of that suggestion. Of course, I knew I could use google. It's just that using google is illegal in the school world. It's like robbing a bank and shooting the teller just for the heck of it. It's cheating, and somehow, the school always finds out. It has happened to numerous people that I know including but not limited to Kayla, Jose, Rosalyn, Ellie, Jacklyn, Brianna, Carrie, and Kyle. That's just from homeroom. You can't even imagine my math class. I would guess about two-thirds of the class has been caught. I am NOT going to become one of those statistics.

"I can't," I said sharply. She jerked back slightly and an emotion I can't quite place flashed through her eyes. It left as quickly as it came, but still, I felt badly. Jerry seemingly caught on to the obvious tension and stepped in.

"I can help you. I could show you a few things and even some tricks you might use." I smiled and nodded. He pulled over a stool I had in my room and started to read over my math homework along with my science. Before I knew it, I was writing down the answers and completing all of my homework including the classwork that we would be working on tomorrow.

"And that's all there is to it." Jerry put his hands on his knees and stood up. I gave him a hug as a thank you not only for helping me with my homework but also assuring that I would get to Ricky's on time. He tensed up the second my arms wrapped around him. He quickly recovered by wrapping his arms around me. I pulled back and smiled at him as I left my room dressed in my outfit for my date tonight.

"You're early," Ricky said as I opened the front door and stepped inside. I turned my head to see him crossing his arms like he usually does. I rolled my eyes at how impossible he was. If I'm late, that's a problem. If I'm early, that's a problem. I never get a break.

He gave me a quite conspicuous once over. A small smirk played at the side of his lips. I put my hand on my hip not understanding what was humorous about the way

I was dressed.

I was wearing a navy-blue dress with gold jewelry. It would be considered somewhere between casual and fancy. In my opinion, perfect for a date with an unknown location. My sandals with gold straps were made from a cork material. I was comfortable and that's all that matters to me personally.

"What?" I asked skeptically. My eyebrows shot up at the sound of his laughter.

"You going on a date or something?" His tone sounded almost disbelieving. That made something inside of me hurt. Is it really that unbelievable that I was going on a date?

"For a matter of fact, I am. His name is Carter, and I don't think he would appreciate you insulting me." Something flashed in his eyes at the sound of my confession but cleared quickly. He put his hands up in surrender.

"I wasn't insulting-"

"Yes, you were," I spat back flatly. He turned away quickly and wheeled into the family room. I've been planning on asking him about how he was feeling with all of the physical therapy but something always gets in the way and by something, I mean his precarious mood swings. They're all over the place. One second he's laughing with me about a funny video we searched up on YouTube and the next he's shutting me out by exercising tirelessly.

A great example of this took place when we were watching *Obstacle Course Fails*. We laughed as hard as toddlers cackling over the word "duty." It was truly hilarious how incapable these people were at completing the obstacle courses. That moment lasted for all of six minutes until something clicked and he went right back into his exercise room and ignored me for two hours.

"Whatever. Have fun. You don't look like trash," he yelled from the family room. I decided not to respond to that comment and took a seat at the kitchen table. I pulled out one of my many motorcycle magazines and got completely lost in them. I've been going absolutely insane not being able to ride my motorcycle. I'd earned enough money to upgrade it but it's been sitting at the shop for almost a week now. It makes me sick that I can't go get it myself. I looked down at my hand and internally cursed at Amber. I guess she did bring me closer to Ricky, but still, I hate her for ruining my hand. It will probably never feel the same ever again.

When I got to the back of the magazine I noticed a paragraph written about this guy named Trevor Rollins and his untimely death. He was 38 when he crashed into the side of an 18-wheeler. Seeing the word *death* made the day I walked in on Ricky with my medications and alcohol flash through my mind. I have been doing my best to ignore the uneasiness that washes over me whenever I take my pain medications and when I see Ricky taking his pills. I've been lucky the last couple of nights. I haven't had nightmares for a little while now.

It's hard not to ask him about his emotional state every day, but he told me that I shouldn't bring it up with him or his mom if I want him to remain stable. When he told me that I nodded but almost everything inside of me said otherwise. I wanted to scream at him and tell him how dangerous it is not to get help. I couldn't live with myself if I just sat back and waited until he killed himself. I would go completely mad if that happened. I've recommended therapists and suicide support groups but he shuts me down every time I bring them up.

"I never knew it was eating you up that much." My heart almost stopped at the sound of Ricky beside me. Dang it! I was talking out loud again. I hate it when I do that. People don't need to know what I think, they really don't.

"You heard all of that?" I asked worriedly. I was praying that he didn't. My fingers were crossed along with my toes. I needed all of the luck that I could get.

"Well, you did just have a conversation with yourself out loud. I'm an expert eavesdropper," he said as though it were a fact that he has good eavesdropping skills.

"You know, the whole eavesdropping thing is considered rude," I stated, finding my eyes locking with everything but his.

"It's rude when the person is talking to another person. I don't believe there's anything against listening to a person who is, not only alone, but also the only other person in my house right now. I'm pretty sure that gives me specific listening rights." I finally turned toward him to give him a look. It didn't work because at that same moment the doorbell rang. I looked over to the clock and saw that it was 8:50. Caroline is never early, ever.

It must be Carter.

I stood up and ignored the look Ricky was giving me, thankful for the interruption. I don't have time for his complaints, and it's rude to keep people waiting at the door. I hesitated at the door, waiting to open it until I heard Ricky wheeling over. I put my hand on the golden door knob and pressed the thumb press down.

"Hey." Carter greeted me with a giant smile.

"Hey. Come on in. You look nice." He was sporting a black dress shirt with beige khakis and black converse. We both looked borderline casual to fancy. Perfect.

"Well you definitely one-upped me in that department. You look fantastic." He smiled at me as he entered Ricky's house. I giggled when he tripped on the welcome mat.

"Carter, I would like you to meet Ricky. Ricky, this is Carter Jones," My eyes widened as I waited for them to shake hands. Carter stuck his out and nodded at Ricky. Ricky continued to sit there and stare at him.

"Well, it's nice to meet you." Carter retracted his hand awkwardly and took a step back. I rolled my eyes at Ricky and turned my back on him, stepping in between the two of them so Carter was looking at me and not the hormonal, moody, delinquent behind me.

"Is he always-"

"Yup. So, don't take it personally. His arms are actually functioning, in case you were wondering. It's his legs that have the problem." Carter nodded. We smiled at each other and then, that's when it got awkward. We all were just kind of standing there. In an effort to ease the tension I got Carter a Cherry Coke and explained that we needed to wait until Caroline got back.

"You guys really don't need to wait." Ricky tried hard to convince us to leave but I refused to leave him alone for even five minutes. That's all it would take, really. Ricky would only need a few minutes to do something to himself. He explained to me that his medications had crazy side effects, and occasionally they malfunction and make him impulsive. I told him that's even more of a reason for me to make sure he's never alone.

Ten minutes passed as we dove into a heated discussion about frozen yogurt compared to ice cream. I tried not to stab my eardrums when I heard that both Ricky and Carter thought that frozen yogurt tasted better than ice cream.

"It's thicker and more substantial. Plus, it's probably ten times healthier for you. It tastes just like ice cream. I really don't understand how you don't agree with us." Carter looked to Ricky who nodded at his points. I wanted to hurl spoons at them at this point. I couldn't believe my date was ganging up on me with the guy I take care of every week.

"Not everything is about health, guys! Have you heard of the phrase 'guilty pleasures?' Yeah, well, that's a phrase for a reason. People call them *guilty* pleasures because they aren't healthy. It can't be considered a guilty pleasure if it's healthy for you. It's insane that you guys think it's okay for people to substitute ice cream for this dairy joke." I scoffed in disgust at the mere thought of frozen yogurt. The world would be just fine without frozen yogurt.

I heard the sound of metal on metal coming from the front door. The unlocking sound meant Caroline was home. I grabbed Carter's hand and pulled him up off the couch with me. I met Caroline at the door and helped carry some of the groceries.

"Hey, Gwen. Who's this?" she asked, grinning at Carter as she shut the door behind her.

"Caroline, this is Carter. Carter this is Ms. Knoll,

Ricky's mom." I looked at Carter who smiled as he stuck out his hand. She waved her hand at his gesture and immediately went in for a hug. He didn't hesitate at all which was good, especially for her self-esteem.

"Okay, well, I don't mean to leave in such a rush but we have to get going. I'll see you guys on Monday." Caroline frowned at my sudden goodbye but recovered quickly by giving me a hug. I hugged her back, and like I've been doing for days now, restrained from hugging her angrily.

We stepped outside and I almost died when I saw the car that Carter drove. He had come to pick me up in a black Chevrolet Corvette Z06. That sports car was one of the highlights in 2016 with up to 650 HP. It's a beautiful car and it is definitely respected in my books. I'm not going to mention it because I don't want him to know how much-

"You love cars, huh?" Darn it.

Yes. "No."

"But you're staring at it."

I know. "No, I'm not."

"Okay whatever you say. Will this do?" He pointed at the black sports car that was currently sitting in my parking spot.

It is more than okay. "Yeah, it's very good." I smiled and suppressed the fan girl giggling that would've come out of my mouth otherwise. He chuckled, clearly not believing my claimed "disinterest" in cars.

"So," I climbed in and shut the door while pulling out my phone, "Where are we going, Mr. Jones?"

"Mr. Jones, huh? Is that what American people call others?" I laughed at his assumption because it seemed genuine.

"No, I just like to mess with you." He glanced at me to make sure I was joking and that's when my laughter broke out. I laughed for probably five minutes straight alongside Carter who seemingly only laughed to make me feel better. I'm not sure what was so funny about him but everything he did was hilarious.

"Are you good now?" he asked skeptically looking between me and the road.

"I would be better if I knew where we were going." I raised an eyebrow, expecting an answer from him right then.

"You'll find out soon enough," he replied with a mischievous smirk.

In that moment, I should've felt uneasy. I should've gotten this sense of uncertainty as the roads and highways passed and faded into towering trees. I should've called someone to let them know that I was being driven to an unknown location with someone who's basically a stranger. The thing, though, was that I felt great. For once, I felt like normal teenage things were happening to me, and for once, I felt okay to be associated with society.

Right now, in this moment, I am just some naive 17-year-old girl, and do you know what?

I like it. I like it a lot.

18 NOT UNDERSTANDING

"If I was meant to be controlled, I would have come with a remote."

"Here we are," Carter stated excitedly. I looked over to the driver's seat to see him already hopping out and hurrying to my side of the car. As he opened my door I suppressed the many questions that were swirling around in my mind.

He had driven us about an hour away from where we live. We had come upon this small trail and he'd driven right up it. I'm going to go out on a limb here and say that, just beyond that small grove, there is a gigantic cliff that looks onto our town. That's just my guess.

"Come on. Oh, and bring your camera." He pointed to the Nikon D3400 sitting in the backseat next to my bag I had brought from Ricky's. I always take that bag and camera to Ricky's so I had to take it on this date. I'm starting to think that was a good idea.

"Okay," I said questioningly. I grabbed his outstretched hand and let him lead me past the grove just like I had suspected. What I didn't suspect was to see a decent sized waterfall flowing in the background. There was a cliff just like I had thought but the waterfall is what took my breath away. I smiled and looked between Carter and the beautiful landscape, all the while knowing that the entire time he was looking at me. I put my camera up to my eye and started doing what I do best.

Some time had passed, and it finally hit me that I was being rude. I turned to Carter who, surprisingly, looked like he was enjoying my little photo shoot. I smiled sheepishly and put my camera down, not before taking one last picture of course.

"What's wrong?" He sounded concerned of all things.

"Nothing I just feel badly that I kind of ignored you for the last half hour. Sorry." It was really bad manners on my part. He shook his head and chuckled.

"Don't apologize. I liked watching you take your pictures. I'm no photographer but I know for a fact that, just by the different angles you were shooting from, you're very talented. I'd love to have some of those pictures if that's cool with you?" I smiled at his compliment and nodded when he asked for some of the pictures. I print out every single picture I take. Whether it is good, bad or somewhere in between. I print out everything. It's kind of self-motivation for me. I know that, either way, no matter how the picture looks, I am going to be printing them out. So, they better be good every time so the money I use to print them is well spent.

"This is beautiful. Thank you for showing me this." I smiled at Carter and followed him back to the grove where two stumps were sitting. We sat down, and almost immediately, started getting to know each other.

"So, what's your story?" Carter asked from his seat on the wood.

"My story?" Confusion was clear in my voice. I'm not understanding what he means by my story. Is he expecting me to have some mysterious past?

"Yeah. Like what interests you? Where you were born? I don't know, what's your family like?" He was giving me suggestions for topics I could only imagine he was curious about.

"Okay. You go first though." I smiled when he gave me a look. He can't just expect me to tell him everything about myself without knowing anything about him.

"Well, I have two brothers, Aidan and Calvin. I'm the oldest at 18. They are twins and 15-years-old. My mom divorced my dad when I was 11 and she's been alone ever since. My whole family was born in Australia, and I didn't want to stay there like they all did. I got my passport, filled out a foreign exchange student application form, and made my way over here alone. It was hard to leave my family alone but Aidan and Calvin are old enough to look after my mom. The only one I was really worried about was my dog, Thor. He's an Australian shepherd but we got him only last year so he's still pretty young. I was the one who mainly took care of him so, I was a little hesitant when my mom offered to help me travel. She was the one who showed me the form and told me about the schools in America that support the exchange program. Thor is great," He pulled out his phone and showed me a picture of his puppy, "And I felt really badly about leaving him. Aidan and Calvin promised me they would take care of him but it was me who rescued him from the sewers. I feel like it was my responsibility to take care of him, but now I'm here, and not taking care of him."

"I can understand that, but I'm sure, your puppy understands." I laughed alongside him when I replayed how that sentence sounded in my head.

"Now it's your turn, Gwen. Who is Gwen Brady?" He crossed his arms and looked at me expectantly.

"That's a really complicated question."

"I've got time."

"Oh, I'm sure you do." I smiled but decided that I would tell him at least as much as he told me. I owed him that. "I was born in the hospital right down the road from my house. My family and I have been in our house since before I can remember. I had a brother named Jett and a Father named Shawn. They both left me two years ago. My mother's name is Marissa and she's actually engaged right now to Jerry Lawson. They are scheduled to be married next month believe it or not. I love to ride motorcycles, and I would say that I know a good bit about cars. I love photography and to stay active, pay for my bike, and pictures I kick-box. I've been kick-boxing competitively for a little over two years now. I started kick-boxing when I was 13 though." I shrugged not convinced that anything I do was all that remarkable.

"And you and Ricky are...." His voice trailed off. I'm guessing he wanted me to fill in the blank.

"I'm basically his babysitter. I call myself his caretaker but really, I'm just there to make sure he isn't alone and takes his medications. It's nothing really."

"But, you two spend a lot of time together I'm assuming." The way Carter looked between my eyes made me wonder if he was jealous of all things.

"Well yeah. I go over every Monday, Wednesday, Thursday, and Friday at 4. I stay till 9 and I get paid daily. At first I was doing it because of my hand." I lifted it up to show him the splint I was sporting at the moment. "I broke it when Amber slammed my locker door on it. I needed money and that same day, ironically, Caroline contacted me and told me that she'd love it if I could keep him company. I make a good bit of money with them so I'm probably still going to take care of him even after my hand heals."

"Are you two.... like.... together or-"

"If we were together, do you think I would've come out with you?" I asked, a little hurt that he thought I'd do that to him or Ricky.

"I guess not," he replied sheepishly. I giggled at his discomfort. Boys are so funny.

"Anyway, it's been really hard for me not to ride. You don't know how much I love it. I'm not sure if you've seen my bike but it is like my pride and joy.... what?" I was curious to see why he was looking at me like that. His face was weird.

"I think it's really cool that you have hobbies like that. Especially since so many people try to put you down for it."

"Where did you get that idea from?"

"Well, in addition to the people at our school, I got that idea from you. The way that you talk about what you like to do like it's a problem, concerns me."

"Concerns you?" I laughed disbelievingly.

"Yeah. It makes me worry that you don't realize how totally awesome it is that you have all of these different interests and hobbies that make you happy. Not everybody has that luxury."

"See, that's what you think. The only reason why I like doing these things is because they make me stronger. Honestly, most of the things I enjoy doing make me happy because they help me cope with the stupid people in my life. The kick-boxing, for example, is a defense mechanism against the football team. It's really hard for me, Carter. So, please, don't tell me my interest are luxuries. They aren't. They're escapes." I looked into Carter's eyes for only a second until I heard something in the trees above us. I looked up and saw a hawk that looked frighteningly similar to the one I saw in the woods closer to my house. I reached for my camera and stood up, taking 4 or 5 pictures as I did so. I ended up getting 18 pictures before it flew away. Once again, grateful for the interruption.

I scrolled through my album until I found the picture of the hawk from before. I compared the two and came to the conclusion that they were the same exact animal. I smiled and looked down at Carter who was studying me intently. I bent down and showed him the pictures of the hawk from a few minutes ago and the one of the hawk from days ago. He agreed that it was the same animal.

"It's really strange that that's the same hawk but yeah it has the same eyes and everything." He pointed.

"Yeah," I said whimsically. I was just so excited to show Ricky my pictures. This was another opportunity to prove him wrong.

"Are you ready to get some food?" Carter asked.

"Yeah. Where would you like to go?"

"Well, I don't really know the area that well so I was

hoping you'd have a few good ideas." He looked almost embarrassed that he was asking for my help. Sometimes boys have too much pride for their own good. If he was anybody else I would've yelled at him for not being comfortable enough to ask me without looking like he was going to pass out.

"I'm really in the mood for somewhere casual if you don't mind. Maybe the café in the town square would be a good idea?"

"That sounds great." He took my hand in his and walked me back to the car. He opened my door and handed me my bag I had left by the trees. I smiled, grateful that he didn't ask why it was so heavy. He doesn't really need to know that I don't go anywhere without extra memory cards for my camera. I would, figuratively, die if I didn't have enough space to take a picture of something like the hawk for example.

We pulled up to Brigg's Café at 10:22. The stars were drowned out by the street lights and stores that were packed inside our little town square. I really never had respect for towns and cities that had too many lights. So much so, that you couldn't even see the stars. The stars deserve to be seen in my opinion. They are only around for a number of hours until they dissolve into the gigantic yellow one we call the sun. They deserve to be acknowledged.

"What can I get you two this evening?" The waitress asked us from behind the counter. There was barely anyone in here and this café didn't have a specialized bar for alcohol so there weren't any age restrictions on it. The waitress was a heavier woman I'm guessing to be about thirty five years of age. She had raven hair and bright red lipstick that made it hard for you to focus on her eyes. I smiled and looked at Carter who was already looking at me. I took that as an invitation to talk first.

I really like it when guys let you decide what you want to get for yourself. There seems to be this misconception that girls like it when guys decide for them.

"I'd like a Dr. Pepper and cheese fries. Do you like those?" Carter nodded when I asked him. "Make that for two people please." She smiled and looked to Carter, not bothering to write down anything I said.

"And what would you like to drink?" She studied him carefully, giving me the feeling that she thought she's seen him before.

"I'll take a coke, thanks." He smiled and turned to me. I waited for her to leave and then did the same.

"So...." His voice trailed off once again.

"So?" I smiled at him and tucked a piece of my hair behind my ear.

"Could I ask you something?"

Not thinking, I answered rather quickly. "Sure."

"What happened when your brother and father left?"

I didn't say anything and that's when realization flashed through Carter's eyes. "Oh, I'm sorry I didn't mean to overstep. Forget I asked."

"Thanks." Only a few seconds passed before our waitress set the fries and drinks down on the counter. I looked at her name tag and saw that it read Maggie. She smiled and turned back into the kitchen. I popped one of the fries in my mouth and almost died when the heat got to my tongue. I didn't choke or make any noises but I could tell that my face looked like a fish. As soon as I swallowed the fry I looked at Carter, and we both started bursting out laughing.

We eventually started playing "never have I ever". All you have to do is hold 5 fingers up and listen to the other person make statements about what they've never done. You put a finger down when the other player says something you have done. We started playing and let me tell you, Carter has done A LOT more than I thought. Good and bad things.

"Never have I ever-"

"Sorry to interrupt you guys, but I was just coming over to check and see if you would like to order your meals now?" Maggie spoke up from behind the counter. I was so focused on what Carter was saying that when Maggie started talking she actually startled me. I looked to Carter who nodded and beckoned for me to order first.

"I would like to get a BLT with extra bacon and mayo. If you could, I'd like to substitute the fries for chips please." Maggie nodded, still not making an effort to write down what I ordered. Usually, this means that the person has worked here for a long time but I haven't seen her in here before so she just must be lazy.

"And for you." She turned her attention to Carter. He smiled.

"I'd like to get a cheeseburger with no onions."

"Fries good?"

"Yup." He smiled and handed Maggie both of our menus. As soon as she left, we picked up from where we left off.

"Never have I ever gone out with someone more than 3 years older than me." I laughed but kept all of my fingers up. I have never done that either.

"Never have I ever been to the zoo." Carter looked at me shocked and lowered one of his fingers. I laughed at his facial expression but didn't elaborate.

"Never have I ever been physically abused." He turned the nature of the game serious by asking one question. I lowered one of my fingers and broke eye contact with him, finding myself staring at a random picture over his right shoulder. He didn't push me about it which I would be forever grateful for. I've never liked talking about my complicated history.

"Never have I ever...."

The game went on for about 15 more minutes. Both of us saying random things that we have never done. I got a little skeptical when he lowered his fingers at a few of my statements but I tried to let it go.

"Here you are." Maggie set down our plates of food and waited there for a second to see if we needed anything else.

"Thank you. It looks good." I smiled, agreeing with Carter's comment. Maggie turned around, and the second she did, I dug into my food. I was starving.

"That was fun." The dinner continued and it went smoothly. Nothing too exciting happened until we got into the car. The song, I'm Still Standing by Elton John, came on and we both started singing our hearts out. We sang all the way home and by the time we were sitting in my parking space, which we are right now, we were out of breath from all the singing. I smiled and looked over to Carter who had just snapped me back to reality by saying exactly what I was thinking.

"Yeah it was. Thank you for tonight." I put my hand on the door knob but didn't open it because Carter had started talking.

"We should do this again. Maybe next time we could go bowling? There's this great bowling place that some of the football guys showed me, and I thought we could go together."

"I'm not sure I can do that when I'm taking care of Ricky though. I mean I could ask him but-"

"Does Ricky own you or something?" I snapped my head towards Carter when he asked that. I wanted to slap him for saying that. How dare he think I can be controlled by a guy of all people.

"What is that supposed to mean?" I asked, annoyed that I wasn't understanding what he was insinuating.

"It just looks like you spend a lot of time with this guy and if we are going to date I'm not sure how comfortable I am with you spending all of your free time with him." I blinked at the boy I clearly don't know as well as I thought I did. I replayed what he said in my head, making sure I was hearing him right.

"From the looks of it, I could say that *you* are trying to control me. I will spend my free time with whomever I want to and NO ONE is going to tell me otherwise. Are you my mother? Are you my father? No and no so I suggest you restart this whole conversation before I get out of this bloody car and never look back," I barked. He looked a little surprised that I got so defensive. I just don't do well with boys trying to tell me what I can and can't do.

"I didn't mean to offend you it's just that I don't really like the thought of you around some other boy every day."

"I'm around boys all day at school."

"You know what I mean."

"You're going to have to spell it out for me because I actually don't know what you mean." I crossed my arms and kept my eyes dead set on his.

"I like you, a lot, Gwen, but I have to make sure that, if we do become something more, you are mine and nobody else's."

"I don't belong to anybody, Carter. The fact that you supposedly like me SO much but can't trust me enough to stay loyal to you worries me. We are talking about a relationship that isn't even off the ground yet, Carter. For you to take me out on one date and already start dictating what I can and can't do concerns me."

"I don't think you understand what I mean."

"No, Carter. You're just not listening. I don't want to go out with you ever again. This would never work, and clearly, your ideas of property and a girlfriend fall close. Thanks for today, I'll, unfortunately, see you on Monday." I put my hand back on the door knob but was surprised when it didn't open.

"Carter open the door."

"I'm not done talking to you though."

"You really think I give two craps about what you are. Open the door Carter!"

"Gwen," he said a little too calmly for my liking.

"I will call the police in 30 seconds if you don't open this door." Anger consumed me in less than a minute, and by this point, I could almost guarantee I was seething.

"Gwen."

"1, 2, 3-"

"Please."

"7, 8, -" I stopped when I heard the click of the car unlocking. When I shut the car door I was surprised I didn't break the window.

I stormed into my house and slammed the front door behind me, setting my bag and camera down on the table.

Me, not understanding.... please.

19 ANGER TO DANGER

"Control your anger, it's only one letter away from danger."

Waking up in the morning usually gets me mad. Today, though, it made me furious. I usually don't like to get up because, usually when I do, I get up too early and cut my sleep short. Today, I was mad because I woke up in the middle of beating up Carter. It was a great feeling really. I may sound sadistic but it felt amazing to show him exactly how he made me feel last night. Telling me that I should stop hanging out with Ricky, come on. Who does he think I am? Some slave he can order around? He's in a new country for all of two minutes and he's already bossing girls around. He can just take his crap and go back to Australia for all I care.

"Honey! We have a date!" My mom exclaimed bursting into my room, slamming my door against my wall in the process. I looked over to my glass display case and let out a breath of relief when I found none of my pictures had fallen. I looked back to my mother who was practically jumping with joy. Jerry wasn't with her which probably explained how jumpy she was. Jerry is usually pretty good at calming her down.

"Good. Go have fun," I said snippily. My voice came out harsher than I had intended. My suppressed fury towards Carter didn't help my situation.

"No not that kind of date. We finalized when the wedding is going to be! It's next month on June 26th! It's a Saturday like you suggested and you're out of school so it all works out!" She exclaimed. Her eyes were wide with excitement and joy. I couldn't help but smile at the sight of her.

"Well, that's great Mom! I'm really excited!"

"Have you already sent out the invitations to everyone?" She nodded diligently before practically skipping out of my bedroom and down the hall. I was quiet for a second and heard her bedroom door open and then close.

Her happiness wasn't enough for me to stay excited forever, though. After she left, I quickly fell back into that fit of rage and annoyance. For Carter to have the insolence to talk to me like I was 5 made me absolutely furious. I wish I never met him and I wish Ricky never had to talk to him. I feel badly for everyone who has ever had to talk to him. There is something missing upstairs when it comes to Carter. It's clear when you realize he didn't know how insulting he was being.

I needed to walk it off. Usually, I would ride it off but no. My hand is currently preventing me from doing everything I love to do so I am forced to walk. I put on a green crop top and some high-waisted jeans. Throwing on some sunglasses to hide the atrocity that was my face at the moment, I jogged down the stairs and out of the house. I waited a second to make sure my mother didn't come running outside to look for me. When she didn't, I walked, relatively fast, all the way to the woods. I had brought my earphones along just for the heck of it. So, I plugged them in and turned Lord Huron on full volume. I was in the mood to drown out everyone that was around me.

Obviously, I took my camera and ended up taking pictures for about three hours. The walk back home was eventful because I had a chance to look over the pictures I had taken. There were tons of trees but the lighting at the time made it look foggy. The dust particles that were visible floating in the sun light would normally make me turn away, but there was something mystical about the few pictures I took with them in it. It probably sounds weird, but if you were to see the pictures, you'd understand. Something inside of me clicked when I saw the one picture I took of a single daisy sitting in the middle of a small pile of stones. That click turned my legs in the direction of the photo developing store.

Before I knew it, I was looking up at the sign for 'Clicks 'n' Pics'. Don't ask about the name. The owner clearly didn't want a lot of business to begin with.

"Hey, Gwen!" Eddie, the cashier, greeted me. I took in his usual low-key persona while eyeing his brown, shoulder length hair. His flannel shirt was tucked into his navy-blue jeans that covered the majority of his work boots. Eddie was a kind soul who always helped my family and me. He had a good relationship with my brother so, of course, he had a good one with me. He's in here almost every day, so I usually talk to him when I need my pictures developed. He knows exactly how I like them so they come back perfect every time.

"Hey Eddie! How's it going?" I asked him politely, walking up to the counter and taking a seat on the stool they had situated there for customers.

"Liana has been getting all these crazy ideas that I've been sneaking around and lying to her. She gives me headaches, Gwen," he said jokingly, rubbing his forehead for effect. Liana was his wife who has been with him for almost 15 years now. It's funny to hear about the struggles they have. I always know how they end though. Eddie ends up buying her something and apologizes for things that 99% of the time he doesn't do. I've come to the conclusion that Liana likes all the gifts so she just makes up random problems that Eddie, supposedly, causes. One day, though, I'm worried Liana is going to say something that really insults Eddie.

"Well, I know you'll figure it out, Eddie. You always do." I nodded showing him just how much I believed in his capability to make his wife happy. He smiled before directing his attention to the memory card in my hand.

"These the pics?" He asks taking the memory card from my outstretched hand.

"Yup. They're all recent so there really is no rush."

"Oh, please. You always say that. I'll have them done by tomorrow morning."

"Awesome, you're the best Eddie." He looked up and waved to me as I walked out of the store. I heard the bell they attached to their door jingle when I walked out. I made a left down the street and started for my house. Hopefully, Jerry was keeping my mom preoccupied because I don't think I can handle her long lecture about leaving the house without talking to her first. She should be able to understand my grave need for a breather.

Almost an hour later, I made it home. It was 2 and I felt extremely exhausted. Anger and exercise, I find, consumes your energy twice as fast when they work together. It's really hard to pin point what is taking the most energy out of me but I'm pretty sure it's the anger. I'm angry all the time but this time, I wasn't expecting it. I'm usually expecting anger to come up at some point during the day when I'm at school. I was ignorant and thought that my new-found happiness from being around Ricky would keep me from getting hurt by people. I've enjoyed the challenge that is Ricky Doone, though. I've enjoyed looking after him and also learning how capable he is all on his own. He is 18 you know.

"Where in GOD'S NAME were you?!" My mother yelled from across the family room. I had made it about 2 minutes before she realized I was back. Luckily, Jerry came down and took over the conversation.

"What your Mother is trying to ask, is where did you go?" He said that 50 times more calmly than my mother did. I find it easier to talk to someone who is calm so I turned all of my attention to Jerry.

"I was really upset about something this morning, so I needed some air. I thought getting in my steps for the day would be a good distraction. I ended up taking a few pictures while I was out and decided to make it easier on everyone and just run them over to the developing store myself. I was in there for all of 15 minutes, and I came straight home after that." I kept my gaze on Jerry who was still as calm as a cat.

"Well, next time sweetheart, if you could just let us know that would be great. Come on Mars let's go." He pulled my mother alongside him all while keeping his eyes locked on the stairs. I blinked and they were walking up the stairs and into their bedroom. I let out a sigh of relief and silently thanked Jerry for coming to my rescue. I'm really liking this idea of marriage now. I could use someone to back me up like that. And did anyone else catch that pet name? Relationship goals right there.

I went to the freezer and pulled out my personal carton of cookie dough ice cream. I jumped on the couch and turned on the TV to a random spy movie. This was another one of my tactics to calm down and reflect on life and the crap that creates it. It usually works.

Crack! Crack! Crack! I smiled when the antagonist was finally taken down by the detective. Wait. I paused the movie when paranoia set in.

The sound of glass breaking came from the front of my house.

I ran up to my bedroom and looked out the window so, whatever it was that was breaking the glass on the first floor, wouldn't see me looking at it. I saw two tall figures circling my house. One of them was breaking our ceramic flower pots in the drive way. The other was.... spray painting my motorcycle. At the sight of that I started shaking. They, as in the football team, had just recently started to mess with me again. I think it's been long enough since Amber broke my hand that they don't feel badly for me anymore. I tried to take deep breaths and let them finish. Unfortunately, one minute turned into three and three turned into six, and the next thing I knew I was grabbing the brown bat I had stored in my room for times like these. I was usually pretty good at controlling my anger towards them, but today, it was different. There was something else there that I just couldn't turn away from. I put on a hat and fixed my hair in a way that made me look like a different person. I felt like fighting and I knew they wouldn't touch me if they thought I was a girl. I put on a big sweatshirt, an old pair of Jerry's shoes and made my way to the front of the house. The second I opened the door they looked up. They didn't walk away like they normally would if they knew it was me. Instead they all looked straight at me. I had sunglasses on so they didn't see me making a mental note of exactly who was on my property at this moment. Zack and Carter. This must be some stupid form of their ridiculous initiation to the football team. Carter told me how badly he wanted to be a part of something. I didn't think he would go this far just to be on the football team, though. Either way, his presence only fueled my fury. It was as though I was the fire and he was the 1000 liters of gasoline.

To get the boys to come at me first I stuck up my middle finger at them.

"Oh, you shouldn't have done that little boy." Zack smirked and waved at someone behind him. I didn't even realize the other two boys standing in the shadows watching. It was Brett and Troy who were there as lookout.

They came up two at a time which didn't seem fair to begin with. I almost laughed when they said they wanted the fight to be fair. It's not fair if it's two against one, but

I honestly couldn't care less. I dropped the bat and put both of my fists up.

Bring it on.

Zack took the first swing and I easily dodged it.

"Guys it's Gwen! It's Gwen and you all know it's her!" Everyone snapped their heads toward Carter. He looked straight at me and, for a while, no one said anything. "Come on! You guys know it's her! Her brother is gone and he's her only sibling."

"You're walking on very thin ice Jones," Zack growled. He was speaking low and extremely sternly. When Brett and Troy looked at me I knew what they were thinking. They just wanted an excuse to see a fight and Zack just wanted one to hit me. That's when I took off the hat and sweatshirt.

They didn't look surprised.

I watched as Zack walked right up to Carter and punched him straight in the face.

"If you think you'll ever be on the team now then I didn't punch you hard enough. Don't even bother turning in your forms." Zack walked down the street and hopped into their car. He drove back up to where we were and let Troy and Brett get in. He spit on Carter from the open window and drove away.

"Gwen-"

"Don't. Just don't. If you expect me to feel badly for you, I don't. If you're expecting me to thank you, I won't. I don't know what you want me to say."

"Gwen just listen to me." Blood spat out of his mouth every time he tried to talk. I turned my back to him so I wouldn't have to see how pathetic he looked. "I didn't realize they were taking me here. It didn't register to me that there isn't an off-campus tryout for the team."

"Carter how stupid do you have to be to not realize that initiation is code word for sabotage. There are 3 people that the football team doesn't mind hurting and I am on the top of that list." I started walking towards my front door.

"But why you? I mean you're a conservative girl who keeps to herself. Why would they mess with you?"

"Jett. It's because of Jett. The only difference now is that he isn't here to clean up their mess and get them back for it."

"At least take some money for the damage." He started to cough after he spoke. I turned around reluctantly and saw a couple one hundred dollar bills he had placed at my feet. I picked up the money and bat I had dropped before. I picked up all the articles of clothing I had taken off to show them my true identity. Stomping up my steps, I opened the door and slammed it all in one motion, making sure never to make eye contact with the boy laying in my driveway. At the sight of my empty family room I called out to my mother. She came barreling down the stairs and before I could even think I was collapsing in her arms. She held me tight and let me completely break down in front of her. This must've been just as scary for her as it was for me because today is the first day in years that I have cried in front of her. And, she doesn't even know why.

I cried for my mother.

I cried for Ricky.

I cried for Jett.

I cried for my father.

I cried for Amber.

I cried for my hand.

I cried for Ty.

I cried for Caroline.

I cried for Carter.

I cried about my inability to make friends.

I cried for that dog down the street.

I cried about all of the times I lied to my mother.

I cried thinking about how Jerry was kind enough to get my bike from the shop.

I cried for every person that was ever dragged into my mess of a life.

I cried because I knew deep down that I would always be the girl that everybody picked on.

I cried at the thought of never seeing Ricky walk.

I cried thinking about how I could ever explain what the boys were about to do.

I cried about all of the expenses I would have.

I cried because I realized Ricky wasn't going enough to fix all of my insecurities.

I cried for the sole purpose of crying.

20 LEARNING TO ACCEPT

"Whatever good things we build end up building us."
– Jim Rohn

It's been three weeks since the boys came over and we are finally on the last week of school. I've gotten all of my acceptance letters except for one and I honestly couldn't be happier. I had a talk with my parents the afternoon the guys came and broke some of our belongings. They told me that they wished I had come to get them for help but were glad that I came to them afterwards. Somehow, a video of the whole thing got around and now everyone is leaving me alone. In fact, most of the school is disgusted with the boys for even trying to start a fight with me. I couldn't be happier. I got my bike and driveway cleaned up with the money I got from Carter. My days have been so much better now that all I have to worry about is my school work and Ricky. It's been pretty amazing watching how he improves because of the physical therapy. Don't get me wrong, most of it has only given him more flexibility in the parts of his body he could already move. That being said, we still have to keep in mind that he hasn't even gone for a full month yet. Today is not only Sunday, but also a special occasion for me. Today is the second to last day of my splint. Tomorrow I get to take it off! That also means on Wednesday, I get to take Ricky on that special motorcycle ride that I promised him. We both came to the agreement that we needed to start constructing the seat so we could start to test it out and all that jazz. We needed to make sure it worked before we actually turned on the motorcycle and started driving.

When I got into that mess with the boys I felt a lot of things. I also cried for a lot of reasons but I was wrong. At least I thought I knew what I was crying about but now, looking back, I realize that I was only crying for one thing. One person really.

Ricky.

When I saw the guys at my house my mind somehow went back to the day Ricky tried to overdose. That day he told me that he didn't deserve me. I guess, the reason why I was so upset was the fact that someone as amazing as Ricky actually believed that they didn't deserve me. He's never treated me the way almost every guy in my life has. I guess, it just made me a little sick to think that Ricky believes he doesn't deserve everything this world has to offer. I believe that with all of my heart and seeing those bimbos acted showed me that. If anything, it's the other way around. I don't deserve him.

"What time are you going over to Ricky's, dear?" My mother called from downstairs. From the sound of her voice I could tell she was lifting something heavy.

"What time is it now?"

"12:30"

"Then in about two hours."

"Okay. Would you like to go to lunch with Jerry and me?"

"If you don't mind, I'd like to stay here."

"That's fine, Gwen. We'll be back soon."

"Bye."

"Bye, love." I waited until I heard their car start up and drive away to go downstairs and blast my speaker. That's my home alone tradition, really. Blast the music and dance around the house like a crazy person. It's fun and I would definitely recommend it.

I eventually fell down on the couch and turned on a movie. The main character was a girl who owned a museum who- wait. Museum. Oh, my God! I never followed up with Jerry about the museum. He probably thinks I don't want to go. I knew I should've left myself a note. I'm so stupid. The one chance I have to bond with my father-to-be and I don't even talk to him about it. So much for telling him how much I 'love' it. I rolled my eyes at how pathetic I was. I keep have dreamed of going to this museum, and I totally blew off the one chance I had to go.

The thoughts about Jerry and the museum were still swirling around in my mind when I heard the door being unlocked. I shot up and decided to give begging Jerry a try.

"Hey Jerry." He gave me a look when he heard the sound of my voice that was currently three octaves higher than normal.

"Hello, Gwen. Let me go out on a limb here, and say that you're getting ready to beg me for something?"

Yes. "Of course, not. I was just going to ask you if your offer for the Roundel museum was still on the table. I never really got back to you about that. I'm pretty sure my hand appointment was one of the reasons why we couldn't go, but I don't know. I would still love to go if you still want to take me." I smiled innocently up at Jerry who looked like he wanted to laugh. He gave me a smile instead.

"Yeah, it's still there. I was just waiting for you to bring it up again. I didn't want to pressure you into going somewhere with me." I wanted to pass out in disbelief. Did Jerry really think I didn't want to go because he was taking me?

"Are you crazy? I wouldn't want anybody else to take me!" I exclaimed, giving him a hug. I didn't have to look at my mother to know she was just beaming at the sight of us. I was the one to pull back and ask him one more clarifying question.

"So, this Tuesday?" He laughed and nodded. I gave him one quicker hug before smiling at both Jerry and my mother and turning for the stairs.

"You only have 20 minutes young lady," my mother called after me. I made a noise to let her know that I already knew about the time dilemma I was currently in.

I pulled on a tank top and black skinny jeans. I was in the mood to be comfortable so I decided to wear slides. I may look like a slob but that's okay with me. I was in one of those 'screw the world' moods. I put my hair in a sloppy bun and threw on sunglasses. I had this feeling that Ricky, and I would be finding our way out and about one way or another.

"You're late." Even though today wasn't a day that I got paid everything was the same. Ricky still pointed out my arrival and Caroline was gone. I told her I was coming over and she asked me if it was alright if she went and did a few errands. I told her it was fine but got this extremely selfish urge to ask for my pay.

I didn't ask. But, I wanted to.

"You're annoying. Good we've both gotten the obvious out of the way." I couldn't help but smile when I saw Ricky. The excitement from everything that was coming up this week was just too much to handle.

"Why are you looking at me like that?" He asked suspiciously. I giggled at the confusion written on his face.

"I'm just so excited man! Aren't you?!" I waited patiently for an answer but only got a shrug out of him. "Whatever. Let's just get started."

"Follow me." I followed Ricky to the elevator and was a little surprised when he told me to get in it with him. He hit the number 3 and before I knew it, the doors for the basement level were opening. We walked into this giant workshop. There were tools, grid paper, calculators, rulers, saws, wood, and more all around the room. I noticed that none of it was placed up high. There were things on the walls and there were tables but everything was lowered. I envied Ricky's determination to design things even with his condition. I found his entire life extremely inspiring.

"So, here are the blue prints that I edited. This one is the final draft, but I wanted to see what you thought of it." He handed me the design, and I looked it over. The thing that I was really curious to see was how he connected the seat to my motorcycle. The motorcycle had enough room for two people but we had to reinforce the seat with extra support for Ricky's legs.

"Can I change a few things?" He nodded and handed me a pen. I smiled and got to work.

Two hours had passed and we had finally agreed on the final product. We kept going back and forth about a few of the measurements but everything was sorted out when I brought my motorcycle into his garage so he could see it and physically touch it. We argued for about 30 minutes about the kind of material we needed to use for the latches and seat belt. I eventually won when I brought up the point about heat safety. We couldn't use any material that would overheat and melt onto the seat itself.

It was a lot of fun to design it but I had a feeling that actually making it would be a little more challenging. I can fix engines and stuff on my bike, but I've never made anything that involves a vehicle from scratch. The parts and pieces have always already been there.

"Do we need to run to the store?" I asked Ricky who had gotten two drinks for us out of his fridge down here. The basement was one of those basements that was partially underground. Half of it was fully embedded in the ground but the other half gradually surfaces until it's completely out in the open. The part that is out in the open is where the garage is, so it was fairly easy for Ricky and I to go back and forth between the garage and the basement to see my bike.

"It's alright. I asked my mother to go to Home Depot to pick up the few materials I didn't already have."

"Where did you find the metallic color coating?"

"Auto body. We are going to stick it to the seat with heat like people do when they customize their cars. It's going to be hard but I can almost guarantee that it will look incredible." I nodded and turned my attention back to the table.

"Let's get started then," I smiled picking up the blue print we had been looking at intently only a few minutes ago. Ricky nodded and wheeled over to his other desk and pulled out the cushion for the seat.

Techno Pop started blaring from my pocket making me jump back in surprise and drop the screw driver I had been holding. Ricky chuckled at my clumsiness but kept on working. I looked down at my phone and realized that I had set an alarm earlier. I needed to be home today, according to my mother, but I really wanted to finish this project. We were so close to finishing it. All we had to add was the extra black leather to support it.

"You're not going to answer that?" Ricky asked, nosily butting into my business.

"It was an alarm genius," I snapped.

"What for?"

"Someone is nosy today," I pointed out, picking up the screw driver and setting it on the table. "My mom had wanted me home now but we're so close I really think we can finish."

"No, you should go if your mom said so. I know how anxious she can get. Trust me, it's not just you who can hear her incessant screaming." He chuckled and rubbed his head as if just thinking about her yelling gave him a headache. I laughed sheepishly, extremely embarrassed that other people could hear my mother. I'm going to talk to her about that.

"Are you sure?"

"100%. Go. I'll see you tomorrow after your splint is taken off." He smiled and wheeled over to the elevator, pressing the up button and ushering me inside. I waved to him and pressed the button that read **main** for the first floor. I'm not going to lie and say that I didn't think this elevator was the coolest thing ever. I did, but my severe fear of elevators got in the way.

"Wow. You actually came home like I told you to. I'm happy." Mom and Jerry were sitting at the kitchen table seemingly having a very important conversation.

"What did you want me back for?" I looked between the two of them and sat down at the head of the table. They both took sips of their coffee instead of answering me.

"Hello? Did you guys hear me?" I waved my hands at both of them. I was about to stand up when they both started laughing. I put my head in my hands and sighed. This is going to be a long dinner if that's how all of the conversations are going to play out.

"Jerry has some great news." I snapped my head up and looked at Jerry excitedly. Jerry was the one person I really liked getting surprises from.

"Yes," I said in a sing-song voice. He smiled at me before handing me a small piece of paper. I picked it up and almost screamed when I read Roundel Museum. It was for tonight!

"How did you.... doesn't it.... what?" I couldn't form a sentence. My excitement was overpowering my better judgment. I already knew we were going at some point but to actually have the ticket in my hand, that just made it 1000 times more real.

"I know the guy that happens to own the place. He owes me one so I asked for a free pass after hours. Nobody but us will be there. Tonight." He tried to suppress the smile that was on his face but it kept getting bigger and bigger as my shrieks of excitement got louder and louder.

"Well, then. What are we waiting for? Let's go!" I jumped up from my chair and bolted for the door, grabbing my bag and camera. As I've said before, I don't go anywhere without my camera. I could hear my mother and Jerry laughing from the kitchen, but I honestly couldn't care less. I was too excited to see the museum that held some of the most famous photos of all time. The thing about this museum that made everything that much more special was the fact that every photo was the first one that the photographer ever printed out. It was the first copy... ever.

"Why did you use that guy's favor for me?" I asked Jerry from the passenger seat of his Land Rover Range Rover. The thing that I really envied about Jerry was his eye for quality things. Everything that he had down to his watch was good quality.

"Why wouldn't I? I thought this would be a great way to get to know you even better and I'd give anything for that," he said smiling over at me for only a second until turning back to the road. He kept smiling even though he was looking ahead.

"Well, thank you," I said graciously. He'll never

know how much it means to me to hear him say that.

"No problem." He nodded at the end of his sentence. I smiled when I saw his fingers start to drum on the steering wheel when "Crazy" by Gnarls Barkley came on. I turned it up and let the song take us all the way to the museum.

"Hey, Jerry! It's great to see you, my man!" The stubby man, whom I'm assuming is the owner, said to Jerry. It's weird and I never understood why men did it. What was the point? Do a handshake or a hug. Why do you have to combine it?

"And who might this young lady be?" The chubby man directed his attention to me. His red mustache moving whenever he spoke.

"This is my daughter, Gwen." I smiled when Jerry introduced me as his daughter and stuck out my hand for the chubby man. "Gwen," I said for myself.

The chubby man smiled and said, "Scott Mooney. It's a pleasure to meet you." He gave me a little wink before turning back to Jerry and embarking on a conversation with him. I tried to tune in to their conversation but I couldn't get over the fact that a grown, fat, man just hit on me. I wanted to slap him.

"You two can follow the signs into the next room and feel free to look around. There are three floors. The first being landscapes. The second being animals and wildlife. The third being human life and candids. Have fun and just please don't touch anything. The photographers sometimes like to stop by the museum and they absolutely hate it when they find fingerprints on their work." He smiled and turned around but not before giving me one last wink. I returned his gesture with a scowl of my own but he turned too quickly.

"Don't mind Scott. He's a flirt and goes after anything that is relatively close to the female species. That's probably why his wife left him." I looked up at Jerry who had taken it upon himself to explain to me why his 'buddy' was basically a pervert. I snorted when I heard him say that Scott's wife left him.

Laughing, we made our way to the first floor. I gasped when Jerry opened the door and I took in all of the pictures that currently surrounded me. There were waterfalls, cliffs, forests, streams, oceans, fields, mountains, and so much more. The colors were vibrant and made this shabby white room come to life. I honestly didn't want to leave.

I thought that way until we made it to the second floor. I shrieked this time instead of gasping. The animals looked so clear that, at first glance, you could mistake them for being there in real life. It was amazing how much emotion these pictures captured from the animals. A lot of them looked excited or curious but there was one that caught my attention. There was a picture of a baby sloth that was hanging from a single tree branch and I couldn't shake the feeling that it was looking for someone. It looked so lost and alone that it made me want to jump into that scene and help the poor baby out.

Excitement and shock hit me in waves when we moved onto the final floor of the museum. I had never seen so many amazing candid photos at one time. The photos inspired me. There were so many ways to take pictures of unknowing subjects, but there were ways that

I hadn't even thought of. Most of my pictures were of one person with a relatively pretty background. I never thought of backing up to the point where you can see who the busy shopper is trying to meet across the street. I never thought of focusing on the businessman behind the elderly beggar. It was amazing. I went down the line and stopped practically breathless when I saw a picture of.... me. I was leaning on my bike and looking down the street at a car. It was the black corvette. I didn't say anything to Jerry but rather focused on the name of the photographer. It was Rick. Trying to stay calm, walked down the line of photos. I came to a silhouette of a girl sitting on a fence with the moon in the background. I wrote the photographer down just like I had done with the last 20. Their pictures were phenomenal. I walked farther writing down every other name until I came to this picture that looked oddly familiar. The boy in the picture was handsome and had green eyes. The only person I know to have green eyes like that....

"Gwen is that Ricky? Is that your picture? That's your work, isn't it?"
It was the candid picture I took of Ricky.

21 NOTHING CHANGES

"You're always one decision away from a totally different life."

Techno.... techno.... techno.... I really need to change my alarm. I shot out of bed this morning forgetting the fact that today was Monday the day that every human is supposed to hate. I'm not sure if anyone has realized this, but Monday has become the day that everyone hates because everyone says that's the way it's supposed to be. Sometimes I wake up on Mondays and I feel amazing. So, no, today isn't the dreaded Monday but rather the dignified Monday. Today is the day I get my splint off. Today is also the day I get to try out my motorcycle for the first time in 6 weeks.

So, no, today isn't a bad day. It's a glorious, liberating, delightful day. That's what I've decided.

"Someone looks chipper this morning." My mother said happily making pancakes and bacon for breakfast.

"I am. Thanks to Jerry, I've gotten so many new ideas about different types of pictures I can take. I found so many photographers that used natural light to make shadows exactly where they wanted them. It was amazing and I HAVE to try it."

"Well, I'm glad you enjoyed our little adventure yesterday, Gwen. I had fun as well," Jerry said smiling, while taking a sip from his coffee. I looked at my mother who was glowing.... again. She has never looked happier than she has in the last few days. It truly makes me wish she had married Jerry earlier.

"I'm so happy that my most favorite people in the whole wide world are getting along." She clapped her hands together and turned back to the stove.

"I think you'll be even happier to hear about Gwen's picture that was showcased in the museum! Can you believe that Mars?" Jerry exclaimed. I couldn't help but to smile when my mom dropped the spatula she had been holding. She started screaming before she ran over to give me a hug. My smiles and laughter were my only explanation as to how they got in there.

Before I knew it, I was hopping in the car with my mother who drove me to school. The whole way there she talked about how amazing Jerry was. In the beginning, it was sweet, but after about 10 minutes it got extremely boring and a little nauseating. You would've thought Jerry was sitting where I was by the way she was talking. When she pulled up to the school I practically jumped out of the car and made a bolt for the door. I heard my mom beep before she drove away. I let out a sigh of relief when I turned around and saw she wasn't there.

"Running from someone, Brady?" I snapped my head to see none other than McKenna standing in front of me and blocking my locker. I rolled my eyes and physically slid her out of the way. She made a little sound that could've been mistaken for a dying squirrel, but I don't judge.

"You have a lot of nerve to put your hands on me freak. After what you did to the football team I'm surprised you would even show your face here."

I turned around and laughed when I saw she was being serious. "What.... I DID? Do you seriously have that little intelligence to stand there and blame me for what I DID to them?"

"You are the one who beat them up-"

"Yeah, because they came and vandalized my house. What did you expect me to do? You know, I don't even know why I'm talking to you about this. You'd never understand what position I'm in so it really doesn't matter."

"You could've called the pol-"

"For the eighth time in the last month? Yeah, I don't think so. I've called them more times than I can count on all of my fingers and toes. Do you really think I'd call them even one more time?"

"You are always such an exaggerator, Gwen." I spun around when I heard her last comment and stomped over to her so my nose was practically touching hers.

"Don't you DARE tell me what I am. You don't know me. You don't know what I go through on a day to day basis because of you and all of your crazy antics. Do you remember that time you told everyone I stole that stupid motorcycle from your so-called 'boyfriend'? Yeah! They sent me away for two weeks. Do you see this?" I lifted up my shirt on the side of my body so she could see the 7-inch scar that ran across my hip horizontally. "Yeah, those thugs in that detention center smashed the mirror in the bathroom and used it to cut me. And do you know who I blame?" I watched as her eyes dropped.

"Me," she filled in quietly.

"No. I blame myself for believing that any of you would ever have my back. I blame myself for being so naive and going against my better judgment. I blame myself for covering for you and your entire god dang 'group' when the police came around asking who knocked down that bloody fountain."

"It wasn't you?" McKenna asked shocked. She probably was surprised that I didn't turn them in a year and a half ago when she, Amber, Amber's group, and the football team got rowdy one night and knocked down the fountain in the park. The repairs cost over $50,000 and that entire group blamed me for turning them in. I knew it was them but I didn't say anything. I thought since, no one got hurt, it wouldn't be that bad if they got off with a warning this time around. I guess a neighbor saw them because they all eventually got caught.

"No, it wasn't me and you all would've known that if you had come and talked to me about it instead of starting this war. It's ridiculous and immature I'd honestly be fine if I never saw any of you ever again. Don't come find me McKenna. Don't talk to me. You know what, don't even look at me." I gave her one last glare before turning around and heading to first period. I walked in and the second after I sat down the bell rang. I let out a breath of relief when it finally registered that I wasn't late.

Being late is probably *one* of my most feared nightmares.

"Are you ready?" I was sitting on the examination table in Dr. Lucero's room. The school day had gone by pretty quickly especially since I had to get out early, so I could see Dr. Lucero on time.

"It won't hurt, will it?" I asked Dr. Lucero who was currently hovering his hands over my damaged one.

"There may be a little pressure when I remove the splint from your hand, but if everything healed smoothly, it should be just fine." I nodded and bit the inside of my cheek to prepare myself for the pain as he took off the splint. He pulled it off rather quickly and it took everything in me not to tear off the inside of my mouth. He didn't tell me that relief of pressure would make my hand tingle. It felt similar to when your hand falls asleep and you feel all the tingles run through it. When I was younger I compared the feeling to ants crawling on you.

"There we go, all done. Everything looks great, Gwen! You should be back to full activity by the end of the summer." I choked on air when I heard him say the end of the summer.

"Wh-what do you mean end of the *summer*?" Trying my very best to keep the frustration and anger out of my tone.

"Well, your hand needs time to rest without anything on it. The bones need to settle, and we need to make sure that they heal correctly. It would be awful if you went back to kick-boxing and your finger ended up curling over permanently."

"Well, I can stay away from the kick-boxing. I just

need you to say that it's okay for me to ride my motorcycle and take pictures."

"I don't have a problem with the pictures but I'm not sure about your motorcycle. It's a very dangerous vehicle and I'm afraid you could further injure your hand."

"I could get hurt just by walking on the sidewalk, so unless there is an irrefutable reason for me to not ride then I'm going to ask you to let me. It's been killing me that I haven't been able to ride." He sighed when he realized that I would not be leaving here until I heard what I wanted to hear.

"Fine. But you have to be careful, and I'd recommend staying away from rough terrain like forest trails. Please be careful Gwen. I'd hate to see you back here too soon." Dr. Lucero's eyes showed that he was speaking against his better judgment. All I knew was that I was thrilled to get permission to ride on my bike so, I just rolled with it.

"Thank you, Dr. Lucero. I'll see you right before I go off to college."

"Yes, and I hope not any sooner than that." He smiled and ushered me out of the room.

I zoned out of the conversation at the thought of riding again. I was going to have to make up for lost time.

"Honey, please be careful." My mom and Jerry were standing in the doorway of the house watching me get on my bike. I didn't respond but rather, kicked the engine to life. I let the roar from my bike drown out my worried mother. Jerry seemed to understand that I liked to ride without an audience because the second I gave him my 'please get Mom away' look he put his arm around her and directed her into the house. I smiled when the front door closed and I was all alone.

I sat there for a few minutes, reveling in the feel of my bike. I tightened my hand around the handlebar and tested out my strength. I needed to make sure I could hold my handlebars securely. If I couldn't, I wouldn't be comfortable riding. I love to ride, but not so much so that I'd die to do it one more time. Yeah, no, that's not happening.

I pulled out of my parking space and turned left down the street. The second I hit the main road, I was gone. I rode like I'd never stopped.

The road began to feel endless so I turned off of it. I wasn't really thinking when I went back to the forest. I got back on the trail, and when it was too late, I realized I had gone against Dr. Lucero's recommendation. I've been down this trail millions of times, and I have never run into any problems. Well, except for that one guy who slapped me. Something inside of me said that he had something to say so, I took the same trail that I did that day and ended up in front of the man's house. He was, once again, outside but this time, instead of stomping over to me, he walked over slowly and quietly.

"You never called the police on me," he stated.

"I didn't think it was necessary for you to go to jail because you were drunk and are incapable of making smart life decisions. That's not really what I came to talk about though. I came back here to make a deal with you."

"Whatever you want, I am willing to do. I am so sorry

for what I did and I-"

"Yeah, I didn't come here to have a full-blown conversation about it. You were drunk, and you got mad so you slapped whatever was in front of you. Trust me, I'm in high school. I know how this stuff works. So...." I let my voice trail off. I was asking for his name.

"Bruce Sanders."

"Bruce, I would like to have the permission to ride on this trail whenever I want. I never have races with people so you don't have to worry about other bikes. It will always be just me and maybe a friend on the back of my bike. Can we agree on that?"

"Of course. Yeah, and even if you do have races I don't mind. As long as you don't have them too late at night, you can drive here whenever you want." He smiled and that's when I noticed the multiple teeth missing from his mouth. I smiled and put the sunglasses I took off, back on. Starting my bike, I drove off and didn't look back once. I'm going to try my best to forget him. He gives me weird vibes.

"So, how was it?" I only had one foot in the door when the questions started coming. Of course, they were from my mother.

"Fine."

"Nothing hurts?"

"Nope."

"Nothing felt different while you were riding?"

"Jerry?" I looked to Jerry for help but he gave me the 'she'll kill me if I talk' look so I guess, I'm on my own for this one. Thanks Jerry.

"Don't look at him. Talk to me Gwen."

"Mom, I'm fine. I drove just like I normally do and now it's time for homework. I have to go over to Ricky's in 30 minutes, so I really need to step on it," I said quickly. I dropped the bag and camera I'd be taking over to Ricky's on the couch and headed up the stairs. I waited a few seconds before I closed my door to make sure my mother wasn't going to yell for me anymore.

Now, all I have to do is find something to wear that says 'my splint was just taken off'. I smiled when my eyes landed on a red romper.

"You're early." Once again, Ricky was sitting 5 feet away from the door with his arms crossed. I rolled my eyes when I saw him and immediately went for the elevator. I didn't wait for Ricky to get in to press the 3rd button. The doors closed before he could make it in and I laughed. My laughter echoed in the metal chamber and my childhood nightmares came back. I had never told anyone this but I had been deathly afraid of elevators since I was 8 when I got trapped in one. Yesterday, when Ricky brought me in it, I wasn't afraid because he was here with me and my mind didn't have time to think about what happened to me 9 years ago. Now I'm alone and there is nothing distracting me from the memory. I was trapped in there for four hours and then some.

When the doors to the basement level opened I practically jumped out of the elevator. I closed my eyes, and let out a deep breath, refusing to let Ricky see that I was afraid of elevators.

"You scared of elevators or something?" I literally jumped when I heard his voice coming from behind. I spun around and threw the roll of paper towels I had been holding at him. He easily deflected the roll with a wave of his hand and laughed.

"God don't DO that, Ricky. You're going to give me a heart attack!" I said, almost breathless from the jumping and fright.

"I'm pretty sure the elevator already did that to you," he said as he laughed and wheeled over to the work table. I almost gasped when I saw the finished project. It looked just like I wanted it to.

"It looks great, Ricky!" I exclaimed happily, bending down to give him a hug.

Ricky mumbled something and I could've sworn he said *'I couldn't have done it without you'*.

"What was that, Rick? Was that a compliment coming out of your mouth?" I laughed when his eyes locked onto a spot on the floor. Making him uncomfortable has become one of my many talents.

"Your head is already too big for your own good." I rolled my eyes at his comment and lifted up the seat. Before I came over I had driven my motorcycle into his garage so now, all we had to do, was take the seat to the garage and attach it.

Walking into the garage, I flicked the lights on and set the seat on top of my bike. The dimensions were perfect which only reiterated just how smart Ricky was. I smiled when I stepped back and took in how good it looked.

"You ready to attach it?" Ricky asked, from the doorway to the garage. I walked over to him and helped him get his wheelchair down the few cement steps that stood in his way. He had the box of tools so we were set.

I looked at him and nodded.

Let's do this.

Almost two hours had passed, and I was screwing in the last nail. When I stood back I almost cried. It looked great and it gave you the impression that the seat came with it. I looked at Ricky who was looking at the bike with just as much pride.

"It looks great," I spoke up after the long minutes of silence. We had been staring at the bike for long enough so I decided that it would be a good idea to test it out. Without waiting for Ricky's consent, I hopped onto the seat. It was extremely comfortable which was great for Ricky's spine. The backrest, luckily, provided even more support. The exterior was the same bronze-metallic color that my bike was so, all in all, the seat was great.

"I guess, it worked," Ricky said unenthusiastically. I whipped my head around to make sure I heard him correctly. His mood had changed all of a sudden.

"What's wrong?" I hopped down from the seat and walked over to Ricky. His eyes were filled with nervousness.

"I've never done something like this before, and I'm just worried that something is going to go wrong."

"What are you talking about?" I asked disbelievingly. I couldn't believe the words that were coming out of his mouth. "Ricky, I know that's not what this is about. What is wrong?" I bent down, so we were both on the same level.

"I've never done anything different than my normal routine. I do the same thing every day and nothing changes."

"Are you happy 100% of the time?"

"Well, no, but no one is."

"But you've never tried to see if something else could make you happier."

"But I'm sure one day I will be content-"

"By doing the same thing and expecting your feelings to change? Nothing changes if nothing changes, Rick. It's absolute craziness to think that living your whole life the same way, everyday, will ever make you happy. You need to try something new, and I'd be honored if you let me help you do just that."

"Wednesday, then?"

"Wednesday." I smiled and turned my attention back to the bike.

It truly looked amazing.

22 ONE JOURNEY

"We must embrace pain and burn it as fuel for our journey." – Kenji Miyazawa

Tuesday couldn't have been any longer. The entire day, all the way up until I fell asleep last night, was filled with my obsession over the ride with Ricky. It may seem silly to get so excited about something like this but the point of the ride is to show Ricky that he can have just as much fun as everyone else. He gets to enjoy what people take for granted every day.

It was a statement.

"Gwen, are you taking your bike, or am I driving you?" My mother asked from the kitchen. Today, Jerry had taken it upon himself to cook us breakfast. It was great, but I was beyond surprised. He made us egg omelets filled with amazing veggies and special 'secret ingredients'. They were cooked perfectly. I guess my mom really struck gold in the husband department this time. He was wealthy, polite, caring, smart, and he knew how to cook. Currently, he was cleaning up the dishes because he refused to let his 'loving fiancé' clean them up herself. When he said that I internally barfed, but at the same time, I was grateful for the help with the chores. Usually, I would be the one to clean them up, but he didn't need to know that.

"I'm taking my bike." My mother breathed in sharply, giving me a good reason to turn on my sympathetic face. She never liked it when I chose my bike.

Many things inside of me told me that my plan was a bad one, but today was about being fearless. Ricky was trying to be and so would I. Last time I took this thing to school my hand was almost dismembered. Today could go either way.

I pulled into the parking lot 10 minutes earlier than usual. I had been making it easy for people to target me because my arrival and departure time almost never changed. At least, this way, I could prevent the usual encounters I would have before 1st period. I smiled when I realized no one had parked near my spot. It was nice because this way I didn't have to worry all day about people scratching my most prized possession.

Opening my locker rather quickly, I took out the textbooks I would be needing. I hate that I need those textbooks.

"We wanted to say sorry." I almost jumped when I turned and saw seven people standing to the right of my locker. I blinked to make sure I was seeing right. Standing before me was McKenna, Amber, Jay, Kent, Carter, Monica, and Lily. Some of the few people who have wronged me at least once in the past four years. I smiled at how ironic it was that they were apologizing to me.

"Why are you smiling?" Monica asked with an attitude. She lowered her voice when she said the word apologize as if it were a curse word. I rolled my eyes and looked at each and every one of them. When I met each of their eyes I tried to remember every single thing that person did to me. McKenna was leading the group. In freshmen year, she ambushed my cheerleading tryout. I'm not going to get into the details of it, but I ended up walking off the field with flour lodged into my eye sockets. Ever since then, she has aided Amber in whatever cruel prank she decided to try on me. I was smart enough to check my shampoo bottles before using them, but once, she filled it with hair removal. McKenna was also the one who told everyone that I stole her boyfriend's bike. I have respect for people who ride motorcycles, so I definitely wouldn't be stealing anything like that.

My eyes landed on the person directly behind McKenna. Jay. He is one of those people who, instead of doing something, does absolutely nothing. He knew that his whole team was emotionally torturing me and did nothing. He let them walk all over me, and I blame him for that. He's the team captain. He should've done something.

Standing to his left was Amber. She has found little ways over the years to get to me. Sometimes she's written just one word on a sticky note and stuck it on my gym locker. Other times she would get a whole group of girls to yell some crude name at me down the hallway. Whatever it was, the underlying message was cruel.

Kent and Carter were standing side by side, and basically, all they've done is vandalize my personal belongings. Carter also made me feel like a possession for ten minutes but that was only for ten minutes. I shut that train down the second it pulled into the station. Sometimes, you have to just go with your gut feeling. It takes you down a better path most of the time.

Monica really hasn't done much besides team up with Amber. She's one of Amber's 'partners in crime' so she is wrong by default.

Lily's icy grey eyes were the ones that held mine for the longest. She was at one point my best friend. We had known each other since the 7th grade, and we promised each other that we would be friends forever. She would help me with my family issues, I would help her with hers, and we use to always find comfort in each other. She had no sympathy for me when Ty, Jett and my father left because, by then, we hadn't been on speaking terms. The summer after freshman year she told me that I needed to become friends with Amber to keep her by my side. Obviously, I told her to go jump in a ditch and take Amber and her posse with her. After that summer, she and Amber were inseparable. Their hate towards me definitely brought them closer. They even went as far as to say that they would figure out a way to ruin my relationship with my brother. I knew that Lily had told them how much I adored him because she was the only one on this Earth that knew just how much I looked up to him. The only one. That's why I have never told anyone else about how close I was to Jett because the one person I trusted used that information to get back at me. Whenever my mother brought up Lily, I made up stupid things that she supposedly did to me. I just try to make up things to tell my mother that wouldn't be too alarming. She's done much worse than spreading a little rumor around.

She's made me question life all together.

"Well, usually the people who are apologizing don't have the attitudes, *Monica*," I said her name with as much anger as I could muster. She doesn't deserve my forgiveness and honestly, I'm beginning to wonder if any of them do. I crossed my arms, waiting for one of them to make the next move.

"Look, Gwen, we didn't come here to start something," Amber said sounding quite tired. It was as if this whole conversation was exhausting to her. Funny.

"You all made my life a living piece of crap for 4 years. You made people believe I was a criminal. You made people believe I was a murderer. You made people believe I was a push-over. You made people believe I was weak. You made people believe I was nothing more than a possession. You made people believe that I was jealous of Amber. And you.... you took the one family relationship that meant more to me than this entire world and destroyed it. Completely annihilated it." Every accusation I made I pointed at the person who I was accusing. I let all of their heads drop in shame just to make what I was about say a little easier on me.

"But," I can't believe I'm saying this, "I forgive you."

The surprise written on their faces made me laugh to myself. Something about this week has gotten me in a good mood, and honestly, I'm ready to let it go. It felt good to finally call them out on what they did to me, but I think it was time.

I looked at all of them one more time before closing

my locker and heading to Mr. Wells' class. For once, I was happy to see my science teacher.

"You're-"

"I know I'm late. You don't need to tell me." I was walking into Ricky's house with a huge smile plastered on my face. I had never been more excited to drive my motorcycle into his garage in my entire life.

"I was going to say on time for once." He smirked when he saw the shock covering my face. I can't believe he actually told me I was on time. He must be just as excited as I was to ride my bike.

After our legendary greeting, we both headed for the elevator. I let him get in first so I would be sure he wouldn't try and pull something. He smirked when he realized what I was doing. I pretended not to notice and pushed the number 3. Within seconds we were in the basement and heading to the garage. I noticed something changed in Ricky's eyes when I opened the door to the garage and let the 4 o'clock sun spill into it. His look was a mixture of determination and confidence, and I decided that it looked good on him. It looked really good.

"Are you okay, Gwen?" I turned, surprised that Ricky was actually asking me how I was. He almost never did that, and he told me that he only does that when something is 'obviously ticking me off'.

"Yeah, why wouldn't I be?"

"Wouldn't it be called hypocritical if you told me to be honest with you, but yet, you weren't honest with me?"

"I don't know what you're talking about."

"Gwen. Please," he pleaded. I've only seen Ricky beg a few times but this time, it looked like he was serious and genuinely concerned. Something inside me broke at the sight of him being completely vulnerable with me.

"The people who jacked me up came to apologize to me today. Well, a few of them did." I looked over to my bike and wished that we were already on it so we didn't have to talk. This was turning into one of the few conversations I didn't want to have with him. This conversation is going to change the mood of the whole day and it's going to ruin it.

"I hope you didn't automatically forgive them." I looked at him shocked when those words left his mouth. I laughed at the sight of his serious face and the sound of his monotonous voice. He smirked when he heard the laugh that escaped my lips.

I shrugged not wanting to be straight forward with the news. Both of us had grown quiet after I spoke. It wasn't a comfortable silence so I decided that I would break it. "Well, we should get going. Come on." I waved Ricky over and was surprised when he obliged. He wheeled over to the right side of my motorcycle, and waited for me to come over. We brought over his portable chin up bar so he could assist me in the great task of getting him actually onto the bike.

I put the brakes on both his wheelchair and the chin up bar so, when he tried to lift himself up, it wouldn't slip. He raised his arms and latched onto the bar. I let him lift himself out of the wheelchair before I intervened and swung his legs onto the seat. I put each leg over either side of the bike and strapped him in using the seat belt we had created just for him. We had made it thick and wide so it would give him as much support as possible. The seat belt was almost half an inch thick and 5 inches wide. It was perfect and made it so I didn't have to be on the bike to provide him with support. The second I fastened the seat belt I tapped him, letting him know he could let go of the bar.

I squealed in excitement when he let go and didn't fall off. He looked at me, frightened of all things.

"God! I thought you hurt yourself. DON'T do that!" He yelled at me angrily. I laughed when I realized how worried he was.

"Don't worry Rick. I'm sure you would've helped me." I smiled innocently and patted his head. He swatted my hand away but not before I could give him a little pinch on the cheek. He hated it when I pretended to treat him like a child. That's why I did it so much.

I hopped on my bike, still laughing from the death glares Ricky was throwing my way. The second I put my foot on the kickstand I realized that this was it. This was the moment that I had been waiting for this entire time. It was finally going to be the day that I drove Ricky Doone on my motorcycle. I smiled at the thought, and all in one motion kicked my bike to a start. The engine roared to life and just like that, we were driving out of the garage and onto the street.

Before I knew it, I was turning onto the main roads and flying through our small town. I laughed when I felt Ricky jerk at the sudden increase in speed. My laughter was carried away in the wind and muffled by my helmet. I looked in my rear-view mirrors and saw Ricky shaking his head back and forth. At first, I thought he was shaking his head in fear, but when we pulled up to a red light, I heard his melodic laughter coming from behind me. The sound of it alone always made me smile because he rarely laughed. My smile grew when I realized just how much he was enjoying it. I got the crazy idea to take him on the forest trail, but I knew that it was rough. The polite thing to do would be to ask. I pulled over directly in front the crossroad that led to the forest. I flicked up my face shield and turned around to face Ricky. I pointed at the picture of the tree, asking whether or not he wanted to go that way. He nodded, rather enthusiastically, and laughed when I jolted the bike forward.

The paved asphalt quickly dissolved into dirt, rock, and grass. I looked around and decided that I would take him down the prettiest trail. The prettiest trail, of course, had to be the way that Bruce lived. I knew it wasn't a problem but I really wasn't in the mood to see Bruce. This moment was supposed to be just for Ricky and me. Not Ricky, Bruce, and me. It just doesn't have the same ring to it.

Shaking the thought of Bruce away I focused all of my attention back onto the trail. It would be absolutely awful if anything-

"GWEN!" I heard a muffled scream before my entire field of vision went black.

There was nothing but black.

"Gwen? Gwen, honey, please get up." My eyes flickered open and the second they did I regretted it. The light that was blaring down on me made my head feel like it was about to explode. It was like the light triggered the pounding sensation that seemed to only get worse by the minute.

When my eyes finally focused, they landed on my hyperventilating mother and a very frightened Jerry. It took a lot inside of me not to smile at the sight of them hovering over me with those faces.

"I'm up." My voice came out quiet and shaky. I looked around the room to see that I was not in my bed but rather a hospital gurney. I rolled my eyes and sighed at the sight of the I.V bags hanging beside me. I looked back at the only two people in the room to find them still staring at me intently.

"Yes?" I asked in a sing song voice. I still wasn't quite sure why neither of them were speaking to me. I wasn't sure until something clicked.

"Where is Ricky?" My mother didn't answer. I looked to Jerry who had all of a sudden found the floor incredibly interesting.

"Mom, I'm going to ask one more time. Where.... is.... Ricky?" The amount of warning that was ringing in my voice seemed to click with her because she finally opened her mouth.

"He's here." My eyes started to fill with tears at all of the possible scenarios that could be occurring right now. The most alarming being the possibility that I killed him.

"And...." I let my voice trail off as I searched my mother's eyes for anything that could tell me what I wanted to know.

"He's in critical condition, Gwen." The first tear slid down my cheek when I heard my mother say that. Instead of showing him how great life could be I basically showed him how fast it could end.

"Mom, tell me all of it. You're killing me. What is it?" I begged her with every last ounce of energy I had left. The idea of Ricky being taken from me made my body physically weak.

"He's in a coma."

That's when the dam broke. I felt the tears on my hands before I really registered the fact that two pairs of arms were wrapping around me and holding my shaking body. My eyes burned with the sadness that I had brought on myself. Looking back on today I realized just how selfish I really was. Instead of just accepting the fact that Ricky was happy the way he was living I had to go and screw it up all together. The idea of never seeing him again made it feel like pieces of my heart broke off and sunk into the pits of my stomach. This feeling makes me wish that I was back in that nightmare. Back in Ricky's house where he was dying in my dreams. I would choose to suffer through those nightmares everyday if it meant that Ricky was back at home, safe.

"He's in a coma" she said. My mother forgot to add the part about the fact that I put him there.

I put Ricky Doone in a coma.

23 STAYING

"Nobody is ever too busy. If they care they will make time."

I was being discharged from the hospital today, but I knew I really wouldn't be leaving until Ricky woke up.

It was Saturday but I couldn't care less. The school year was over, and I had already gotten my high school diploma. The hospital allowed me to go to my graduation for literally 30 minutes just so I could pick up my diploma and 'officially' graduate from high school. It didn't feel like I graduated though. If anything, it felt like the first day of school all over again. Ricky still hasn't woken up, and it's been three days. Three days and there hasn't been the slightest movement.

Caroline has been, understandably, furious with me since the second she found out I took him riding. Since Ricky was an adult she couldn't charge me with anything but I knew for a fact that should would have if she could've. My mother and Jerry left a few hours ago and promised to be back really soon with food for me. Every time they leave, Caroline takes it upon herself to come into my room to yell and scold me about how bad of a person I am. She's even gone as far as to say that she should've never let me into Ricky's life. I can see why she wouldn't want me in his life. Clearly, my impact on Ricky's life was for the worse and it was only a matter of time until something bad happened.

The doctors and surgeons explained to me what happened but I still don't fully understand it. Somehow, the seat belt we designed snapped, causing Ricky to fly almost 20 feet away from the bike. He hit pieces of his lumbar and cervical spine. I, on the other hand, got a mild concussion and a little scratch on my hand. Yes, I did have to be tested for drugs and alcohol, but of course, they came back negative and all the charges were dropped.

It isn't fair.

That's the conclusion that I've come to, and to punish myself, I've decided that I will stay in the hospital until he wakes up. That is the least that I could do for him.

I snapped out of my thoughts when I heard a gentle knock on the door. It was the doctor, Dr. Bowers. She had asked me to call her Lacey, but I was in no mood to be friendly. I hadn't really been in a good mood since the accident. How could I be? I could've killed him and no one is admitting that to me. Well, except for Caroline. She's made it very clear that I will never be seeing Ricky again unless it's outside, accidentally. That means I'm basically never seeing him again.

"How are you doing?"

"Well, besides the fact that no one is telling me about my, possibly, dying friend, I'm good."

"He won't die Gwen." She said almost as if she believed it.

Almost.

"Don't lie to me, Bowers. You and I both know there is a high probability that he won't make it through this. That's the truth and not even my parents can deny that." I sighed and dropped my head back on my pillow. I couldn't live with myself if he doesn't wake up.

"I'm not lying to you. I came in here to let you know that his vitals are stable. Despite his present state, and the fact he's in a coma, he looks good. I wasn't supposed to tell you that but I like you, Gwen. And, I'd hate to see you freaking out unnecessarily. You are finally being discharged." She smiled as she busied herself with organizing the folder she had in her hands.

"Thanks. Would it be possible for me to wait here until my parents get back, though? They're supposed to be here any moment now."

"Oh, yeah, of course. When they arrive, though, I'm going to ask that you go out to the main lobby or waiting area." She smiled once more before leaving. The second the door closed I saw her sprint towards the door to the emergency room.

Fifteen minutes had passed and my parents were walking in with pizza. I smiled the second the smell hit my nose. The cheesy deliciousness made my mouth water uncontrollably. I had gotten way too accustomed to the hospital "food" they have here. Well that and I stress eat.... a lot.

"Thanks, guys." I smiled at Jerry and my mother who were skeptically watching me as I put on my shoes. "Oh, I was discharged while you guys were gone. You're going to have to go to the nurse's station to approve it or whatever." I got my shoes on and let out an accomplished sigh. It's a lot of work putting on shoes from the hospital bed. I guess, I could've stood up but I was too worried that I would get dizzy and fall back down. I have a concussion, and at the moment, the only thing I've been focusing on is making sure I stay in as good of condition as I can so I can sit and wait for Ricky. I'm not exactly sure how long that will be, but I plan on waiting until the end.

I looked over at the door and saw my parents walking back in. They both nodded letting me know that they had approved my discharge and that we were all set. I smiled and picked up the pizza. My mom held the door open for me as I led them into the waiting room. I set the pizza down and finally turned to Jerry and my mother who had struggled to keep up with my fast pace.

"So, I need you all to hear me out before you say anything." I waited until they both nodded. I needed to make sure I had their undivided attention. "I have to stay here. I don't feel right about leaving Ricky. I'm aware that he wouldn't know I was here, but honestly, it's more for me than for him. Caroline still won't let me see him, and I understand that, but I don't feel right about leaving. I need to stay to be able to live with myself and if I need to handcuff myself to one of those chairs out there and swallow the key then I will. I need to stay and I need you all to understand." I breathed in the second I stopped talking. I talked so fast that I forgot to breathe in the first place.

Minutes passed and still, no one had answered me. I looked back and forth between Jerry and my mother awaiting the answer I was dying to hear.

"I don't know about this, Gwen. I mean, our wedding is coming up and I need you there-."

"Mom, I wouldn't miss your wedding for the world. Whatever you need me for I'll be there. If you need help decorating, I'll help. I want to make that day the best day of your lives, but I need you both to let me stay here whenever I'm not helping you. Whatever happens, by the end of it all, I need to be able to live with myself and the only way I know how to do that is if I stay with him throughout this," I let a few seconds pass before adding, "Plus, this hospital is small so you'll always know where I am. There is only one waiting room and that's where I'll be." My mother's eyes searched mine before she let out a shaky breath. When her eyes dropped, I knew she'd given in.

She looked to Jerry who gave her a 'it's up to you' look. Classic fiancé move.

"Fine, but you have to come home for lunch and whenever you need to sleep."

"Mom-"

"NO! That is final. I'm not debating this. Take it or leave it, and if you don't take it you're coming home with us now." She crossed her arms and gave me the 'eye'. When she did that everyone within 100 feet was automatically put in danger. I stared at her for about 30 seconds until I finally realized she would be winning this fight. You have to pick and choose the battles you fight with her.

"Okay. I'll see you tonight." I gave her a small smile before giving both of them a hug. I turned around, getting ready to head to the waiting room when I felt a hand on my shoulder. I turned around and met my mother's eyes. She handed me my charger before turning and leaving with Jerry. I smiled at her receding figure.

Thanks, Mom.

"Who are you waiting for?" I jumped, startled, when I heard a small voice coming from beside me. I turned to the chair to my left to see a little girl with pig tails and two missing front teeth, looking up at me expectantly. She was the epitome of adorable. I smiled at her before thinking over the question she asked me.

"His name is Ricky." Her eyes sparkled with something before she opened her mouth to speak.

"He your boyfriend?" My mouth dropped in shock when those words left her mouth.

"Are you crazy? No. I've been taking care of him and we got into an accident."

"Do you want him to be your boyfriend?"

"I-"

"Because I have a boyfriend. Mommy told me that if I wanted to be with somebody I had to go get him myself." She nodded after reciting her mother's words. Something told me those weren't exactly her mother's words. I smiled and laughed to myself at the thought, looking down at the little girl.

The attitude coming from the little girl was enough to rival Amber's. I could definitely see her being the next queen bee.

"What's your name?"

"Mommy told me not to talk to strangers, but since I started talking to you first, I'm going to tell you. Zoey Mays. I'm 6."

"Nice to meet you, Zoey. I'm Gwen."

"Yeah, yeah. We need to go back to your boy problem though."

"I don't have a boy problem, Zoey."

"Keep saying that. Anyway, the way that you know he likes you is if he gets you stuff. Nathan gets me stuff every day."

"Well, Ricky doesn't get me stuff."

"I think you are lying. You're so pretty. He should be getting you expensive stuff like those candy bracelets."

"Candy bracelets?"

"If he gets you a candy bracelet you guys are going to get married. That's what my best friend told me. She has a boyfriend too and he got her a candy bracelet and now they are going to get married. It's law."

"So, if he never gets me a candy bracelet then what?"

"Well, then I guess someone else has to get you a candy bracelet." I had to hold back the laugh. Zoey was being completely serious throughout this entire conversation which only showed how young she was.

"Well thank you-"

"I'm sure somebody will. Like him." She pointed to a tall boy standing near the vending machines. I shook my head in disgust. He was probably 5 years younger than me!

"Nope. I don't think I would accept the bracelet." She let out a gasp as the words rolled easily off my tongue.

"WHAT?! When someone gives you a candy bracelet you HAVE to take it."

"I have to?"

"You HAVE to. It's law."

"Hmm." I put my hand on my chin pretending to

think over the entire thing.

"Fine. We'll find somebody better." She looked around the waiting room until her eyes landed on a tall woman with the same dark brown hair as her. Her face exploded into a cheeky grin that made its way all the way to her eyes.

"MOMMY!" She squealed and jumped down from the chair. As she ran over to her mother, I noticed the pink tutu she was sporting. I looked to her mother who mouthed a 'thank you'. I'm guessing that was for keeping her little girl occupied but I wasn't quite sure. Zoey jumped onto her mother and eventually bribed her to come and meet me. I stood up when they reached my chair.

"Hi, I'm Gwen." I smiled and stuck out my hand for Zoey's mother. Zoey was still in her arms so, to enable her to shake my hand, she had to reposition hers around Zoey.

"Avianna. Thank you for keeping Zoey company. She doesn't get along with too many people." When her mother said that we both looked at Zoey. She shrugged, getting us both to laugh.

"It was no problem. Zoey gave me a lot of useful tips that I definitely will be using in the future." I gave her a little wink. Her mother turned her attention to her and tickled her stomach.

"Is that so?" She asked happily. I smiled when Zoey started to giggle. "I hope I'm not intruding when I ask you who you're here for?"

"No, you're not. I'm actually here for a friend. Ricky. We were both in the same accident so it's only fair that I wait until he wakes up." Her mother nodded, approvingly. She gave me an apologetic smile before setting Zoey down.

"Well, we're sorry to hear that. I hope that he gets better quickly. I think it's very kind of you to stay here and wait for him. Zoey and I are also waiting for someone, isn't that right Zo? Her father, my husband Cedric, was hit by a drunk driver. He's been in here for 4 days now so Zoey and I have been coming out here to get some fresh air."

"I'm so sorry. I hope he can go home soon."

"Yeah," Zoey interjected, "We do too. Daddy keeps telling me that he's fine here but I know he's lying. Daddy never offers to do my hair." She pulled on her pigtails showing off the hair job that her father did. I laughed when she showed me how lopsided they were.

"Zoey, I think your father did a great job," her mother chimed in. I didn't totally disagree, but you could definitely tell that her hair wasn't done by her mother.

"Mommy don't start lying too. Even you said a blind woman could've done it better." She looked up to her mother with an innocent smile. I could tell that, if Zoey was any older, her mother would've been furious. Being young definitely has its perks.

"Well, I'll let you two get back to him. Please tell him that I said hi, and that I hope he gets better soon." They both smiled and nodded at me before turning and walking down the hallway. I saw them turn the corner before I lost sight of them.

I sat back down and looked down at my watch. It was currently 4:35 and I still hadn't seen Caroline. I was hoping that she'd come out and see me waiting for him. I really wanted to try and persuade her to let me visit him.

I think it's completely unfair for her to forbid me to see him. Since I'm not family I have to listen to her but there have been multiple times where I have wanted to totally forget what she says and walk back there. That would probably get me thrown out, though, and I'd rather wait out here until he wakes up than at my house. I couldn't handle seeing his house or my motorcycle every day for that long. I would constantly be reminded of exactly every way I had let him down.

This is probably the first time in my entire life that I didn't want to see my bike. It was a feeling that I thought I'd never grow to have. Then again, I never thought I'd care about someone as much as I care about Ricky so, I guess anything can happen.

"Gwen." I heard my name being called and I immediately looked up. Normally I would've stood, but I didn't have the energy at the moment. Seeing her and being completely bored out of my mind was enough to knock the power out of almost anyone.

My eyes focused on Caroline who was, now, making her way over to me. She took the seat next to me, and for a while, we both sat there staring into oblivion, and undoubtedly, thinking about Ricky. She was the one to break the silence.

"I know you didn't mean to." I turned to her, surprised to say the least, when I heard her soft voice play next to me. I'm not sure what changed in the last three days, but she looked as though the mere sight of me was tiring.

"Really?" I asked her quietly. Tears started to collect in my eyes.

"Yeah. He would hate me until the end of time if he woke up and heard that I didn't let you see him. We both made mistakes when it came down to what was best for him. Now I know how you felt when you learned why I didn't get him into physical therapy." She wasn't looking at me but rather a seemingly interesting spot on the floor. I could tell by her body language that it was killing her to not have anyone to talk to. I haven't seen anybody come in here asking for Ricky.

I thought over what she had just told me, and I guess, she was right. I had never compared the two situations, but looking back, one could say they were relatively close. When I found out that she didn't take him to therapy the first thing that I thought of was how selfish she was being for only worrying about how *she* felt. When someone looks at what I've done, can they really say that we, Caroline and I, are much different? We both only worried about what *we* thought was best for him and not what he actually wanted. In hindsight, you could say that I was being selfish and demanding.

"So, are you saying I can see him?" I asked cautiously. Lowering my voice with every word that I spoke. I was walking on dangerously thin ice here and anything I said could break the thin layer of vulnerability Caroline had opened up within herself.

"Yeah. I am. I'll be out here when you're done." I smiled, grateful for the permission that she'd granted me.

I walked up to the desk and told the nurse that Caroline was giving me her approval to see him. The nurse smiled and gave me the room number. It was on this floor so I didn't have to go very far.

I walked down the hall and stopped when I saw Ricky lying on a hospital bed through the glass window of his room. I entered, cautiously, almost as if his thoughts were enough to scare me away.

Before I took in the sight of him, I looked around the room. He was connected to a countless number of machines that constantly beeped. The ugly hospital gown they had put him in didn't mask his attractiveness one bit. I was smiling at the thought, until I looked over to him and met.... nothing. His eyes were closed, and expecting to see bright green ones, I sank into the chair adjacent to his bed in shame.

"Hey." I tried to remember the article I read about how, in some cases, the coma patient could hear what was going on around them. I tried hard to keep my hopes up but it was virtually impossible. When he didn't reply with one of his snarky comments, like how my voice sounded like a frog dying from mycobacteriosis or how I looked like a homeless guy from New York City, that's when the tears came. I sat there crying, shaking, with the sadness that will never be lifted off of my shoulders until I know that he's okay.

I stared at him for almost an hour straight trying to push down the guilt that came with the sight of him. I kept thinking about how I was the one who put him there and how he didn't deserve it. He didn't deserve it at all.

"Hey, Rick." I sniffed once to get my crying to ease up for a few minutes so I could actually get a sentence out. "It's Gwen. I know you probably don't want to see me now so it's probably a good thing that your eyes are closed. I just wanted to let you know that I saw the pictures at the Roundel museum. How and when you got them there is a mystery to me but they look phenomenal.

I love the picture of me by my bike. How you took that one is an even bigger mystery, but yeah, they look amazing. I still haven't been able to understand why you did that, but it's always been a dream of mine to have pictures make it into that museum so, thank you. You have no idea how much that means to me...." My train of thought was cut off by the sobs that came after I spoke of his kindness. I couldn't help, but cry at how ridiculous this was. He's given me so much and what do I do? I put him in the hospital.

"I'm so sorry, Rick. I don't know what happened.... I just.... I've driven down that trail more times than I can count." I waited a moment before a sad reality came rushing to me. "You told me Rick! You warned me about that stupid seat belt when we were making it, and what do I do? I change it to that stupid polyester material. I'm so sorry." A few tears had fallen when I admitted the truth to him, and ultimately, myself. It might as well have been me throwing him off the motorcycle. "I know my apology probably means nothing to you but I want you to know how awful I feel. We still have to do so much. You still have to show me your obstacle courses. I still have to show you my school." I waited a few seconds in an effort to try and get my voice back. It had literally died down to a whisper. "When you wake up don't get mad at your Mom for not letting me see you earlier. I completely understand, and I probably would've done the same thing if I was in her position." I wiped the tears that had stained my face and stood from the chair. I looked at Ricky one more time before brushing the single strand of hair that always seemed to cover his left eye out of the way.

"You look better when your hair is out of your face."
I tried to laugh, but it came out as more of a whimper. I
don't know how people get through things like this, but
no matter how hard it is for me, I'm staying.

I won't leave until I know he's okay.

24 WITH EXPERIENCE

"It takes one to know one."

It's Wednesday now and that means that there are three days until my mother's wedding. I've been obeying her rules by going home every day at lunch time and whenever I need to sleep. She hasn't asked me for any help with the wedding, and at this point, I think it's for the best. I feel like I would ruin the happy mood that weddings are supposed to create. My mother has taken it upon herself to pick out the bridesmaid dresses even though I told her I could do it. So far, she has sent me 30 different pictures of possible dresses that the bridesmaids could wear. Thinking of the bridesmaids, I have vetoed probably 20 of them. I'm sorry, but who wants to wear a dress that has a flower bigger than your head attached to the shoulder? I really don't think anybody would want that.

Anyway, that's what has been going on lately. My routine really hasn't changed over the past few days. I get to the hospital around 9, have my normal two-hour conversation with Zoey, visit with Ricky for about 30 minutes before and 30 minutes after lunch, sit and talk with Caroline for a little while and then play on my phone until dinner time. It's not the most exciting plan, but it's worked for me.

I was sitting in the waiting room playing on my phone. It was 3:15 now so, unless Ricky got up, I would be sitting here until around 8. It sounds boring, but I've come to terms with the feeling. In my opinion, I deserve to be everything that's coming for me.

I failed the battle so I put my phone away and decided to reflect on my life at the moment. I put my head in my hands and tried to control the feeling of guilt that washed over me in waves at random times during the day. I couldn't handle sitting in Ricky's room for more than an hour when I wasn't sure if he wanted to be near me. I didn't want to force him to hear the voice of a person he most likely hates right now. He deserves to be as comfortable as possible.

"Miss." My eyes landed on an older woman who was sitting across from me on the other side of the waiting room. I had come to learn about almost all of the people in this waiting room because most of them were like me; constantly, sitting in one of these chairs for hours on end multiple days of the week. Reflecting on the disasters that happened to them. There was Kaitlyn Douglas who was waiting for her 15-year-old daughter who had epilepsy and had seizures almost every two days. I didn't talk to her all that much, but whenever she came in, we always said hello to each other. Wyatt Fisher was waiting for his sister who had complications with her alcohol withdrawal. Then Mariah Hicks who was waiting for her cousin who accidentally overdosed on her pain medications. Chad Salas was waiting for his best friend who fell asleep and hit a tree around the corner from here. Orion Booth was waiting for his wife who was currently undergoing a brain tumor surgery. Elisa Hensley was waiting for her boyfriend who got ink poisoning from one of the tattoos he had gotten from the tattoo parlor by the local supermarket. Franklin Weiss was waiting for his son-in-law who was getting one of his toes amputated because of his diabetic foot. I know it sounds weird, but yes, there are such things as a diabetic foot. Tucker Burnett was waiting on his twin brother who was getting a heart valve replacement. Tucker was hyperventilating and talking to himself about how worried he was one day, so I took it upon myself to talk to him about it. I think my advice helped him because he stopped the heavy breathing and one-sided conversations. The last 'usual' person I met in the waiting room was Abagail Pollard. She was waiting for three people who all happened to be in her immediate family, her son, daughter, and older sister. They had been driving back from a vacation that Abagail couldn't attend, when they hit a deer and rolled into a nearby lake. Thank God they had been right around the corner from the hospital because officials were notified within minutes and they were helped almost immediately. It was hard to see Abagail so upset and so vulnerable. I was sending good thoughts to all of them.

So, the older woman definitely caught me off guard. I took in her rose-colored dress that went perfectly with the red hair clip she currently had placed in her silver hair. I probably stared at her for one second too long because she tilted her head in confusion.

I smiled, embarrassed that I had been caught staring. "Sorry. Yes?"

"May I sit next to you?" Her gentle voice barely made it across the waiting room.

"Of course." I smiled and touched the seat next to me, signaling for her to come sit in the leather chair that was unoccupied to my left. She came over rather quickly and sat down.

"I couldn't help but notice that you were alone. A girl your age shouldn't be, are you alright dear?" She positioned her body so she was facing me. I did the same thing to show her respect.

"Oh, yeah, I'm alright. You don't need to worry about me," I reassured her. I didn't want her worrying about me when she probably had problems of her own to worry about.

"I always worry about people whom I don't think should be alone," she said matter-of-factly.

"I definitely deserve to be upset. My friend, Ricky, is in a coma right now because of me."

"I'm sure it wasn't your fault, dear."

"It was. I was driving him around on my motorcycle and we got into an accident." Every time I told someone about the accident, Ricky's voice played in my mind. The last thing I heard him say, or yell rather, was my name. Gwen.

"It was an accident correct?"

"Oh of course. I would never-"

"Well, then there's your answer. It wasn't your fault if you didn't purposefully crash. It looks to me as if you truly care about this.... friend.... of yours." The look in her eyes gave me the impression that she didn't think we were just friends. I'm not sure why but I'm seeing this pattern of people constantly thinking everything is more than it is. Let's not get ahead of ourselves here.

"I do."

"Well then you shouldn't feel so awful. Can I tell you an experience I had with something similar to this?"

"Sure." I could tell the story was going to be a long one so I positioned myself comfortably in the chair, anticipating the idea that I would be sitting here for a while.

"It was the summer of 81 and I was on my way to the beach with my husband, his brother, my brother, and his son. I was driving because I did not want any of the men to drive my new VW Vanagon. It was my latest obsession at the time and I was very protective of it. We were on the highway when a truck was getting off at an exit. I overestimated the speed of the 18-wheeler and ended up clipping the bumper. We went spinning into the oncoming traffic and ended up causing a 5 or 6 car crash. It was awful, and it was all my fault. Many were injured but everyone survived. Everyone except for my husband that is." She went quiet for a second and that's when I paid her my condolences.

"I'm so sorry." Her eyes were still on mine, so I could tell she was grateful for my apology. She gave me a sad smile before continuing.

"Thank you, dear. But, yes, for the longest time I blamed myself for his death, and I punished myself for it. I stopped eating for a while and ended up losing 50 pounds or so. I was not in a good place. When I got taken away to a treatment center I got the help I needed, and I was released feeling like a new person. The thing about that experience was the fact that I almost died. When I was on the bed that was supposed to be my death bed I realized something. Emmitt, my late husband, wouldn't want me to go like this. He would want me to live for as long and as healthy as I could. I came to the conclusion that blaming myself for something that was an honest accident wouldn't get me anywhere. It would only make me relive that moment over and over again and never move on with my life. Eventually I moved and started over. I re-married and have two beautiful step children whom he had when I married him. They're all grown up now while my current husband, their father, is here for his annual heart check-up. So, what I'm trying to say is that something good can come out of every situation no matter how bad it is. Based on your age I wouldn't be surprised if your friend walked out of this healthier than ever."

"Well, I really do appreciate your story but you don't know all of Ricky's health.... complications." I tried to give her a genuine smile but her story was still taking a toll on my spirit. That's absolutely awful.

"Like I said, I wouldn't be surprised if he came out of this hospital feeling healthier than ever. Take my advice...," her voice trailed off, letting me know that she wanted to know my name.

"Oh, Gwen."

"Gwen. Take my advice and have hope. I'm not going to say everything happens for a reason and I'm not going to say it's going to be easy but sometimes the journey makes the destination all that much prettier. My name is Ruby." I smiled and leaned over to give her a hug. She was a small woman which made it easy for me to wrap my arms around her. Something about her presence made me extremely calm and hopeful.

"Do you have any advice for the wedding I am supposed to participate in three days from now?" I laughed, sarcastically, not truly believing that she would give me advice for that too.

"Leave the chair to your right empty and imagine him beside you. That imagination is what lights the path for reality."

"I think that's a great idea Ms. Ruby." She smiled and laughed.

"Please, call me Ruby. I hope to see you again Gwen." She squeezed my hand briefly before standing up and heading into the main part of the hospital where the patients were. I could only imagine she was heading to her husband's room. I smiled at her receding figure before pulling out my phone and texting my mother.

I needed to make sure that she still had a place for Ricky and if she had enough for Zoey and Avianna. I had talked to them so much this week that I didn't feel right about not inviting them. They have definitely made my time here a lot more interesting. Especially little Zoey. She really knows how to make conversation interesting. We've talked about many different things including, but not limited to: boys; candy; pollution; princesses; colors; friends; stars; lipstick; me; mothers; dogs; the economy; the president; braids; ice cream; the sun; the moon; and zippers. Her mother claims to not know where all of this comes from, but I'm going to guess that most of it comes from her father. You know children, they can't let anything go.

Before I knew it, my alarm to go home was going off. Luckily, I changed it to a more appropriate ringtone so people around me wouldn't think the fire alarm was going off or something. The new alarm is a lot less, well, alarming.

My mother refused to allow me to ride my bike, but honestly, I wouldn't want to ride it now. I am still in shock from the accident to drive anything at the moment. For the past few weeks, Jerry has come to pick me up. He's clearly gotten the hint that talking about Ricky was the worst thing he could choose to talk about, so he's kept the conversations lighthearted. Most of the time I end up talking about the people that I meet in the waiting room. I've gotten to know all of them so, evidently, they all know me. I thought the only thing to do would be to tell Jerry and my mom about them.

The people in the waiting room are all going through hard times, but we all found a way to grieve together. It's kind of like our own private support group. They all have helped me accept what I did to Ricky. Ruby was probably the most influential out of all of them but every single person in that hospital has taught me that we all go through hard times. The survivors are the living, breathing proof that you can get through whatever it is that you are going through.

I smiled when I saw Jerry's car pull up in front of the hospital. I opened the door and threw my bag in the backseat. I kept my camera on my lap because occasionally I'll take pictures while we are on the road. The trees are usually the main focus of the picture. I'm never going to understand why my eyes always seem to lock onto the trees. It's like, they are drawn to them.

Sitting in one spot for as long as I have over the past few days really has made my love for the outdoors grow. Every time I step outside I take one long deep breath and let the smell of nature completely override all of my other senses. Nature has never been something I take for granted, but rather, something I choose to cherish and revel in every day.

"Meet any new people today?" Jerry had chosen to speak first. Usually, he would let me talk first, but I guess, today he was feeling a little daring.

"Actually, I did. Her name is Ruby and she told me about how her first husband died. It was very moving and similar to mine." I told him with a small smile. I had been trying hard not to let my sadness show through because that would ruin the entire 'wedding' mood that was currently surrounding my parents. If this were a child's movie, they would be skipping around the house.

"Well, I'm glad that she helped you." I let a few moments pass before I changed the subject completely.

"Jerry?" He made a noise to get me to keep talking. "How are you doing with my mother being pregnant and all?" The way he looked at me got my heart rate to spike.

"Did you think I didn't know? I'm ecstatic! But, he or she will never replace you." I smiled when I heard his reassuring words. It's nice to hear that at least once.

"Did you see Caroline?" He asked, curious, most likely, about how Caroline treated me today. Both of my parents know that Caroline is similar to a ticking time bomb. One second she is apologetic and the next she is exploding and obliterating every possible bridge that I have tried to create to bring us closer. It hurts to say the least.

"She was good today. She bought me a hot chocolate, and we talked about jewelry." Jerry laughed when he heard the topic of our conversation today. I laughed along with him because now, that I'm thinking about it, it truly sounds ridiculous.

"Jewelry?" He asked, laughter playing around his words.

"Jewelry." That was the last word that was spoken before our favorite song came on, 'I'm Still Standing' by Elton John. We both looked at each other and smiled before belting out all of the lyrics.

Every. Single. One.

"Well, there are my two favorite human beings!" My mother said happily before rushing over and giving us a group hug. Jerry and I both laughed and wrapped our arms around her.

"So, I thought we all could watch a movie together?" My mom offered up. Jerry and I both looked at each other, then to her, and then shrugged.
Who knows? Maybe this movie will be a good way to get my mind off of everything. Besides, I haven't spent enough time with my mother. Her words, not mine.

25 BELLS AND BURGUNDY

"Marry the one who gives you the same feeling you get when you see your food coming in a restaurant."

I decided not to go to the hospital today.

It was the day of the wedding and my mother couldn't be more anxious. She told me that I didn't have to meet up with her until 3 but I didn't feel right about that. I was the maid of honor so I felt like I should be by her side starting at the crack of dawn. Granted the wedding wasn't until 7 tonight, but still, I didn't feel right about leaving it all for my mother.

We were currently running through the checklist of every possible thing my mother would need. This list had about 80 items on it, starting with her wedding dress and ending with a box of tissues. It took hours to get through the checklist but at least, now, we could finally get to the fun stuff. The full day of pampering.

Our first stop was the nail salon and spa. My mother got a full-blown skin rejuvenation treatment while I just stuck with the simple mani-pedi. The time flew by as we went to every shop that could offer my mother even the slightest help with her wedding-day-beauty mission. By the end of the day we had been to a total of 7 different beauty shops. I had promised my mother that I would check on the bridesmaids and their dresses so I was heading to the changing rooms now.

The wedding was located on this cozy little farm about an hour away from our house. There were multiple barns and stone buildings scattered across the 100 acres of green field that made up the farm. My mother had her own little barn to herself while the bridesmaids and I were in the stone cottage closest to where Jerry and the groomsmen were. My mother and I had decided on burgundy colored dresses for the bridesmaids so I was currently helping everyone with their burgundy lip stick. You could tell just by the way the venue was set up that it was going to be a great night. No one seemed to mind the fact that golf carts were needed to get from one side of the farm to the other.

"How do I look, Gwenny?" I looked down at Trina who was currently playing with the end of my dress. I smiled and bent down so we were eye to eye. Trina was going to be our flower girl.

"You look like a princess," I said happily. She was dressed in a burgundy dress as well but it had this puffy, Cinderella feel to it. She looked even more adorable than she usually did. Called it!

"You really think so?" She asked hopefully, her eyes sparkling with the light only little girls possess.

"I do." She giggled when I spun her around like a princess at a royal ball. I couldn't help but laugh along with her. The second the laugh escaped my lips, though,

I immediately felt the pang of guilt that came almost every few hours at this point. How could I be happy when Ricky was in the hospital unconscious?

I looked over to the clock and then back to all of the ladies standing before me. My mother had four bridesmaids, including myself. Jerry had the same number of groomsmen so everything would be even. Since every person was important to Jerry and my mother, they decided that everyone would eventually take their seats before the actual ceremony started. Basically, the only people standing will be my mother, Jerry, and the wedding officiant.

"Okay, ladies, this is it!" I called out to everyone who was currently in the room with me. I smiled when everyone smiled back at me. It was so nice to see my family and friends just as excited as I was. The bridesmaids included me, Eva (my mom's best friend), Carina (another one of my mom's best friends), and Aunt Angie (my mother's brother's wife). Jerry had asked his two best friends and two of his brothers to be in the wedding. Theo (the youngest of Jerry's siblings) is the best man.

The entire venue was exploding with this sense of happiness, and I was hopeful that, even if only for a moment, it would take my mind off of Ricky.

"Your mother is so lucky to have such an organized daughter." I smiled at my Aunt Angie and pretended to not hear the mumbled, "I wish my daughter took that trait."

I clapped my hands and got all of the bridesmaids into the golf cart. It was time to check on the bride.

"You look gorgeous." My mother turned at the sound of my voice. I smiled at her until I noticed her eyes filling with tears. "Mom," I took a few steps towards her and put my hand on her shoulder, "What's wrong? You're supposed to be smiling. Did I forget something? I knew the whole Ricky thing would distract me-"

"Gwen. I'm crying because you look so beautiful, and I can't really believe that I'm getting married." I let out a sigh of relief when I heard my mother's words. I thought I had done something wrong.

"Oh good. Well not that you're crying, you're going to ruin your professional make up, but I'm glad that you're happy. Jerry really is great."

"Oh, he is Gwen. You know, he was the one that was there for me when everything went down with your father."

"And Jet," I spat.

"And Jet." The sound of his name alone was enough to make me sad, so I decided to change the subject. I also had to remember that we had company. I turned around and beckoned for the bridesmaids to come and pose with me and my mother for a picture.

"You guys look AMAZING!" She squealed before pulling us all into a group hug. I laughed when Carina tripped and almost fell into the huddle of bridesmaids.

"I'm going to take a peek at the finished venue. I'll be right back." They all smiled before turning back to talk with my mother about God knows what. At moments like these, I feel more mature than the grown women standing behind me.

I had to hold back the gasp when I saw the decorated field. It took even more strength to keep quiet at the sight of the alter and the aisle leading up to it. There was a wooden frame that held up gladioli and dangling white lights. It wasn't completely dark yet but I knew that, when it was, this entire field would look like New York City at midnight. There were a few people already seated on the benches along with the wedding officiant who was already at the podium. I smiled when I saw Zoey running down the white aisle yelling my name.

"GWEN! GWEN! IT'S SO PRETTY HERE!" She jumped into my arms and toppled me over right there in front of my family and friends. You've just got to love the timing of little children. Avianna laughed and made her way over to me as well, a little more gracefully might I add.

"Well, thank you Zoey. Have you ever been to a wedding before?" I positioned her comfortably in my arms.

"Nope. This is my first!" She giggled when her mother came up behind her and tickled her. I handed Zoey back to her mother and said hello.

"You look gorgeous Gwen. I wanted to let you know that Zoey and I are so grateful for the invitation. This is exactly what we needed." She smiled appreciatively.

"No problem. I hope you guys didn't feel pressured to come. I know that your husband is still in critical condition and-"

"Actually, that's what I wanted to talk to you about. He is doing a lot better and we talked all day yesterday about today. Yeah, he told us to come and have fun and not worry so much about him." Something inside me clicked, and I'm afraid that calling it jealousy wouldn't be too far from it.

"Oh, wow! Avianna that's great! I'm really happy for you." I waited a second before something else hit me. "Oh, my God, did he want to come?! Oh, Avianna I didn't even think to invite him, I am so sorry. I could-"

"No, Gwen, please. No, I'm glad you didn't. He's not in any condition to come, and he would've if a sweet girl like you asked him to. He would've claimed it due to chivalry that it would be rude if he turned down your invitation. No, he needs to stay in the hospital." I laughed at how frazzled Avianna had gotten just thinking about how her husband acts. Zoey's head tilted to the side in confusion. Oh no, here comes the long string of questions.

"What does shi-va-ry mean?" I couldn't help but giggle at the sound of her tiny voice trying to sound out chivalry.

Her mother's head dropped in defeat. She knew she wouldn't be able to get out of this one.

"It's basically a person's morals and how they-"

"What are morals?"

"Morals are your values like what you-"

"You mean like jewelry. So, I have shi-va-ry because I have jewelry?"

"No. Values are what a person believes is important. Kindness and manners are good examples. When someone says that they won't go to the bathroom until everyone has their food at dinner, that's a-"

"So, I have to WAIT to go to the bathroom at dinner? I really don't think that is fair Mommy. When I have to pee, I have to pee." She crossed her arms and looked to me as if looking at her mother was tiring. I used every ounce of energy I had to keep a smile from breaking out.

Avianna looked like she was about to "blow a gasket".

"No, Zoey I really think we should have this conversation with your father. He's better at explaining things to you."

"Yeah, tell me about it," she mumbled loud enough so we both could hear it. Her mother's eyes darted down at her, shocked by her attitude.

"What was that young lady?" Zoey immediately put on her guiltless puppy dog eyes and smiled innocently up at her mother. I laughed and decided that this would be where I leave the two of them to go back to their seats.

"Well, I have to go but I'll see you two later. Save me two seats, okay?"

"Will do. Zoey tell Gwen how beautiful she is." Zoey looked at me and smiled.

"Gwen, you are the prettiest person I have ever seen. Don't tell anyone," She leaned in and whispered, acting as though she had a secret to share, "But you are even prettier than sleeping beauty."

"You really think so?" I whispered back.

"I know so." Zoey cupped her hand around her mouth in an effort to only let me hear what she was saying. The second I turned around I let out a silent laugh. She was one of the cutest little girls on the planet.

More people started to make their way to the benches, and that's when I knew it was closer to 7 than I thought. I took one last look at the venue and couldn't help the anticipation that climbed its way through me. Both families love music so we even set up a portable dance floor closer to where the groomsmen were. I just knew my mother would love it.

On the way back to the cottage where my mother was, I got another one of my many waves of guilt. The problem with guilt is that, no matter how hard anybody else tries, nobody else can relieve it but you. You have to accept what you did and move on yourself. By yourself.

I felt a small breeze run over my bare shoulders but I didn't feel the coldness. I was too hurt on the inside to feel anything physically. How could I be laughing and smiling while Ricky was in the hospital, possibly *dying*. What kind of person does that make me?

"Gwen?" I looked up, dazed. I didn't even realize that I had made it back to the bridesmaids.

"Yes?" I asked quietly.

"Your phone is ringing. Are you going to answer it?" I blinked at my mother's observation and looked down. I had a small black purse with me so I opened it to get to my phone. I clicked the power button so it would stop ringing.

"The wedding is supposed to start soon. I shouldn't be on the phone-"

"Take the call." I listened to the serious tone my mother was carrying and decided to step out and take it. I clicked the green button and put the cell to my ear.

"Hello?"

"Yeah, Hello. Is this Gwen Brady?"

"Yes."

"Hi, Gwen. I got a request from a Ms. Caroline Knoll to let you know that, and I quote, "he is moving." I am guessing she is referring to a Mr. Ricky Doone."

Silence.

More silence.

"Hello.... Hello? Well, I am going to hang up now but that was the message. Have a good day." I let the hospital's side of the phone cut off the call. I listened as the static sound on the other end of the line drowned out everything around me.

I couldn't believe it. He's moving! He was actually moving! Well, I guess, as much as Ricky can move but still. No one will ever know how grateful I was in this moment. I didn't kill him.

"Honey we have to go now." I smiled at my mother who came out to get me. I ran over to her and gave her a hug. She didn't ask me what it was for, but instead, returned the gesture. I knew we both were smiling at this point.

"Let's tell Trina she can get her flower basket ready."

The wedding was absolutely beautiful. I'm not going to go through the entire thing but here were some of the highlights. So, instead of having the boring piano 'here comes the bride' music we got in touch with a radio station. We called them, and we asked if they could play a good love song that was upbeat and extremely optimistic. It wasn't exactly a love song but it was perfect. Literally, "Perfect" by Pink.

It was great because everyone danced down the aisle. Even some of the guests were rocking to it. It was fun and everyone seemed happy.

Zoey was sitting to my left and Avianna to hers. Originally, I had a chair to my right but I eventually scooted over one. Ruby told me to imagine that Ricky was here with me but I didn't have to. I didn't have to imagine him moving because he was! I trusted Caroline enough to know she wouldn't lie about something that revolutionary.

My mother had beautiful vows prepared and so did Jerry. Everyone was crying by the time they both finished. The thing that really struck me was the fact that Jerry told my mother that she was the strongest woman he had ever met. I completely agree. I also think that she's been strong for a couple of years too long and Jerry was there just in time to rescue her. I will forever be grateful for the comfort that he has provided her. It has helped everyone.

After Alvaro, the wedding officiant, pronounced them husband and wife and he officially became my father, we all headed to the dance floor and danced for, literally, hours. A few people got up to the microphone to say congratulations to my parents and now, it was my turn. I had this entire speech written down on a piece of lined paper, but I eventually came to the conclusion that speaking from my heart was the better way to go.

I walked up to the microphone and got everybody's attention. It was quite nerve racking to have everyone in my family staring at me but that feeling quickly dissipated when I met the eyes of my mother and Jerry. I smiled and collected my thoughts.

"Mom," I took a breath before I called Jerry the name I know he has been dying to hear, "Dad. I just want you both to know how grateful I am for both of you. I have been to hell and back over these past two years and both of you have helped me through it all. I wouldn't want anybody else as parents, and I hope you all know how much I love you both. You both always find a way to put me first and I still wonder how you do it. Jerry," I locked my eyes with his, "You have always acted like my father even before you knew me. Mom would come home with gifts for me, from you, and they were always meaningful. I remember when I broke this pen that I had used for 3 years straight. It was my lucky pen and I remember you went out that night and got me a custom one that had my name on it and everything. You do so much for me and I want you to know how much that means to me." I looked to my mom who already had tears in her eyes, "Mom. You have saved me from so many difficult situations, and have protected me from so much pain. Every day you get up and put aside all of your own problems for my own. You constantly worry about me and you always have my best interest at heart. When I get hurt you are always the first one to care. I am so happy that you found somebody that deserves you. You are too special for just anyone." I appreciated the few guests that laughed at my comment. Smiling at the thought, I continued, "I love you so much and I couldn't be happier for you. For both of you." Everybody clapped, as I made my way over to them and hugged them both. I was the last person to speak before the music started up again and we danced as if we had never stopped.

It's a lot of fun when you have a family who enjoys music. It makes everything better in my opinion.

By the time I got home, it was almost 3 am. My parents had decided to go on their honeymoon right after their wedding so, they packed their bags a few days before the wedding and kept them in the car. They were taking a trip to Aruba and wanted to leave directly from the wedding, leaving me alone for the next week and a half. Great!

I told my mother I was okay with the trip, but now that I'm alone, I can't fight the uncertainty that constantly makes me question my communication skills. I mean, what was I supposed to say?

Luckily, Darren and Trina have offered to do things with me this week so I wasn't alone 24/7. That was extremely nice of them, and honestly, I don't know who else I would've turned to. My family lives almost 10 hours away so we weren't exactly just 'one call away'.

It was nice to see everyone again. I'm not going to lie; my cousin was a little mischievous. He was the ring bearer and decided that it would be a good idea to put the rings on the stray cat that lived on the farm. Apparently, the cat was 'extremely friendly' but something about the way it's piercing yellow-green eyes stared me down gave me mixed signals. We ended up having to chase the cat for almost half an hour when he took off running with the rings around his tail. Tony, my cousin AKA ring bearer, is 3 so I guess he had an excuse. I'm not going to lie and say that watching him study the cats tail like it was an alien wasn't adorable, because it was. But it stopped being adorable when my parents' vows were cut short and the cat was wearing the rings as he ran across the farm.

I clicked my phone off but not before setting my alarm for 6:30. I know I probably wouldn't be getting anything more than 3 hours of sleep but that's what I get.

Hopefully, Ricky will be conscious tomorrow and not just 'moving'.

I'm not sure how much longer I can take the silence.

Silence, in my opinion, is the heaviest, most heartbreaking form of human communication.

26 THE CANDY BRACELET

"Pretty much all the honest truth telling in the world is done by children." – Oliver Wendell Holmes

The subtle alarm sound came from my phone at 6:30 in the morning. Naturally, I groaned and rolled out of my bed onto the floor. At this particular moment that t-shirt that said "I'm allergic to mornings" wouldn't be too far off. I quickly threw on a tank top, my leather jacket, and a pair of boots. Darren had been nice enough to offer to drive me to the hospital all week because I was too scared to drive myself. I knew I had to get out of the funk I was in sometime soon but today was definitely not that day.

Stuffing some cereal in my mouth, I grabbed my charger and opened the door. Darren was already waiting for me when I opened it. Obviously, I looked to see if little Trina was in the back seat. No matter who was driving, I would always look for Trina. I frowned when I realized she wasn't there. Hopping into the front seat, I instantly asked Darren what he thought of the wedding.

"You want my honest answer?" He asked as he

turned onto the highway.

Only if it's positive. "Definitely."

"That wedding was better than the one I had imagined in my head." I laughed when his face broke out into a gigantic smile, projecting from not only his wide grin but bright eyes. Truly beautiful smiles are the ones you can see through the eyes, in my opinion. The guilt came soon after my laughter died, but it was good while it lasted.

"What's the matter?" I looked over to see Darren alternating glances between me and the road. Concern and worry were written on his face.

"Oh, it's nothing. I haven't felt the same since the accident so it's probably just my concussion." I shrugged and looked out my window, not thinking twice about blaming my mood on my injury. Avoiding the conversation about Ricky altogether.

"Well, if you ever want to talk about anything, just let me know. You've been pretty distant over the past few weeks so I just wanted to make sure you know I am always here for you."

I smiled at his comforting words. "Thanks Ren. I know you are. For the record, I haven't even been talking to my mom so it's nothing personal."

I turned up the radio and let the sound of Imagine Dragons take us all the way to the hospital.

"Thanks." I waved to Darren as he pulled out of the parking lot of the hospital. I hadn't even made it through the doors when Zoey wrapped her arms around me. I laughed when Avianna ran over and detached the child from my body.

"Hello Gwen," Avianna breathed the words as she tried to catch her breath from having run after Zoey.

"Hey Avianna. How's Cedric?"

"He's good. He still has that ridiculous idea in his head that he's fine and shouldn't still be here. He's been giving the nurses a little bit of a hard time but I usually try to stay around to protect them." She rolled her eyes while talking about her husband. It was funny to see her reaction whenever she brought up Cedric's immaturity.

"Did you have breakfast?" I looked down to see Zoey tugging on my leather jacket. Clearly, someone was hungry.

"Zoey!" Avianna gasped at her comment.

"What? I just wanted to know if I wasn't the only one who didn't eat."

"I offered you food this morning, and you told me you weren't hungry."

"Well, now I am."

"Excuse me? Who do you think you are talking to with that tone?"

Zoey looked up to her mother innocently and confused. "What do you mean? I am talking to you and Gwen." Avianna sighed before looking to me. I took that as a cry for help, so I took over the conversation.

"How about this.... I'll take you to go get food in the food court while your mother has some alone time with your father. Does that sound good?" I looked between Avianna and Zoey to make sure they were alright with that plan. I definitely needed to make sure Avianna was okay with it.

Avianna nodded quite enthusiastically while Zoey started squealing. I smiled and took Zoey's hand. "So, what would you like for breakfast?" I asked Zoey as we walked away from her mother and towards the doors leading to the food court.

Zoey and I sat down with a big plate of waffles and multiple containers of powder sugar. Ironically, Zoey and I both have a sweet tooth for powder sugar. What can I say? I love eating sweet stuff that looks like snow. I think it is the best invention yet.

"So, who was that boy who dropped you off? He your husband?"

I almost choked on the waffles that I was eating. I'm never going to get use to Zoey's incessant talk about marriage.

"Nope. He hasn't gotten me a candy bracelet and I don't want him to." The second those words left my mouth Zoey snapped her head towards me and stared at me for a good 3 minutes.

"Then who DO you want to give you a candy bracelet?" She asked sternly. A better way to describe the look on her face would be disappointment.

"No one."

"NO ONE? So, you want to be.... *alone*?" She whispered the word *alone* like it was a bad word.

"Being alone isn't a bad thing, Zoey."

"But someone as pretty as you can't be alone. You'll be a cat lady!"

"I don't think being alone is based on how pretty you are Zoey."

"Yes, it is."

"Well, then I guess you will never be alone. I'm sure you have all the boys chasing you."

"Chasing me?! WHY would they CHASE me?!" She cried out worriedly. This little girl was priceless.

"I mean they all will like you."

"Oh," She shrugged, "Okay. I can deal with that. Besides, I *know* Nathan will get me a candy bracelet soon."

"Oh, is that so?"

"Yup," she guaranteed. I smiled and put another piece of my waffle in my mouth to stop myself from laughing. I really should be videotaping this conversation.

"How about we talk about your mother?" I offered. I don't mean to change the subject on her but talking about boys is extremely tiring.

"Oh, okay. Mommy. Yeah, what about her?"

"Well, what does she like to do with you?"

"Well, we go all over the place. She takes me on the plane all the time."

"Oh, really, where do you guys go?"

"The beach a lot. Daddy tries to come too but he usually has to go to work."

"Do you miss him a lot?"

"DUH!" She said loudly. I'm not sure where she gets her attitude from, but it's certainly prevalent in most conversations.

"Does your Mom go away a lot?"

"No, she's always home. It's nice. She bakes with me, and even helps me when I have play dates."

"You need help on your play dates?"

"Yeah, my friends are very confusing."

"I see. What about when you don't have friends over. What do you do then?"

"Let's talk about you. What do you do?" I blinked at

her, obvious, change in subject.

"Well, I like kickboxing, photography, and I consider myself a pretty good motorcyclist."

"What's all that?"

"You don't know what any of those things are?" She shook her head and looked up at me expectantly. Oh, God. This was going to be one long conversation.

Our conversation finally ended when I looked at the time and told Zoey I had to take her back to her mother. She whined for a few minutes until I bribed her with ice cream. I had to get her to leave somehow. As we walked back I realized that Zoey has been the only one who could make me laugh while Ricky's been in the hospital.

"Thank you, Gwen." I smiled at Avianna as she took Zoey's hand. "Did you have fun Zo?" Zoey nodded before rushing over to me and giving me a hug.

"What's this for?" I looked down to Zoey who held onto me like I was disappearing.

"I've always wanted a sister." She looked up at me with her big puppy eyes. It took everything in me not to break down into tears.

"Me too, Zoey. Me too." I bent down and hugged her more comfortably. Before I knew what was happening Avianna was telling Zoey that they had to go back to her father. I smiled at her but got distracted when Caroline's voice came from behind me. I had so many people talking to me at once that it made my head hurt.

"Gwen! Gwen!" I met Caroline's eyes and got this great sense of hope when she ran towards me, smiling.

"Yes?" I asked eagerly. She couldn't have been

running any slower.

"He's up!" She exclaimed.

"Your boyfriend?" I looked down at Zoey and laughed when she asked her question. I turned back to Caroline, who was completely ignoring Avianna and Zoey.

"Ricky's up?" I asked quietly. Not wanting to get my hopes up for something I could've easily misheard.

She nodded, enthusiastically, before beckoning to me to follow her to Ricky's room. She put her finger up to stop me. She was telling me to wait a second because she had to use the restroom. I guess she wanted to be there when Ricky and I saw each other. Something inside of me was a little disappointed that she was going to be there but I quickly brushed it off. Heck, I was seeing Ricky!

"So, Ricky is your boyfriend?" I turned to Avianna, who seemed to be amused with the whole scene playing out before her.

I laughed. "Oh, no. Zoey just wants that to be the case. He's a close friend. I've been taking care of him for a little while now, and I had just felt horrible when we were in the accident because of me. I don't even know how he is or what's wrong with him now. He has cerebral palsy and is paralyzed from the waist down so I don't know how the accident affected him." I tried to keep the concern out of my voice when I explained to her what happened. She looked at me apologetically, but quickly broke eye contact with me when she saw Zoey making a dash out the door. I'm pretty sure she was chasing a butterfly. I laughed when Avianna caught up to her and locked her in her arms.

I saw Caroline come out of the bathroom and immediately bent down to pick up my bag and camera. I was so excited to show Ricky his finished collage. I had spent hours a few nights ago working on it and it was, finally, complete. Many different pictures flooded the page including some of the places he's always wanted to go to. Not that long ago he told me that he's always wanted to go to Ireland, New Zealand, and Australia. He didn't tell me why but I have a feeling it's just the idea of getting away. Getting away, specifically, from the confines of his house and lifestyle.

As I was picking up my things I heard the tapping of little feet running for me. I didn't have to look up to know that Zoey was standing above me. I smiled as I listened to her heavy breathing.

"All that running tired you out, huh?" I asked, looking at all of my stuff on the ground.

"I think he should give you the candy bracelet."

"Zoey, I really don't want to play the candy bracelet game with you right now-"

"No, seriously. He's cute and he's staring at you." I breathed in trying hard not to get mad at the 6-year-old who was currently distracting me from seeing Ricky. When I finally got all of my stuff in order I turned around to see who Zoey was talking about. If I was bending over, and they were looking at me, the likelihood they were looking at my butt was high. I was preparing myself to confront whomever it was that was staring.

I caught my breath when I saw who was standing in the middle of the blue double doors that separated the patients from the waiting room. I tried to move but my feet and legs just gave out. I landed in the chair behind me and stared. I couldn't form words and even if I could my mouth wouldn't move. I was shocked, completely and utterly frozen. I looked down at my hands when they started shaking because that seemed to be the only thing that was moving. I didn't even hear my heart beat. At that moment, I knew everything was going to be okay. I knew that I wouldn't blame Amber for breaking my hand and making me believe I was worthless. I knew I wouldn't blame my brother for leaving and my father for hurting my mom. I knew I wouldn't blame Ty for coming back and expecting everything to be the same as when he left. I knew Caroline and I would one day see eye to eye and be able to put aside all of our differences. I knew that Ricky and I were both going to get past this accident. I knew a lot just by looking at the person standing on two feet, 10 paces away from me.

I knew then that we would both be more than the shadows that hid behind the wheels.

Artist rendition of Gwen by Dasha Didenko

ABOUT THE AUTHOR

Brooke L. Smith was 13 years old when she started writing *The Shadows Beyond These Wheels*. (She completed the book when she was 14.) She really wanted to make this a teen project that inspired young teens to try things they've dreamed of doing. Now a 9th grader in her home state of Maryland, Brooke and her family live in the suburbs of Washington, D.C.